Praise for *Learning to Breathe*

A 2019 YALSA Best Fiction for Young Adults Selection

Amelia Bloomer's 2019 Top Ten Recommended Feminist Books for Young Readers Selection

A Junior Library Guild Selection

Governor General's Award Finalist

"A love letter to girls—bittersweet and full of hope."
—Ibi Zoboi, author of National Book Award finalist *American Street*

"This is a stellar debut."
—Brandy Colbert, award-winning author of *Little & Lion* and *Pointe*

"A vibrant, essential story of healing, resilience, and finding one's family."
—Stephanie Kuehn, author of William C. Morris Award–winning *Charm & Strange*

"A raw, beautiful, unforgettable must-read."
—Tiffany D. Jackson, author of *Allegedly*

"Poetic."
—Angela Johnson, award-winning author of *Heaven*

"If you want to understand #MeToo for a sixteen-year-old growing up on what many Americans know mostly as a tourist paradise, read *Learning to Breathe*."
—Terry Farish, award-winning author of *The Good Braider*

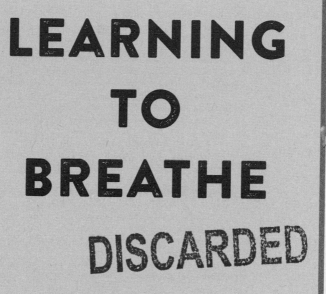

LEARNING TO BREATHE

DISCARDED

JANICE LYNN MATHER

SIMON & SCHUSTER BFYR

NEW YORK   LONDON   TORONTO   SYDNEY   NEW DELHI

SIMON & SCHUSTER BFYR

An imprint of Simon & Schuster Children's Publishing Division
1230 Avenue of the Americas, New York, New York 10020
This book is a work of fiction. Any references to historical events,
real people, or real places are used fictitiously. Other names, characters, places, and events are
products of the author's imagination,
and any resemblance to actual events or places or persons,
living or dead, is entirely coincidental.
Text copyright © 2018 by Janice Lynn Mather
Cover photograph copyright © 2018 by Ali Smith
Cover illustration copyright © 2018 by GreedyHen
SIMON & SCHUSTER BFYR is a trademark of Simon & Schuster, Inc.
For information about special discounts for bulk purchases, please contact
Simon & Schuster Special Sales at
1-866-506-1949 or business@simonandschuster.com.
The Simon & Schuster Speakers Bureau can bring authors to your live event. For more
information or to book an event,
contact the Simon & Schuster Speakers Bureau at
1-866-248-3049 or visit our website at www.simonspeakers.com.
Also available in a SIMON & SCHUSTER BFYR hardcover edition
Interior design by Hilary Zarycky
Cover design by Krista Vossen and Lizzy Bromley
The text for this book was set in New Caledonia.
Manufactured in the United States of America
First SIMON & SCHUSTER BFYR paperback edition August 2019
2 4 6 8 10 9 7 5 3 1
The Library of Congress has cataloged the hardcover edition as follows:
Names: Mather, Janice Lynn, author.
Title: Learning to breathe / Janice Lynn Mather.
Description: First edition. | New York : Simon & Schuster Books for Young Readers, [2018]
| Summary: Sixteen-year-old Indy struggles to conceal that she is pregnant by rape and then,
turned out by relatives, must find a way to survive on her own in Nassau.
Identifiers: LCCN 2017047526| ISBN 9781534406018 (hardback) | ISBN 9781534406032
(eBook) | ISBN 9781534406025 (pbk)
Subjects: | CYAC: Pregnancy—Fiction. | Rape—Fiction. | Family life—Caribbean Area—
Fiction. | Homeless persons—Fiction. | Yoga—Fiction. | Caribbean Area—Fiction.
Classification: LCC PZ7.1.M3766 Le 2018 | DDC [Fic]—dc23
LC record available at https://lccn.loc.gov/2017047526

For every Indy
(and each Smiley, too)

PROLOGUE

HOME LOOKS SMALL FROM *here, crammed in the backseat of Mamma's latest boyfriend's car. A clapboard house painted a tired blue, missing shingles on the roof like snaggled teeth, overgrown yard full of stubborn guava trees, and herbs sprouting in haphazard patches. Behind, the ocean stretches out, land dropping off to docking-deep water. Grammy sits on the old porch, shelling peas into a bowl balanced on the straw bag at her feet. As usual, a book lies open on her lap.*

"Hurry up," Mamma says from the front seat. She leans back and puts her feet up on the dashboard. She's not speaking to Grammy since they argued about sending me away to Nassau for school. The boyfriend is skinny, his face covered in pimples even though he's older than she is; he shuts the car engine off, his eyes darting nervously toward the house. "Five minutes." Mamma swigs from her beer bottle, settling deeper into her seat.

"*Give the girl time to say bye, at least. The boat ain going nowhere yet,*" the boyfriend says as I get out and start up the pathway. I glance back to see if he's staring at me, but he's reclined now too, chugging from his own bottle.

"*Today is the day.*" Grammy nods at the porch step, telling me to sit down.

"*I guess so.*" The wood creaks under my weight. My fingers find the familiar split where, years back, a different boyfriend slipped and fell. His head stitched up nicely but the step has held on to its scar. "*Grammy, I really have to go?*"

Grammy's fingers snap the necks of still-green pods, thumbs nudging the pigeon peas out of their cozy shells and into the bowl. As they land, they tinkle cheerfully. She looks out at the car. "*You know what your mamma said. Better you finish your last two years of high school in the city.*" She looks down again, shelling one last pod, then wipes off her hands on her faded gray dress. "*Remember what I tell you?*"

I hate talking about this. "*Yeah, yeah.*"

She raises her eyebrows, beady eyes peering over her glasses like a mockingbird's, quick and keen, warning that I might get a pecking if I don't look out. "*What's that, now?*"

"*Watch myself.*" The car horn beeps twice, agreeing. "*And stay out of trouble.*"

Grammy nods, glaring over my shoulder at the car. "*Bide your time!*" she shouts, then leans in, whispering, "*I can't be over there. I can't run to you when something go wrong. You can't run to me. You gotta watch out for yourself. And Indy?" Grammy grabs hold of my arm. "Don't let no one take advantage of you. You hear?"

Her fingers dig into me. She won't let go until I nod. When I do, she sighs and reaches for the book.

"What's that?"

Grammy closes it, turning the cover away from me. She wraps it in a clean rag, tying the bundle up with string. She sets aside the bowl of peas and pushes the book deep into the straw bag, then rearranges a piece of white cloth over the top, tucking it in securely. She lifts the bag by its frayed straps. "Take this with you." It's packed so full its sides bulge.

"What's in it?"

"You'll see, when the time is right. Now, Indy? When you reach Nassau, that book? You put it someplace safe, and keep it wrap up, you understand? Don't open it, not yet."

Then what you give it to me for now, I think. Out loud, I say, "Okay."

At the end of the driveway, the car has started up. Mamma leans on the horn, forcing out a long, steady whine. Grammy pulls me in for a rough hug, her arms thin and strong. I bury my face in her bony shoulder. What's waiting for me in Nassau? What's on the other side of the water? Grammy's arms tighten before she lets go.

"Go on, now." The horn's wail grows longer. Grammy won't look at me. "Go. Before your ma bring all the dead people out the graveyard."

I stumble my way down to the car, the straw bag bumping against my hip. Only when I'm three steps away from the car does Mamma ease up off that horn. When I turn back to wave, Grammy's already gone, the porch empty, as if she's left Mariner's too. The front door gapes wide, a shocked mouth.

When we get to the dock, Mamma reaches around her seat and presses something into my hand. An old phone, from two or three boyfriends ago, the body scratched and the screen cracked. I take it reluctantly. While Mamma and the boyfriend argue about how long the boat ride will be, I get out of the car alone and take Grammy's straw bag with me. I leave everything else; the black garbage bag full of hand-me-down clothes, the one box of books and pens and pencils, the other full of mangoes for my aunt and uncle and cousin. I want to be light. Nassau is a new start. A new place. I want to be free.

1

IT'S BIOLOGY WHERE THINGS start to unravel. Mr. McDonald's out getting his cup of coffee and everyone's abandoned their seats. A cluster of boys is huddled around Quetz's phone, peering earnestly at its screen. Some of the girls are flipping through a magazine. Me, I have Grammy's book hidden behind my Science 11 notes under the desk, and I'm thinking about how I'm five periods late and nothing fits quite right anymore. I'm trying to peek at the pages without being noticed when I sense someone behind me. Before I can turn, they pull my bra strap far back, then let it fly.

There's a loud sound, something slapping and tearing at the same time, then brief, unexpected relief, like loosening the waistband on a pair of jeans that's too snug. I spin around to see my cousin Smiley, and am about to say *Why you in my class? What you want?* when I see everyone's paused, mouths hanging open. Then I feel a cool breeze where breeze shouldn't be felt, and look down. My top's popped open, I can see bra and skin and everything. I try to close up my blouse but two buttons are totally gone, ripped right off with the force of my too-big-for-this-bra-and-this-shirt-and-this-life chest bursting free. I cling to the fabric anyway, trying to hold things in place.

Churchy, whose grammy sent him over from Mariner's last August, same time as me, breaks the silence. In Mariner's, we called him Churchy for the way he dressed from before he was in school; pants starched stiff with creases down the front of each leg, shirt collar you could peel fruit on, hair always kept too low, and the way he stuttered out *T-t-t-two t-t-t-times f-f-five is t-t-t-ten* like raspy Bishop Laing. And since Churchy's first act off the boat was to call me by *my* stupid nickname, I made sure everyone at our new school learned his. Now Churchy gets me back. He holds out a white button. "Here, D-D-D-Doubles," he says.

His stutter sets everyone off. Quetz is motorboating *D-D-D-D-D-D-D-D-D-Doubles*, cheeks slack, shaking his head side to side, eyes bugged out like a comic book perv. Bullet's long head is flung back, finger pointing. Mark's turned, his face right on eye level with my chest. "Wow and wow," he's saying in his best Barry White impression, a look on his face like Christmas and his birthday came together, even though

I'm holding my blouse so tight there's not even half a wow to be seen. Samara's trying to hide her laugh behind her hand, and failing.

"Guess that's why they call you Doubles," Smiley says, grinning.

Used to be I'd laugh it off. I know Churchy didn't mean it, and anyway, we're all humiliated at some point: Mark cannonballing into the pool and his trunks sliding off, Quetz—short for Quetzalcoatl—giving a presentation on the rise of the Aztec empire while he tries to fight off a hard-on in his slim-fit pants. I can't laugh at this, though; I'm not normal like the rest of them. Not anymore. Not ever again. I stand up, my face burning, and shove Smiley—not hard, but she's younger than me, and so skinny she goes flying into Mark's desk. I hear her "Owwww!" over the whole class's laughter as I run out, clutching my blouse with one hand, hanging on to the book and the straw bag with the other.

"Excuse me!" I hear, as I run right into Mr. McDonald, hot coffee and all, and there's swearing as I hurl myself down the stairs. I run past the nurse's office, past the art buildings, windows a blur, past the security guard in his hut, talking to the maid. He doesn't stop me, just glances my way, then turns back to chatting her up, as if girls holding their clothes together make a break for freedom every day. I slip into the bathrooms at the bottom of the path. All that running has my chest hurting—my breasts are always sore now—and more than anything, I wish I could lie down, close my eyes, and forget this afternoon ever happened. I always pack comfortable clothes to change into right after school, and today it's a loose T-shirt and one of the skirts Grammy sent over with me: long purple Androsia, wide and soft and elastic-waisted. I lock myself into a stall and take off the blouse. It's been feeling tight for weeks, but maybe I can sew the buttons back on. The skirt, at least, still fits all right; I only begged it off the school secretary last week, salvaging it from the stack of orphaned uniforms in the lost and found. I just wish the bra could have lasted longer. It's the biggest one I have, and still sort of new. I'll have to make it work for now. I tie that stupid busted strap together in a bulky knot, then stuff my uniform into the bottom of the bag. Back in my own clothes, I head outside. Behind me, the school buildings stand placid; meanwhile, I'm falling apart. I turn away, squeeze through a gap in the fence, and step onto the street.

"Ocean water cleanses," Grammy used to say, before she let Mamma ship me off. Whenever I had a cold, after an argument, if one of Mamma's boyfriends looked at me funny—the answer was always the same. "Go in the sea. Put your head in the water. Cool off. Take a swim."

Ocean water can't cleanse everything, though.

I take the bus toward Aunt Patrice's house but stay on it a couple extra stops and get off at the end of the route, where Main Street finishes its run from downtown to the southern part of Nassau. Around the bend is a half-rocky, half-sandy snippet of beach with a rickety dock the boys use to backflip off into the sea. Today, it's empty, not even seagulls perched on the old posts jutting out of the water, where part of the wood has rotted or washed away. I drop my bag on the dock and pull out Grammy's book again. It's disheveled, the edges colored a faint red, pages yellowed with time. The paperback cover has come loose and been reattached with old masking tape that's grown brittle and flaked away. Grammy has joined it once more with a fresh binding, determined to hold it together, to pass it to me, as if she foresaw how much I would need it, that I'd open it again and again. There's no picture on the cover, only its title: *The Pregnancy Book*. Now, like always, seeing those words is a kick in the gut.

I thumb open the book, turning the pages carefully. I navigate the chapters with their soft, hopeful names—"The Story of Conception"; "Early Days"; "Expanding Horizons"; "Preparing Your Home"—and stop at "Signs and Symptoms." I don't want to read what the author says; there's something else I'm looking for. There it is, squeezed at the top of the page. Grammy's familiar cursive, speaking to me:

I knew from the second my mouth itched for ripe mango.

They say when you pregnant you want sour things, but my body didn't care, it craved sweetness and juice. I sent my nephew on a hunt; trees were done bearing, but I promised him a new pair of shorts and a cake for his birthday. I would have given him this same plot of land if I had to, right then. It took him half the day, and where he found them he never told me, but he came back all scratched up and grinning, with two of the saddest past-ripe fruit you ever saw. To me, though, it was better than a six-course dinner after a fast. I ran down to meet him on the path, snatched those mangoes, and bit straight in. It was sugar and sunshine, the best of all things. It completed a part of me I never knew was half-done. Right then I realized I had to be in the family way. That was my first lesson: don't matter what they say you should want. Only you know what it is you need most.

Reading Grammy's words brings her voice back to me as clearly as if she was here beside me. Her stories always used to be a comfort, but as much as I miss her, I'm angry, too. I toss the book down. Why would she have given this thing to me, unless she thought I'd need it? How could she have known? I sure didn't. The only thing I knew was when I got pregnant. I knew from the moment it happened, and there was no sugar or sunshine in it.

One night—like a whole bunch of nights in December, November, October—sleeping sitting up on the couch, cause it feels a few paces closer to safe. I'm knocked awake, thump onto the floor so loud someone has to have heard. Math book pages rustle as I try to twist away. He catches my feet, cursing so quiet I can make out the tone but no words. Face to the wall, eyes squeezed shut, I brace myself and wait, but this time there's no sound of a packet tearing open. I choke out, "You ain gat nothin?" because Gary always does, always says "I gotta be careful, I ain know where you been" or "You sleep around like ya mummy? Everybody know Mariner's Cay Sharice." Only this time, nothing. When I try to scream, his hand covers my mouth. There's that sick salty body smell Mamma's boyfriends always had, only Mamma isn't here, only me. I can't call out, I can't move, I can only think of how I'm letting it happen, letting someone take advantage, and what would Grammy say, and it's happening and all I want, all I want is for it to stop.

I kick my school shoes and socks off. At the edge of the dock, the sea bobs and laps, waiting. What I need is to not feel dirty. I need to be clean. I climb up onto one of the wooden posts, feet barely fitting on it. I teeter for a moment. Then I jump.

There is an instant, sailing through the air, when I am both moving and still. There's no room for the rush of fears and doubts in my head. My breathing stops. I can hear the *poundpound* of my heart. No thinking, I can just be.

Then the smack of impact, the tearing through water, body sucked down down down before the force reverses and I rise. I break through the surface, gasping for air, wet face, drenched hair, eyes stinging from the salt. The dock already seems far away.

I swim. Head underwater, breaststroke style, gliding long, coming up only when I need a breath. My purple skirt pulses and undulates, an enormous jellyfish. The water holds me up, even my heavy breasts and expanding belly; moving easily through the sea, I feel almost like myself, except for the knot at the back of the busted bra and my underwear's elastic, digging in. I am alone; there's a few people farther up on the shore, but they can't see anything from there. What if I could really be free? Pretend there's nothing going on, pretend Gary never happened and I'm a normal sixteen-year-old taking a swim? It's not so private I'd strip down fully, but maybe I could loosen things a bit . . .

I wriggle out of my underwear. The panties bob, brazen and black against the clear blue. The bra is next; I undo the knot holding it closed and my chest celebrates, liberated at last beneath the balloon of my shirt. It's the newest one I have, but it's ruined now; what's the point in holding on? The bra follows me for three arms' lengths, catching my ankles like seaweed, until I kick it free and take off through the water, my skirt billowing around my legs. I come in line with the curve of sand along the shore, smattered with benches, put my head down in the shallow water and glide past like a purple-frilled fish. When I surface again, I glimpse the blur of parked cars, hear the shrieks of kids too little to be in school. *Kids.* I dip my head back under and push off again, muffling their cries.

As I swim past houses, a few with boats tied up, I realize I'm getting tired. It's deeper now, and farther on, the shoreline is rocky. Just ahead is one last stretch of sandy shore, a private beach flanked by a low wall that runs all the way along it, then disappears up into someone's property. From here I can't see a roof, but it's probably some winter home left empty during the hot summer months. Casuarina trees grow on either side, giving shade. I push toward land, feet fumbling for the bottom. When it's shallow enough to walk, I hurry for the shore. Out of water, the skirt and shirt cling to everything, forming a second skin. I yank the soggy fabric away from me, wringing it out. The skirt hangs like spent petals now. I lean up against the wall to catch myself. It's taller, close up, too tall to step over, but short enough to climb. If I can get over it, I can cut through the yard to the road and walk back to my bag and shoes on the dock.

I put my hands on the top, my butt against the side, pull and . . . nothing. My back's hurting, and what was so light in the ocean now feels like a sack of wet concrete. On top of everything else, I have to pee. I try again, using my legs to help launch me up. One extra pull, and I'm up and swinging over, feet touching down on the other side.

As soon as I turn around, I know I've made a terrible mistake. This is no abandoned winter home. Instead, it's a buzz of activity, some sort of exercise camp on cleanup day. To the right is a low wooden building, the open door leading to a small office, and past that, through trees, a large pavilion. Farther along the wall is a big deck standing on its own, with about a dozen people on it, all stretching in unison. They stand with their arms up to the sky, then bend, bringing their hands to the ground, following the lead of a tall woman at the front. To the left are twenty or so miniature cottages. You could fit four of them in Aunt Patrice's living room, but they're scattered across a wide area, separated by trees that defy the salt air; mango, guava, almond, dilly, poinciana. Off the deck, a handful of other people bustle around in staff shirts. A girl on the porch of the cottage closest to me sings tunelessly as she sweeps. A woman with a red scarf tied on her head paints the office wall, her brow knotted in concentration. And not more than twelve feet from me, a guy is weeding around the base of a coconut tree, his fat dreadlocks tied back. He's bare-backed, but so bony even Smiley wouldn't be able to muster a dirty comment. His shirt hangs from the back pocket of his shorts like a dog's tongue while he squats, cutlass in one hand, sending grass and dirt flying.

No one's seen me—yet. I look down and realize one of my feet is planted right on an exercise mat, thin and cushiony like a sheet of rubber sponge. It's bright red. I might as well be standing on a target. I have to sneak away, quickly, quietly. Bonus if I can find their bathroom without anyone noticing. *Please*, I pray, *let me be invisible.*

"Hey!"

Prayer denied. Cutlass Guy stands up, wiping his forehead with the back of the same hand that holds the machete. It's a miracle he doesn't lop off his ear. "Miss, you all right?" He takes a step toward me.

"Sorry. I got the wrong place." I back up against the wall. But where can I go? I can't make the swim back to the dock. Even the beach feels too far.

"You soaking wet. You always swim with all your clothes on? Hey, you ain fall off a boat or anything, right? You live round here? You speak English?" Cutlass Guy takes another step forward. He's only Smiley's height, would have to stand on tiptoes to look me eye to eye, but with that cutlass in his hand, I don't care. "You swam up here? From where? Back that way?" He uses the machete as an extension of his arm, pointing at the ocean; the blade reflects the sun's glare into my face, making me squint.

"I going right now." Forget the bathroom. I decide to

make a run for the path between the nearest cabin and the woman painting. I take one, two steps before I trip, stumbling over the stupid mat. Cutlass Guy reaches out to catch me and I let out a shriek.

I clap a hand over my mouth, but it's too late. A plump woman with a box of groceries on one hip turns midstride to look at me. The sweeping girl drops her broom and stares. The class on the deck has let out and a few of the students pause to look too, their mats tucked under their arms, curled up like long cinnamon rolls. My gaze falls on the woman with the red scarf, paintbrush frozen, like she's touching up the air. She's the first person to spring back to life.

"No! Oh, no. No, no, no, no, no." In a few bounds, she's right in my face, brush still in hand, dripping butter-colored paint. "You the one who went and messed up our walls? You did this?" She points at the area she's patchily repainted. "I should call the police on you. Trespassing and vandalizing and I wouldn't be surprised if you stealing, too. You and whoever else did this, get out. Right now, out. Out, out, out." She jabs the paintbrush at me like she plans to skewer me on it.

"Hey, hey, hold on." Cutlass Guy steps in between us. "Look at her, she ain no vandal. You see her with any spray paint?"

"What are you doing here?" the woman demands, ignoring him. She is short and pointy-faced, younger than Grammy but older than Mamma, her skin dark and glowing from sweat or pure fury.

I open my mouth, but nothing comes out.

"What, you don't talk?"

"Come on." Cutlass Guy crosses his arms. "You ga yell at her while she stand here soaking wet, on a yoga mat?" He turns to me. "Look here, miss, you want sit down? Maya," he calls to the woman toting groceries, "you got any switcher in the kitchen? She might be thirsty. You thirsty?" Maya nods and disappears down the path to the right. He swings back around to the painter, gesturing with the cutlass again. "We can't just throw people out, man. We have to make sure she okay."

"Don't point that damn cutlass at me," she snaps. "You," she says, spinning around to glare at me, "when I come back in ten minutes, you better be outta here. Wherever you come from, you go right back."

"You should spend a minute on the deck," Cutlass Guy shouts as she stomps off, tossing her paintbrush down as she goes. "Need some yoga for that bad attitude." He glances at me. "Don't mind what Joe say. You don't have to rush outta here. How could we kick you out? And this a yoga retreat and all."

"I'm fine," I say, finding my voice again. "Y'all have a bathroom?"

"Yeah, shore. Get it? *Shore?*" He smiles, showing off a

perfect set of white teeth, and laughs. It's a nice laugh. Of course, I know better than to trust a person on that alone.

I shift a little. I really have to pee. "Um—where?"

"Sorry," he says, noticing I'm not amused, and points past the office wall Joe was painting. "Bathroom's over that way."

I barely make it there; inside, I'm so relieved, I don't have time to regret the shoes abandoned on the dock. While I'm in the stall, someone comes in and drapes some clothes over the door. I take them down; loose, faded sweatpants and a saggy T-shirt, still clothesline warm. I change, then wash my hands, leaving my wet clothes in the sink. Outside, someone's set a fresh glass of switcher on the step. I chug it; cool, not too sweet, and just enough sour. I start down a path that leads me past the cabins. The girl with the broom is sweeping one of them; through the open door, I see a nightstand, a bureau, a narrow bed. What I'd give for something so simple, a home that's safe, that's all mine, that's close to the sea. Worlds, or at least streets, away from Gary.

There are footsteps, voices approaching me from the beach. I head down the path in the opposite direction, following it through the dense trees and shrubs until it widens, opening into an unpaved parking lot with a beat-up white jeep and a few other cars crammed together in the shade. I hobble over the gravel and through the black, rusty gates, down a long driveway lined with more trees. That gives way to a badly paved street, then the road curving back to where I began.

My school shoes wait for me on the dock reproachfully. Beside them, the book still sits, blown open, its pages rustling back and forth. I slip on my shoes and think of shoving the book off the edge and into the water, sending it to the same fate as those waist-hating panties and that stupid busted bra. I don't care about the underwear, I have more of those, but I'm starting to regret setting the bra free. Even with the broken strap, it's the best one I had. I peer over the edge, sure it's long gone, but miraculously, there it is, bobbing, curled around one of the dock's posts. I reach down and fish it out. Maybe a few staples could make it wearable again. Or duct tape—that stuff will hold anything together. I wring it out and cram it into the pocket of the borrowed pants, then put the book back in my bag. There's no point going back to school, not right now. I start walking, heading to the only place I have to go.

2

WHEN THE BOAT PULLS into Nassau Harbour, I scan the faces crowded on the dock, waiting to pick passengers up. There: a girl holding a homemade cardboard sign over her head, a stern-faced woman beside her. My cousin Cecile and Aunt Patrice. Uncle should be there too, though I can't see him anywhere. As I step off the boat, Cecile pushes her way toward me and squeezes me in a hug.

"You look just the same!" she says, letting me go to waggle the cardboard under my nose. My name is scrawled in thin pencil and a photograph taped underneath, for comparison, I guess. I recognize the picture; it's the one Mamma sent in the mail, along with the letter asking them to take me in. It was taken two years ago in Grammy's front yard. I'm barefoot, wearing an Androsia skirt and a plain white top, squinting at the camera. Mamma was there too, but before she sent the letter *off, I caught her cutting herself out, making the photo shorter, and jagged. Even now, I can still see her arm around my waist.*

"Your uncle had to work," Aunt Patrice says, by way of an introduction. Instead of a hug, she gives me a sharp nod, narrowing her eyes as if that might change what's standing in front of her: me, fresh off the boat in an aquamarine skirt that's sister to the one I wear in the picture, and a homemade blouse that suddenly feels homely, nothing to my name but the straw bag over my shoulder. She purses her lips, tasting something sour. Looking back at her, in her navy jacket and matching pants and bright red high-heeled shoes, I feel shabby, a stray dog next to a freshly groomed poodle.

"I'm Smiley," Cecile says with a grin that's already decided we'll be friends. It's obvious why they call her that; her smile stretches her long face into a wide one, the happy dancing right up to her eyes. That, and she's skinny and looks like Guy Smiley off Sesame Street; the same dark hair, eyebrows that slope up, and so bright-skinned she's almost yellow.

"This is Cecile," Aunt Patrice corrects. "Where's your luggage?"

I shift Grammy's straw bag on my shoulder. "This all I have."

Her frown deepens as she turns away, making her way toward the parked cars. "But it ain ga be all you need."

"Smiley," the girl whispers. She takes my bag in one

hand, looping her free arm through mine, and smiles even more. I can't tell if she's trying to put me at ease or if she's that unaware. "What your friends call you?"

Just Indy, I'm about to say, when I hear a familiar voice call "D-D-D-Doubles!" I don't have to turn to know it's Churchy from Mariner's Cay. "D-D-D-Doubles, it's me!" He waves before he's swallowed up in the crowd, his own people hugging him, taking his bags. I turn away. New start, I keep thinking. New start. New start.

"Doubles?" Smiley laughs. "That's what they call you? Doubles?"

"Look like a double to me," Aunt Patrice says, unlocking the car doors. "And starting off the same way as Sharice."

I get into the backseat, trying to play it off, but I know that name's going to follow me.

Back at Aunt Patrice's house, I don't shower. I leave the ocean's salt film on me. I'm supposed to keep my things in the living room, but I dump my bag in Smiley's room, beside the bed where Aunt Patrice won't see it, then head back out to the kitchen. On the way there, I glimpse myself in the front room mirror, even bigger in the oversized shirt and pants, then keep right on going.

Gary's been in the house sometime since this morning. His stuff is strung through the kitchen like he's marking territory. A laundry bag full of chef's uniforms from the hotel is dumped down by the washing machine, stinking of sweat, stale cologne, and whatever he cooked at work, a hodgepodge that makes me want to retch. I ram them into the washer, bag and all, and slam the door shut.

I rifle through the fridge, yanking out the disposable aluminum pan he's brought from work. Buffet leftovers: fried rice with egg strewn through like bits of shredded sponge; fried fish; ripe fried plantain, soggy with cold grease. I catch a whiff and my stomach tightens, the inside of my mouth starting to water, warning me. I grab the whole thing and run outside with it, reaching the garbage can just in time to be sick, my vomit splashing over the discarded food. When I'm done, I wipe my mouth with my arm and cover the bin with the plank of plywood we keep on top, weighing it down with a concrete block to deter curious stray dogs. Last thing I need is all this mess strewn over the front lawn. As I rinse my hands at the hose, Aunt Patrice's car turns into the driveway. Aunt Patrice keeps it running while Smiley climbs out, unloading her bags. I keep my head down while my cousin heads for the door, hoping I won't be seen.

"Oh, you home," Aunt Patrice calls through the open car window. She rarely uses my name, as if saying *Indira* comes with a fine. I straighten up awkwardly. "Why you wasn't at school this afternoon?"

"Um—I was feeling sick and they tell me I could go," I fumble.

"You had any boys in my house?" she barks.

"What?"

"Don't answer me 'what.' Your ma ain teach you no manners?"

Grammy. Grammy's the one who taught me. "No," I say, then add, "ma'am."

"Better not. I know everything that goes on in this house." She rolls up the window and toots the horn twice as she drives off. Like she just set me straight. Like she gave me fair warning. Like she's said something brand-new. She must have forgotten the first day I was here, when she took care to lay out the rules. *"You have boys in here, you out. You want sleep out like big woman, you out. You come home late, you out. Understand? Your uncle want you here, not me. I ain takin no wildness from you."* But she can't know *everything* that goes on. If that was true, she'd know all about Gary. She'd know what he did to me.

Back inside, I find Smiley in her volleyball uniform, scowling into the fridge. Must be after four, then.

"Hey." She glances back at me. "What happened to all that food Gary bring home?"

I don't answer. I'm not in the mood.

"He text me and say he brought stuff back from breakfast and lunch today."

I dig through my bag for a ginger mint. "I threw it out."

"What you do that for?" she complains, slamming the fridge door shut.

"It smelled off."

Smiley sighs as she reaches for the house phone. "You mad?" When I don't answer, she shuffles through a stack of takeout menus while I collect up papers scattered over the counter and through the living room—brochures, a work schedule, old flyers—and bundle them into a garbage bag. When I come back into the kitchen, Smiley's hanging up the phone. "Come with me, let's go get dinner," she says, by way of an apology.

"From where?"

"Tasty Spot."

Food's the last thing on my mind right now, but even if it wasn't, Churchy's family owns that place, fifteen minutes' walk away. I turn my attention to the sink and start tackling last night's dishes. I'm not interested in seeing anyone from school. Especially him. "I'll stay here," I say.

"What's wrong with you, why you always cleaning? You worse than my mummy."

That's not saying much. Aunt Patrice will dump bags of groceries right on the floor for someone else to put away, eggs and raw meat and all. Shoes stay in a jumble by the front door. Once every couple days, she corrals us to clean the mess and excuses herself to choir practice, to her women's group, to go hail a neighbor. Still, Smiley's words send an ugly shudder straight up my spine.

"Well, I ain nobody's mummy." I dry my hands on the legs of the borrowed pants. "Just trying to help out." I fill up a pot with water, take a bay leaf and a chunk of cinnamon bark from Aunt Patrice's spice cupboard, and toss them in to simmer. The kitchen still reeks of those sweaty clothes.

"What's that for?" Smiley watches from the table.

"For the stink. You don't smell in here?"

Smiley stares at me like I'm from another planet. What's new?

"Never mind."

Smiley and I, we should never get along, let alone be cousins. She's Uncle's child, fully, unlike Gary, who Aunt Patrice had long before they met. But Uncle isn't my real uncle either; one of Grammy's cousins had him young and sent him to live with her and Mamma when he was a little boy. *Nothing new under the sun, Indy,* I can hear Grammy saying. *"You ain the first baby I brought up for somebody."* Technically, Smiley and I are half cousins once removed. But there's no *technically* in Smiley's world. Only that grin. She flashes it now as she holds up something rectangular and compact.

"Sure you don't wanna come?"

"What's that?"

"A wallet."

I snatch it from her and open it up. Credit cards, work ID, license. Gary's face leers out at me from the picture. He must have left it on the chair.

Smiley's grin widens. "What you say somebody treat us to dinner?" She reaches over and slides out one of the fifties stashed at the back, brandishing it like a trophy.

"Why?" I say, handing the whole thing back. It's been weeks since I got one of Grammy's envelopes with a bill or two folded inside. Aunt Patrice will let me have food, but she doesn't give me allowance, especially since Mamma stopped sending money a few months ago too. Even so, I don't want anything to do with Gary's wallet, though I know later I'll feel hungry. But Smiley gets all the spending money she wants from Aunt Patrice; she doesn't even need to take this.

She gives me a mischievous smirk. "Why not? What are big brothers for?"

That's Smiley. When's she ever needed a reason? I gather up my straw bag from the living room, slinging it over my shoulder. "Let's go."

"You should have heard Mr. MacDonald asking about you," Smiley says as we step into the Tasty Spot. Evening news is on the TV in the corner, and there's Churchy behind the counter, stuffing Styrofoam containers into plastic bags and stapling on the receipts.

Churchy glances up at us and stutters out a nervous "H-h-hey."

Us leaving Mariner's Cay the same time, ending up at the same school, has been like having a funhouse mirror following me. Every time I try to forget how it was back home, Churchy is there, throwing back my true reflection as nothing but Doubles, easy Sharice's chip-off-the-old-block daughter. I slide onto a stool while Smiley asks him how long before our order's ready. I don't acknowledge him; I'm still mad about him calling me *Doubles* in the classroom. Of all the times to dig up that name.

"What'd you tell Mr. MacDonald?" I ask as Smiley hoists herself up onto the stool beside me. She swings her feet, pretending to be a preschooler in a big-people chair.

"He ask me what I was doing in his class, why I wasn't in my own classroom. I told him I came to give you a pad, and you went to the nurse's office cause you had cramps, and he didn't ask any more. I say you'd be back to school tomorrow."

"Oh, so everyone think I have my period," I say, pretending to be annoyed. "Thanks." Truth is, I'd give anything to be getting my period, for my biggest worry to be that I ran out of pads at school. I fan myself with my hand, hot in the borrowed clothes from the retreat.

"What's this crap you got on, anyway?" Smiley asks, reading my thoughts.

I play dumb. "What you mean?"

"What happen to your uniform? Or those old-timey skirts you always wear?"

"My uniform? You forget what you do to my blouse?" I bite my lip, regretting my familiar purple skirt left behind, balled up in the retreat's dingy sink. Smiley's still looking at me sideways. She knows there's a secret and she can't wait to sink her teeth into it.

"But these don't look like your clothes. Indy . . . you got a boyfriend?"

"No." My heart's banging against the inside of my chest so loud she must be able to hear it herself. "My regular clothes in the wash, that's all." It's Smiley, I tell myself. She's not going to go rooting through dirty laundry to check my story. "I found these in the back of the closet."

She tilts her head to one side, skeptical. "Whose closet? Gary's?"

Obviously not hers, and I can't say it was from Aunt Patrice's. The clothes are baggy on me, but way too small to be Uncle's. "Yeah," I say, almost choking on the word. I pray she won't ask anything more. *Just leave it alone*, I plead silently.

"Oh." She sucks her teeth. "I thought you had a boy-friend." She must be satisfied, because she turns away to look out the window. "So what you did after you left school?"

Great. More questions. "Rode around on the bus."

"All that time?"

"And went for a walk."

"Since when you's go for walks?" Smiley laughs. Through the little window into the kitchen, I glimpse Churchy hurrying past, a pot in one hand, spoon in the other.

"Hurry up, man, Churchy," I call, dodging Smiley's inquisition.

Churchy pokes his head through the window; he is tall and wiry. The height isn't so bad, but he's too skinny for someone working in a restaurant, like a bald woman trying to sell weave. He wipes his forehead with his sleeve; he's still in his school pants and shirt, a faded apron tied over them. "F-f-five minutes."

"I bet you I could make Churchy give me his cell number," Smiley whispers.

"What you want that for?" I say, but she's already off the stool, ducking under the STAFF ONLY sign and into the kitchen.

"Hey, Churchy, you here by yourself?" she calls from the doorway.

"J-j-j-just f-for a while."

"You want some help?"

She flashes her classic smile, all teeth. Leaning with one hip cocked off to the side, flat chest stuck forward, head flung back. If I tried the same thing, it'd come off obscene. When she does it, though, it's funny, or so people think. Aunt Patrice, shaking her head, can only muster a muttered half-warning. Uncle breaks into a muted chuckle. Even Gary laughs.

The sofa creaks under me, complaining every time I shift around, trying to get comfortable. The bottom sheet won't stay in place. I don't care about that, I've slept on sofas before, and worse. A different creak; door opening. I reach over and snap on the lamp. It's Gary.

"You up too?" He's in loose shorts and a shirt, ready for bed. "Mind if I watch TV?"

I want to ask why he can't watch something in his own room, or sleep, like normal people do after midnight. But it's his house. I just came here. "Um . . . sure."

He sits down on the edge of the sofa, his behind pressing into my feet. Why can't he sit on the other couch? I pull back, and he eases up.

"You sure you don't mind?" he asks, turning on the TV. He settles on a reality show. "Looks pretty good. What you think?" A line of young women in high heels and short dresses stand in obedient formation, posed for a young man whose job it is to pick three to date. "You wanna turn off the lamp? There's a glare on the screen."

I don't know what to do. I don't want to be in here with the light off, but I'm not supposed to sleep in Smiley's room. He stretches over to turn it off himself, his shirt brushing against me. Settles back into the sofa with a sigh, like he's sitting down with a cold drink on a hot day. It doesn't feel right, him and me and the dark and my sheets. On the screen, the young man presents flowers to one of the girls while she simpers, batting her eyelids. I stand up.

"You ain gotta leave for me. I don't have to watch this." He reaches out fast, his fingers wrapped around my wrist, resting there, holding. This shouldn't be happening. I shouldn't let it happen. I have to get away. But there's no Grammy to run to here.

"I goin to the bathroom," I mumble, pulling away. The bathroom seems too many paces away but I get there finally. As I close the door behind me, I stumble into the garbage can. Under the door, I see Aunt Patrice's light flick on. Footsteps, then her voice, clearing her throat, then nothing. I stay in a long time, but when I finally come out, he's gone and the TV is off. The room, as far as things you can put a proper name to, is just as it was before. But something's shifted, tainting the air.

"Indy! You daydreaming, hey?" Smiley elbows my ribs as she climbs back onto her stool. "Man, he harder to break than I thought. I had to tell him you needed it to talk about homework. I almost couldn't get it."

My tongue feels like a slug in my mouth. "Get what?"

"The number." She rolls her eyes, swinging her legs, a kid again. Lucky for me, the way I feel isn't showing, or she's too caught up in herself to notice. Churchy finally bustles out of the kitchen with our two containers of food. "Doubles, you ain ga say hi?" she says, looking at him. "Churchy, see how stuck-up she is? She don't even talk to people outside school."

"It r-r-ready." He brushes aside her flirty tone like petals falling in his face, pretty but of no real interest.

"Let's see," Smiley says. "What you got for us again?" She's trying to make him talk, so he'll have to stutter his way through another sentence, and another. If it was me, I'd tell her to check it her damn self, but Churchy opens each container to show us.

"One c-c-curry ch-ch-chicken and w-w-white rice."

"Mmmm," Smiley groans, leaning forward, mimicking the women on the late-night TV shows. "What else?"

"F-f-f-f."

"Ooooh. *F-f-f-f-f* smells so good." She looks over at me, giggling. "Hey, Indy? Can't wait to put that in my mouth."

"Stop being so stupid," I tell her, then turn to him. "It's fine, Churchy."

"F-f-f. F-f-f-fried f-f-f-fish."

"That's a lotta effs," Smiley says. I close up the food containers, shoving them into the bag. Churchy's head is down as he pretends to check the register.

"You made it yourself? With your own two strong hands?"

"Y-your bill come to t-t-twenty-one-seventy-five."

"Twenty-one-seventy-five?" Smiley snaps out of her ridiculous act as she pulls out the fifty. "How you get that uneven number?"

"Th-thirteen for yours." He points to the bottom container, then points at me. "H-h-hers is less."

"Why?" Smiley protests, as if she's paying for it, and not Gary.

"C-c-classmate's special." Churchy looks down at the register, counting out the change. He slides a ten, three fives, a few ones, and a perfectly arranged stack of coins over to her.

"Oh, I see," she says knowingly, gathering up the money. "Classmate's *special*."

"Let's go." I grab her by the arm. I'm squeezing so hard I can feel my fingers pressing deep into her flesh.

"Bye, loverboy!" Smiley calls as I drag her out the door, her giggles intensifying as we get outside. "Poor Churchy. Ah my. No wonder he wouldn't even look at me. He got the hots for you."

"What you had to bother him for?" I ask her as we step out onto the road. It's twilight now, darkness closing in fast.

"You bruise me," she complains, pretend-sulking as she rubs her arm. Even in the faint light, I can see the red imprints my fingers have left. I should feel guilty. Instead,

I'm furious. I hate listening to her squeak and moan. I've heard that before, back in Mariner's, those fake noises made for attention. *A strange house, in a room full of kids I barely know, some snoring. Squeak of the mattress springs on the other side of the wall. And noises. Shut my eyes, pretend I don't hear. In the morning, the older boys say, "Morning, Sharice," to Mamma, to show she's not worth being called Ms. Ferguson. "How you sleep last night?" One of them utters a mocking groan before their dad throws a few unaimed slaps and mutters something about respect. Mamma's voice is hard and proud as she answers. "Just fine. Like a big old happy baby."*

"What you so sour for? I was only playing, Churchy know that," Smiley says breezily, turning down a path that cuts between two houses.

"Where you going?" I call after her.

"Hurry up, this way faster." Her voice is muffled by the bush and vine on either side. I hesitate, then step through the narrow opening, the food bag bumping against my legs. A mosquito whines in my ear.

"I'm gonna kill you," I call ahead, speeding up. "Where you is?"

"Right here. Hurry up." Her voice is coming from somewhere over to the left. I take a few more quick steps and falter my way out onto our street.

"Smiley?" I don't see her anywhere. The road is empty; no one could have taken her that quick, but panic doesn't wait for logic. "Smiley?" I call again, fighting to catch my breath.

"Gotcha!" she shouts, jumping out from behind a parked car, her laugh ringing through the air. I push past her and start walking toward the house. "What, you can't take a joke?" she calls behind me.

It's not funny. It's not even scary. It's nothing, a stupid prank from a stupid kid. She's only playing. So why's my heart trying to hammer its way out of my chest? Why are my palms so slick with sweat I can hardly hold on to the bag of food?

A streetlight blinks on and I look back to check that the footsteps behind me are Cecile's. Even though it's only the two of us on the road, I pick up the pace, hurrying away from my cousin, and her joy that nothing can touch. From the jokes she can find funny and I can't, the lightness that comes from being teased for nothing worse than a goofy smile. From that feeling I get sometimes, being around her. Envy. For what I have to carry while she swings her arms, hands free.

3

MARINER'S. MUSIC BLARING, VOICES raised. *Laughter somewhere, and bottles clinking. Me, hidden in the shadow of the trees, as far from it as I can get without leaving. Watching this man, not a monster, just an ordinary man, lean into Mamma until the space between them disappears. Her legs are wobbly; the drink in her hand spills onto the grass, the party swallowing up its splash.*

It's Avery Jones, who's a plumber, sometimes, who says good morning if Grammy and I pass him on the street. Eyes that squinch up, crinkled and happy, when he smiles, large hands I've seen clamp down on his little brother's shoulder, not rough, but firm, when he's been caught smoking in the back of the graveyard. Those same eyes, now hungry, piggy. Those same fleshy hands groping Mamma while she pretends to push him away, her laugh stretched out like a telephone wire. "Trust me, your ma know what she's doing," Grammy said once. "Letting all these men around her." I knew, even then, at ten years old, that Grammy didn't really mean "around her," but something else, something murkier, something harder to put into words.

I see Mamma's head bobbing and lolling, liquor heavy, her neck loose. And that laugh. Too high to be giddy, too loud to be straight, too silly to be sure. Right before Avery Jones carries her around the back of the house, where I don't dare follow, she teeters toward the shadows where I hide.

"That's you, baby?" Her words pile up, one on top of the other. "I know that's you."

"I right here," Avery Jones says, an arm around her waist. "What you lookin at? You see ghost in the bush, ay?" As he leads her off, I swear she looks straight at me, her eyes drained and empty.

I stare at myself in the bathroom mirror, shirt pulled against my body, pants hanging low on my hips. The ruined bra is knotted so tight it digs into my sides, but my chest still droops. "That's how you's carry yourself?" Grammy would say. "That's how I look now," I imagine myself answering. "You let Mamma send me away and this what happen." For a moment, I let my gaze drop to my midsection. Even with my clothes on, I'm reaching the stage where I can't just pass for plump. I remember the one thing Grammy told me. *Don't let no one take advantage of you.* If she meant it, how could she go and give me that book? Was she trying to warn me? Or did she know what I would become?

I turn away from my reflection as I take off the shirt and bra. To look my big, bare self in the eye would make it feel too true. I reach for the roll of gray duct tape I've brought in with me and set it down on the counter. I wrap strips of it around each end of the bra's back straps so the broken hooks can't cut into me. Pull it back on and take one more strip, wrap it around the whole bottom of the bra. Then I pull the shirt over my head.

Okay. That looks better. My belly is still suspiciously large, if you look close, but my chest, at least, is in the right place. Sort of.

The tape gives with an abrupt popping sound. My life can't even be held in place with *duct tape*. The tape that holds *anything*.

I'm desperate. That's the only reason I do it. If I could call Grammy, I would, but she's never had a phone. Crouching down in the bathtub, a towel tented over my head to keep the sound in, I hammer out Mamma's number on the cell phone. My fingers are clumsy and numb. The number is the one she had when I came to Nassau, and by now it's probably changed. Ring. *Come on.* Ring. Pause, then somebody hears my prayer and there's the familiar trill over the crackly line.

"Who's this?"

I haven't heard her voice in months. The time evaporates instantly, and I'm right back there in the next room, crouched in a quiet spot while the party rages. I imagine her laughter billowing, limbs moving, smile blooming, till she gets too drunk and starts to crumple.

"Mamma, this me."

"Who?"

"You only got one child."

She laughs ridiculously, amused by something I can't see. Her voice is too sweet, like overripe guavas hitting cement. "Indy!" She says my name as though she's just discovered it, proud of excavating this artifact. "You bein good? You ain giving your auntie no problems, ay?"

I know right then this call was a mistake, worse than trying to duct-tape my life back together. She's past drunk. But I'm in it now, and I need someone, *really* need someone who might get it, so I keep going anyway.

"Where you is?" I ask.

There's a crash in the background. "Whoops!" She giggles. "I at the house, baby, but I lil busy now. We got company!"

I don't know which house she means. When I left, it was a run-down duplex, her and the pimply-faced man in the one bedroom, me on the sofa out front. By now, it could be some lean-to with four kids in the other room, or the master suite of somebody working in Nassau or Miami who sneaks away from his wife one weekend every two months. I want Grammy. I want to tell her. I want her to know, and want her to tell me what to do. I'm not scared of whether she'll be sad or angry, of the disappointment in her voice. Having her know what happened wouldn't be the worst thing, if I could have a person who knows me, a person who isn't drunk, who'll tell me it'll be okay, who'll help me figure out what to do.

"Mamma, how's Grammy?" The question is hollow, a sucked-out chicken bone. Right now, it's almost implausible that Grammy, in her evening housecoat and a soft-worn head-scarf, glasses on and a book in her lap, could exist in the same universe as Mamma, with the sloshing drink cups and the curls of smoke and the abandoned bottles of rum.

"You call for me, or you call for your grammy? Don't matter, I know you love her more. You ain got time for your old drunk ma. Right?"

I know what that means; they aren't speaking and Mamma has no idea how she is. "I called for you."

"Look here, tell your auntie hold on. I ga send something down there for you soon. I so broke right now," Mamma slurs. A man's voice mutters something. "Stop that, baby," she tells him, but her voice is thick with invitation. "This my daughter on the phone. Yes I did tell you I had a daughter."

The bathroom doorknob rattles.

"Hey, what you doing in there?" Smiley calls from the hallway.

"Hold on," I shout back. I can hear whoever's messing with Mamma, a man with a low voice. Then the line crackles, or she drops her phone, or both.

"I gotta pee!" Smiley shouts.

"Well, use Aunt Patrice bathroom!" I shout back.

"We lil busy, baby. You wanna call me later?"

"You mean me?" I whisper into the phone. That's the thing with Mamma. To her, everybody's "baby."

"Indy, open the door, man!" Smiley's voice pitches to a whine. "Hurry up, I about to pee my pants."

Mamma laughs at some joke I can't hear. Smiley's fist is on the door now, while she complains to Aunt Patrice that I'm hogging the bathroom. The music's louder. Another laugh on the line. So much noise and no one hearing me. I don't know why I say it. Maybe because Mamma's been there, she *is* there, and my saying it won't be letting her down. Maybe because she'll know what to do. Maybe just so the call won't be a waste.

"Mamma, wait," I whisper. "I'm pregnant."

"Indy!" Smiley pummels the door, shaking it so hard it threatens to burst loose. Aunt Patrice's voice booms in, loud and firm.

"Indira, hurry up, you don't own the toilet in there. You know you don't pay no bills in this house."

"Mamma. You hear me?" I whisper again.

In the pause that follows, everything seems to stop. Smiley and Aunt Patrice's talking, the song on the other end of the phone line, the party's din, the murmuring man, they all fade away. Mamma's words come to me, crisp as 6 a.m. air.

"Do what you gotta do."

The line goes dead or she hangs up or my two dollars' worth of minutes run out. I climb out of the tub, and the distance between where I stand, with my slightly damp feet, and the door seems so far. I put down the towel and the phone. I pick up the roll of duct tape, staring at it. It's too weak. Like me.

The doorknob shudders and, with a pop, clicks unlocked and the door opens.

"I thought you was dead in here or something." Smiley stands, victorious, a bobby pin in one hand. "Hurry up, I gotta pee." She squeezes in past me. "What, you wanna stay for the show?"

I half-trip out into the hall, carrying the duct tape and phone with me. No sign of Aunt Patrice—I guess she found something better to do than preside over a bathroom dispute. There's nowhere to go in this place, no space of my own. My legs carry me through the kitchen, out the door, to the back-yard. I climb up into the scarlet plum tree, its bark rough against my hands and feet. I sit on the ledge where its biggest limbs connect to the trunk. From here, I see the bathroom window, a small square of light. Smiley sure is taking her time. What does she need to spend so long in there for, anyway? Who does she need privacy to call? What secrets does she have to tape closed?

"This is it!" Smiley squeaks as we pull up to the house. I gawk at it through the car window; Grammy didn't tell me they lived in a mansion. Later, I'll realize it's only average, an ordinary bungalow in a regular neighborhood. But right now, all I can think is that Grammy's house could fit in the front yard, easy. Smiley leads me in and shows me the kitchen, where half-unpacked grocery bags are scattered on the floor like a bad child's toys. Even so, there's room to do jumping jacks in there, if you wanted. The oven is large, the fridge shiny and new. In the living room are two wide sofas and an armchair, a coffee table crowded with magazines, and a muted TV, images flashing frantically across the screen. Grammy doesn't have a TV, but if she did, she'd turn it off when we went out. We pass the master bedroom.

"Mummy don't like people in there, but I'll show you later," Smiley whispers, taking me to her room next. It's large and bright, a white double bed piled high with pillows. "I wish you could sleep in here," she says, "but Mummy say she want you in your own space."

Last, Smiley shows me where I'm to stay. The bedroom is painted gray, the curtains drawn. Whoever used to sleep here went away and left everything in its place. The closet is half open, crammed with jeans and collared shirts. On one wall, a poster of a rapper half-scowls and half-leers at me. From the bureau's top drawer, a balled-up tube sock peers out.

"Gary used to sleep here. My brother," she says, but from the way things look, Gary might walk through the door any-time, flop down on the bed, and demand to know what I'm doing in his room. Smiley perches on the bed to watch me unpack Grammy's straw bag. "How come you don't have more stuff?" She sounds surprised; she wouldn't be if she knew Mamma, knew about the faded hand-me-downs rounded up and packed into a trash bag. The look on Aunt Patrice's face when she saw my empty hands was bad enough. Imagine if I'd shown up looking like garbage day.

"I have enough," I say, and hope it's true. I lift the fold of fabric Grammy used to cover the bag's contents. Underneath is a spray of casuarina pine needles, still supple and green, to keep bugs away, and a neatly folded sheet, in case Aunt Patrice doesn't believe in clean linens, I guess.

"You bring twigs? What for?" Smiley asks as I pull the sheet away and the smell of home is released; the scent of Grammy's trusty Pears soap, and the saltiness that comes from living near the sea. While Smiley chatters, I pull out *seven handmade skirts, calf-length and elastic-waisted, in seven shades of Androsia: Atlantic blue and ripe-fruit purple, fearless red, June poinciana leaf green, the whole rainbow, each in its own deep, strong color, like Grammy went to the birthplace of every hue and drew out its navel string for thread. Nested in between the skirts are bags of homemade sweets: pink-and-white squares of coconut candy, brick-hard peanut and benny cakes, pineapple tart still soft from baking. Under those are panties, the tags still on, and new bras. Two of the bras are my size, and the third is a little bigger. Smiley snatches the larger one up.*

"You's wear a size 36DD?" She nearly chokes on a mouthful of tart.

Thirty-six D, though I'm not about to tell her that. I snatch it out of her hand and put it on the bed beside me.

"Grammy always buy a size up, in case I grow," I explain. Smiley snickers; clearly, she doesn't have this problem. I keep unpacking: five new toothbrushes, a few sticks of deodorant, six packs of pads, eight soaps, and the mysterious book she tucked in there, shrouded in fabric. The book isn't big; only long as my hand, and three fingers thick. I bring it to my nose and breathe in Grammy.

"What's that?"

"Just something from home."

Smiley screws up her face and goes back to rummaging

through the clothes. She must say something funny because she keeps laughing, but I don't hear. All I can think of is Grammy and that book and how I'd give anything to be in her kitchen, surrounded by the scent of vinegar and thyme leaves and lime, the brisk zing of the house on cleaning day. I can't wait. I yank off the string and pull the cloth away. The book falls onto my lap, cover side up. The Pregnancy Book. *The title stares me in the face, accusingly. I've never seen this book in my life, though it's worn so hard it has to be older than me. I turn it over quickly, hoping my cousin hasn't seen, wishing I'd never unwrapped it.*

Smiley's already distracted by something more amusing; she pops one of my bras onto her head like a bonnet. "Hey, you don't need no grocery bags when you go shopping. Look!" She takes another bra and tucks the sweets into the cup, slinging the hooked strap over her shoulder. It's silly and childish and it's exactly what I need. Her laughter spreads, taking up space in that strange room, swallowing me.

But later, after Smiley leaves, I climb into the closet and shove the book way down deep, at the back. I've already seen how Aunt Patrice looks at me sideways, like a bit of dust in the corner of a room. It won't matter that I never had a boyfriend, never kissed anyone, and never plan to. I know if she finds that book, finds any reason to suspect me of acting up, she'll sweep me right out.

I look up and see that the tree is bearing heavily. In daylight, the fruit will be half green, starting to blush purple and red. In the dark, all I can see is the silhouette of those knobby plums, the branches bare and leafless around them. I slide the roll of duct tape from around my wrist. Balancing on the tree's strong limbs, I hoist up my shirt. No one to see, only the sound of the TV, faint, from inside, and the clatter of the next-door neighbor cooking. I feel for the ridge where the tape begins. Pull out a long strip. Again, I wrap it around the bottom edge of the bra, under my chest, around my ribs. Again. Again. This time, it's holding. I'll have to sleep in it, the stickiness against my skin all through the night. When I take it off to shower in the morning, it will sting, a giant Band-Aid you can't rip away fast. I'll just have to tape it right back on. Mamma's voice plays in my head, bored and flat. *Do what you gotta do.*

4

I CAN ONLY STARE at the biology test for so long before flipping the paper over and putting my pen down. My head hurts, my mouth tastes of breakfast coming up the wrong way, and I don't know any of the answers. I push my chair back, making the legs squeak against the tiled floor. Mr. MacDonald looks at me, then at the inverted paper.

"I'm done."

He glances back at the clock. Forty minutes to go. "You know this is a big part of your grade," he says, but I'm already heading for the back of the classroom, retrieving the straw bag from among the jumble of backpacks and totes. Equation for photosynthesis? I've got duct tape half stuck to my bra and half stuck to my skin. The same blouse that shamed me is patched up with mismatched buttons that can't change the fact that it's too tight. And this morning when I reached down and touched my stomach, I swear it was even bigger than it was last night. Equate *that*.

Outside, the air feels humid and dank. Bag over my shoulder, I head for the bathroom. I lock myself in one of the stalls, flipping the toilet cover closed and sitting down. The bathroom is empty, and blissfully quiet. I have time to kill before three. Smiley doesn't have volleyball practice today, and Aunt Patrice isn't picking us up; we'll head home on the bus together. I pull Grammy's book out of the bag. It opens to a section in "Signs and Symptoms" that's all about morning sickness, which has got to be the most ridiculous name ever, because I puke at all times of the day. *Many women find a few crackers first thing in the morning help reduce nausea,* the book says. In the margin, Grammy's scrawled *Ginger biscuits* and underlined the words three times. Too bad I didn't see that tip right after lunch. I thumb forward to "Expanding Horizons." Grammy's filled half a page with her sloping handwriting. I hunker down, immersing myself in her words:

I was always thin, so I couldn't hide past three months, but some of my friends went four, five, even six months before anybody knew. My auntie Doreen was two thirds of the way through before she even told her husband. She waited until the day before he was to go out to sea and dropped it into conversation, over chicken souse and Johnny cake. "You want hot pepper? You need some lime? You mind another child?"

Poor man. He nearly had a heart attack. She was older, and he already had white hair, and he thought she had seen the change. Of course, as my mother used to say, long as a man and a woman get together, anything can happen.

The main bathroom door bursts open and an army of girls rumble in, erasing the scene Grammy's words painted, making those big-bellied women disappear. The noise shouldn't surprise me—it's the girls' bathroom, not My Secret Pregnant Place of Refuge—but I jump up anyway, the book falling out of my hands. Before I can stop it, it slides out from under the stall's door.

"What's that?"

"Somebody drop a book."

Through the space between the wall and the door, I see a girl bend to pick it up.

"Man, hide that, ain nobody want see no book now," someone says. "I just finish that biology test."

The girl who picked it up tosses it on the counter. "I was so glad when Doubles get up. I didn't want to be the first to leave."

I recognize Brenda, short and nosey; she glances down at the book as she reaches for a piece of paper towel. "Hey, look at this!" She dries her hands off on her skirt and picks the book up, brandishing it like an accusation. "*Pregnancy Book?*"

There's a series of *ooohs* and gasps.

"Let's hear it, man! Who been knocking boots?"

"Bang bang!" someone jokes.

"Ain mine!"

"Girl, don't bring that round me!"

Brenda's peering at my closed door. "Hey, somebody in here."

"Who?"

"I bet you whoever in there, that's hers."

"Hello? Hey, this belong to you?"

"That's Raisin Legs?"

"Don't be stupid, she don't have no bunch of scars on her. That's Raquel?"

"Raquel still in the classroom. Tiny?"

Someone bends down, peering under the door. "Those ankles look tiny to you?"

The girls draw together, making a single, curious body. My head spins. I can't breathe. I back up as far as I can.

"See the shoes, you could tell by the shoes."

"That's Tamika, man."

"Hello, I standin right here. Plus I don't wear black socks."

"And you ain pregnant!"

"Yeah, that too!"

Hands on the outside of the door, rattling it. The stall is shrinking by the second.

"Who it is, man? You think she pregnant for real?"

"Who you know is read pregnancy books unless they pregnant?"

"Maybe she in there trying to take the pregnancy test right now."

The voices start to sound farther away, as if some invisible padding is suffocating me. There's only one way out, and it's through the wall of girls crowded around that door, through the voices and the hands and the questions and speculations and conclusions. I have to escape. But if I open that door, my secret comes out with me.

"Hello? Hello?" Someone bangs on the door. An eye appears, shoved right up against the gap.

"You could see?"

"No. Hello?"

I can't stay in here forever; someone's gonna guess right, or look under the door and see it's me. Why prolong the torture? I take the straw bag by its worn straps, fling the door open, and make a break for it.

The cluster of girls scatters, shrieking as I barrel through them. There's a hollow sound, wood slamming against bone, and a distant "Oww!" Someone cries, "That's Doubles!" and someone else asks, "Her?" I don't stop moving—not till I'm outside.

But it still isn't over. They rush out after me, clustering

like ants around a drop of water. "What wrong with you? You hurt Samara, ya know! Got her right in the head with that door." A sea of different voices all merge into one. My head feels light enough to float right off my body.

"Ladies?" A stern voice breaks through everything. Ms. Wilson, the school counselor. The chatter is silenced momentarily before, like a flock of birds, it changes direction and takes flight again.

"Ms. Wilson, she gone crazy."

"She was in the stall, and she come out and start swinging—"

"And she have this book—"

"No, that ain true, we was by the door and when she come out—"

"She mean to do that—"

"What's that noise?" Ms. Wilson cuts them all off, tilting her head toward the bathroom. Someone's still in there, wailing like they're getting murdered.

"That's Samara—"

"That's what we tryin to tell you—"

"She smack Samara in her head—"

I didn't smack anyone, and if I did, it wasn't on purpose, I want to say, but all I can do is lean against the closest wall, pulling in air.

"Samara's hurt? Show me." Ms. Wilson starts striding into

the bathroom, then glances back at me. "You wait right there, Indira," she calls over her shoulder. "Don't move."

"Come see!" someone says, urging her into the bathroom. Ms. Wilson returns a minute later, leading Samara out.

"Tamika, you take Samara to the nurse," Ms. Wilson says. "The rest of you, get back to class."

"But we had a test and we done—"

"Then wait quietly in the library until time to go home. Almost half an hour left in the day." Ms. Wilson watches Samara retreat down the hall, leaning on Tamika's shoulder as though she may never walk unassisted again. Reluctantly, the other girls start to follow.

Ms. Wilson turns to me, peering over the top of her ancient plastic glasses. "Indira? Why would you hit her?"

"It was an accident," I mutter. "They was all outside the stall."

Ms. Wilson frowns at me. "Why were they outside your stall?"

"I—I—sorry." My head's starting to spin.

"Indira? You don't look good."

"I'm fine," I say. My tongue, my voice, my body all seem to belong to someone else, but I force myself to go on. I can't get sent to the nurse's office. "I didn't hit her, she was just in the way."

"Are you hurt?"

"No, ma'am."

"And do I need to bring Samara in to discuss this fight?"

"It wasn't a fight." I scramble for clear thoughts. "It was a mistake, I hit her with the door when I opened it, is all. I didn't mean to. I'm sorry."

Ms. Wilson weighs my words for a moment, then nods. "You know we don't tolerate fighting."

"It wasn't a fight."

"I'm going to let you off with a warning, and you can write an apology letter to give to Samara tomorrow," she says, and I almost melt with relief. Then she adds, "Someone needs to pick you up, though, and I want to make sure you and Samara are separated for the rest of the day. Go on to my office, you can wait there."

What choice do I have? As I walk away, I feel a tap on my shoulder and turn to look. Brenda holds something out to me.

"I ain mean to get you in trouble," she says. It's the book. She holds it so the cover faces down, its title hidden from view. I take it, and before I can say anything, she's turned away, running to rejoin her friends. I shove the book deep in the straw bag and walk to the office. I should be thankful that no one said that word to Ms. Wilson: *pregnant*. Even so, the talk will spread between them, and out into the whole school from there. But before I can even worry about that, I have a bigger problem to face: who's coming for me.

Aunt Patrice is at work. Uncle is away this whole week. Only one person would answer the home phone now.

"Some girls just can't stay out of trouble." Gary steps into Ms. Wilson's office, his teeth displayed in a wide grin.

"Gary Johnson!" She exclaims his name like a five-foot-eight-inch birthday present just waltzed in. It's been eleven years since he graduated, but she still springs up out of her chair and rushes from behind her desk to hug him.

"Ms. Wilson! Still young and beautiful as ever," he croons as she lets him go. I want to throw up.

"What are you doing these days?" She eyes his chef's jacket approvingly. "Still at the hotel, I see."

"Obviously," I mutter, bending over to fiddle with my shoe buckle so I don't have to watch this charade.

"So you came to get Indira here?"

"Yes, ma'am. Gotta help out the family." I can hear the fake smile in his voice.

"I know your parents appreciate it."

I feel him looking at me again and stay down, pretending to straighten out my socks.

"Is there something in your shoe, Ms. Ferguson?"

I stand up, imagining my shoe bouncing off the panes of Ms. Wilson's owlish glasses. "No."

"Give your mother and father my regards, Gary," Ms.

Wilson says, holding the door open. "Indira, I trust tomorrow will be a new day. And don't forget that letter."

"Yes, Ms. Wilson," I say, gritting my teeth as I follow Gary out into the hall. He walks out to the parking lot ahead of me so no one has to think we even know each other. Fine by me.

"You crave trouble like a fatty crave ice cream, ay?" Gary unlocks his truck's door and takes his time getting in before he leans over to open the passenger side.

I bite my tongue as I sit down and slam the door shut. He never misses a chance to wash, polish, and buff this stupid thing. I wish I could scour it with steel wool. Maybe shine it up with a couple concrete blocks, for good measure. I see him cut his eye at me as he starts the truck up, silent as we drive up to the gate. The security guard is chatting up the cleaning lady again. Without even looking, he waves Gary through.

"Getting sent to the office during your exams. Sharice must be so proud." Gary swerves out of the school yard and onto the road. "Before you know it, you ga be following right in her footsteps."

Nothing. Just pretend he's not here. Pretend I'm not here. Keep my mouth shut, and when we get back to the house, find someplace to walk to. I'm not going inside by myself with him. And if he so much as looks at me wrong, I'll get right out of the truck and walk the rest of the way. Daylight makes me bold.

"Hey, Doubles? That's what they's call you, right?"

I switch the radio on and flip through the stations, stopping at a shrill, grating song being belted out by a girl who sounds airbrushed and chipmunked. Her voice is a chunk of bubble gum, too sweet, too sticky, too pink. I crank the volume up.

"You forget whose car you ridin in, hey?" Gary's voice pitches, a crack in his veneer of pleasantness. He wrenches the radio sound down, reducing the girl's voice to an insect buzz. I want to piss him off. Want him to be annoyed. The truck tears down the far end of Main Street, where homes are set farther back from the road and businesses are all but extinct. He should be turning off toward the house soon.

And then we've passed the street. Is he taking a different way?

"Where we going?" The truck's speeding up. Houses are sparse now, and petering to nothing but bush. No other cars anywhere. An image flashes in my head: his truck, parked by the water. His hands on me and daylight no savior; I could scream for days and no one would hear.

"Let me out." The words come out snagged, as if the inside of my throat is barbed.

Gary swings down a hidden side street, turns so fast I'm slammed up against the door. "Take it easy." His voice is even. The truck slows, but we're still moving. We pass one half-built house, then nothing. The road is potholed. Up ahead it thins to a dirt track, then curves and disappears into more bush, dense and choked in vines. He rests a hand on my leg. Heavy, up high.

"Let me out!"

"I know you miss me." Voice syrup, smothering and fake-sweet. "I know you miss our times. Been a while." Slowing more. "I can't come see you in the night when you all holed up in Smiley's room. What happen, you too good for the sofa? Hey?"

"Leave me alone!" I push his hand away hard and he swerves, then recovers, steering straight again. His eyes are briefly on the road as he grabs out at me. He just misses my arm. I know he was reaching for something else.

"I don't know why you playing cute." He looks over. "You know you like that."

I see dust up ahead first, then a white jeep coming our way, bumper stickers slapped on the hood like tattoos. He is looking over at me again, hand back on my leg, pressing down, eyes on my chest. "You more like your ma than I thought. Only you ain all used up. Still nice and fresh."

I get ahold of the wheel, wrenching it to the right; the truck lurches across the road into the jeep's path, turning sideways, hurtling toward bush and tree trunk ahead. Gary slams on the brakes so hard I jerk forward, and there are scraping sounds, twigs and branches clawing at the front hood, the windows and sides. I wrestle the door open against the leaves, running hard for the jeep. "Stop! Stop!" It's pulling over. "I . . . help me." Panting, fingers fumbling at the passenger door's handle—thank God it's unlocked—and then I'm jumping in, slamming the door shut before I even look at the driver. "Go! Go!" I shout into the face behind the wheel. Startled eyes, mouth an O of surprise, thick dreadlocks, hands raised as if he thinks I might try to rob him.

"Hey, hey, take it easy. Y'all had an accident?" He peers into my face; I've seen him before, can't think where, won't stop to ask.

"Just drive!"

"Hold on." The driver gets out, walking over to the truck. Why doesn't he understand? I could run, except my legs are jelly and I can't seem to move. The driver's pushing his way through the overgrowth, heading for Gary. Idiot. "Chief, you all right?" He pokes his head between the greenery, right into the truck's open door. "You need a tow or something?"

"Don't let him—" I gasp. Everything's closing in, the air fighting me. I put my head against the dash. There's a *ding, ding, ding*; he's left the keys in the ignition. *Drive*, I think. *Just climb over and drive.* Ringing in my ears. My chest is going to explode. "Don't let him—"

"Everything cool, boss," I hear the jeep's driver say,

through a fog. I bring my head up to see Gary fling his truck into reverse, pulling back onto the road and spinning around. He peels off, wheels throwing gravel into the air. I can still feel the imprint of his fingers searing into my leg. "You okay?" the guy asks, his voice closer. The jeep jostles as he gets back in.

I drag air into my lungs. "My chest."

"It's okay, you could relax. Whoever that was, he's gone. Just me and my gardening stuff, and my bougainvillea, and we ain out to bother nobody." He glances into the backseat, and I look too. A lawn mower, shovel, spades, a big pot with a half-wilted plant. Behind his seat, a machete. Cutlass Guy.

"Hey, it's you!" he exclaims, recognizing me at the same time. "Listen, take it easy. You ain dyin, I promise. Keep your mouth closed and breathe through your nose. Deep breaths. Ain no big thing. Like this."

I can't get what he's saying, what he wants me to copy. I close my eyes, willing my heart to stop.

"Good, just keep going, it'll pass," he continues, even though I can't be doing anything right. "Don't worry. It'll pass, okay? Ain nobody here to hurt you. We go way back, remember?"

"Cutlass Guy," I wheeze.

"Ah, there you go." He laughs, an easy laugh, a laugh meant to make me feel at ease too. "I didn't introduce myself the other day. I'm Dion. Remember, from the retreat? But yeah, I normally have a cutlass with me. Can't keep those grounds looking good without it, right?" He starts the jeep up, pulling forward slowly. "You keep breathing, okay? That guy do you something? You know him? You want me call the police? Who he is?"

His questions, too fast to answer even if I had breath to do it, soothe me and give me something else to focus on. Gary's gone. It's okay. For now, it's okay. I reach down and realize something's missing. My bag. It's still in Gary's truck.

"Let me drive down to the retreat. It's a couple minutes away; you could sit and catch yourself." The jeep follows the road's curve, pausing at the same gate I left by, that day. It's closed this time; he hops out, swinging it open. We pull under an aged concrete arch and down a driveway that might have been paved before Independence. Wild grass and trees, short and stocky, tall and wide. He parks the jeep under a shady almond tree. "You doin better? You breathin, at least."

"Thanks." I get out. The earth feels unsteady under my feet. "I'm fine. I better go."

"Oh, no, no, you ain goin nowhere," he says. "Come in the office and sit down." He leads me over to the same building that angry woman was painting. The job is done now, the wall restored to a cheery, even cream. An overgrown hibiscus spills over near the doorway. A potcake dog, lounging in the shade of an out-of-bloom bougainvillea, yawns as we pass.

"Is the owner here?"

"Joe?" Dion nods, clumping up the stairs, lead-footed even in flip-flops. "She's always here. I think she's teaching a class now. Trust me, though, she ain worrying about you."

"What did you come here for, then?" A woman's voice reverberates from inside the office. Joe. Guess she's not in class after all. "You wanna come in and get paid to do nothing?" she continues. "You think that's how this ga work? Get out!"

I stop at the foot of the stairs. Dion shakes his head. "Oh boy. She on the warpath today." He catches sight of me and chuckles. "Don't worry about Joe," he says. "She only carry on that way if she has a reason."

The same girl I saw sweeping barges out of the office, nearly knocking both of us down.

"That woman worse than the devil," she barks at Dion as she passes us. "Not enough yoga in this world to help her."

"Don't let the gate hit you on the way out!" Joe yells after her from the doorway. "Absolutely incompetent," she adds, almost as loudly. She sees me and her scowl deepens. "What? Now you back?" She tilts her head to one side, assessing me. "You sneaking in again? Or you decided to use the entrance this time? Or are you here to do yoga dressed in school uniform?"

"*I* brought her here to use the phone," Dion says mildly.

"Better not be a long-distance call."

Dion brushes past her. "She had a problem up the road, some crazy guy in a truck. So it could be a call to the moon, if that's what she needs."

Joe's frown tells me she wants to say more, but in an instant, Dion's transformed from docile beach hippie to infuriated big brother, and Joe doesn't seem to want to deal with that. "Fine," she concedes. "But I'm not in the mood for no more trouble today." She thumps down the steps and marches down one of the pathways. I feel sorry for any class she's supposed to teach.

"You can come," Dion says from inside. I venture up and into the office. He gestures at the cordless phone on a cluttered desk and turns to a bookshelf, pretending to study the titles. It's his way of trying to give me privacy, I guess, without leaving me alone. "Joe's all right," he assures me, sliding a thick book off a shelf. "Call whoever you need."

I stare at the receiver. Who I need is Grammy, but she doesn't have a phone. The only way I used to get her was through Mamma, but I can't bear the thought of that voice again, all loose and free, only tightening to say those words. *Do what you gotta do.*

"You need a directory?" Dion looks up from his book.

"It's okay." I pick up the phone, cradling it to my chest,

hope it might quell the fluttering in there. If I call Smiley, I'll have to explain what happened at school, if she hasn't heard it for herself by now. I put the phone up to my ear; I have to dial some number. If I call the house, there's a chance Gary could pick up, if he's somehow made it back already. I call my cell's number and listen to it ring six times before the voice mail kicks in. "No one home," I say, hanging up.

"And nobody else you could call?" Dion sets the book down, worried.

"Not really." I head for the doorway. "Thanks."

"Hey, hey, hold on. I can't let you leave yet. Who was that back there?"

"Nobody."

"That wasn't nobody."

"Just my cousin."

"That's how your cousin carries on all the time?"

"He have a temper, is all."

"But how y'all end up in the bush? I almost hit you, good thing I was paying attention. And if that had been up closer by the curve . . . Where y'all was goin, anyway?"

"I guess he got lost." Why am I covering for him? I pass my hand over the sore spot on my leg, pretending to smooth a pleat on my skirt.

"Pretty hard to get lost. Ain nothin else down this road except us and the beach. You sure you okay?" Dion looks at me earnestly, with a truth-getting stare. A Grammy stare.

Six months before I leave Mariner's, Mamma and I are staying on the other side of the island, in a cramped apartment above a restaurant-bar that stays open all night. Mamma's working downstairs to pay for the rent. Grammy's forbidden me to go down there at all. Forbidden me to talk to anyone when I leave for school, when I come home in the afternoon. Down the rickety stairs, then up, no looking, no chitchat, no smiles. "Morning, afternoon, that's it. Not even good evening, cause you ain ga be out that kinda time." Gladys, who tends bar, must have told Grammy about the boyfriends Mamma's started bringing up some nights. I sleep on the sofa, hard and stained, and Mamma closes the bedroom door, pretending that creates privacy. With the shudder of the music from downstairs, the rise and fall of voices, I figure no one can hear the noises coming from Mamma's room. No one except me.

One night when I wake up, I tiptoe to the bathroom, light as I can. Someone stands blocking the bathroom doorway. A new boyfriend. Even though shadows hide his eyes, I know he's staring at me. There's nothing to see, I have on the long cotton pajamas Grammy gave me, the drawstring at the waist double-knotted the way she told me to, and I have on the bra she said I should sleep in. I'm nothing but a wall of cotton with a red scarf tied down over my hair, and bare feet and sleepy eyes, and I have to pee.

"You need something?" he asks. He says it like this is his house and I'm an intruder, a guest in the wrong place. The air around him is stale, a salty swampwater smell laced with something else. I know what it is but I don't have a word for it. They all have that stink. The whole apartment has it, after they've been here. "Or you got a little something for me?"

I stumble back. "Indy, go lay down," Mamma calls out from the room, her voice low. "Baby, you comin back in? I need you, baby. Come on. She ain got nothin for you. She just a child. She ain even fill out yet."

He looks at me longer, slow, up and down, like that doesn't matter, like that might be even better, but finally he turns and goes back in to Mamma, leaving the door open.

My feet carry me to the front door, and I break all the rules. I leave the apartment, I step out into the night. A car's headlights flash just below my feet as it turns, then heads up the hill. The bar's outside lights are glaring. I duck down and sit at the top of the cool concrete staircase leading down to the bar and the street. Bite my lip. Even out in all this air, I can't breathe. I hold my breath. I hold my pee. I stare out into the night, full of music, of voices that swing from anger to laughter, then back again. And in the morning, when Grammy meets me down at the foot of the stairs to walk with me to school, she takes my face in her hands, holding me so tight it hurts. "Why you still in your nightclothes? What happened to you?" Staring deep into my eyes, trying to read them, like she doesn't trust my mouth for truth. "Anyone touch you, Indy?"

I don't know how to answer. He didn't put his hand on me, but he looked, and there was touch in his eyes, and the thing that comes after touch too.

"Hey? You okay?" Dion says again. When I still don't answer, he abruptly switches topics. "Actually, it's good you came back. You left your clothes here." He reaches under a chair, pulling out a cardboard box. He produces my skirt and shirt, folded up neatly. The shirt is streaked and spotted with purple from lying wet against the skirt's strong dye. The fabric, even stained, is familiar and soft.

"Can I use your bathroom?"

"Sure. You know where it is."

In the bathroom, I change into my own clothes, then roll the uniform up tight and tuck it under my arm. Stepping outside into the fresh air, I glance around. Nobody. In the distance, I can hear Joe barking orders. I should leave. But where would I go? Back to the house, to Gary? The house might be empty, if he's gone to work early. I know he missed hitting the tree, but did the branches and twigs scratch up the truck? If so, he could have gone to get it fixed. Or he could be back at Aunt Patrice's house by now, fuming. Waiting for me.

I head in the opposite direction from Joe's voice and take

a path that peters out into sand. The trees fan out and scatter until it's just a few casuarinas growing next to the wall that divides the retreat from the beach. Beyond it, the sea waits. I climb over and step onto the rocks jutting out into the water. I ditch the rolled-up uniform and kick off my shoes, letting the rough, pitted surface poke and jab at my feet. The sea bobs and jostles, smacking the underside of the rocks. I sit down at the edge and lower my feet into the water. Breathing is easy by the sea. My body wants the salt, wants the openness, the freedom ocean air gives. Close my eyes and I could almost be . . .

"You found the good spot."

I nearly fall off into the water. Dion, a few rocks over, stands on one leg, the other bent up, foot snuggled against the inside of his thigh. His body is ramrod straight, hands raised high in the air, palms pressed together over his head. When did he sneak up here?

"What you doing?" I say, trying to suppress my surprise.

"Tree pose. Improves strength, balance, and focus. I thought you went home."

If only it was that simple. I can see him about to say something more, and chances are, it's gonna be about Gary. "What happened with the girl back there, anyway?" I say before he can speak.

"In the office? That was our cleaning lady. Or former

cleaning lady. Turns out she wasn't actually cleaning anything, just spraying Glade and flushing the toilets every once in a while." He makes a face.

"Nasty."

"I know. Especially since Joe only goes for that natural cleaning stuff. Herbs and whatnot."

"Sounds like my grammy. I used to have to help her scrub the whole house down with nothing but baking soda and herb vinegar." I stand up. Normally, I'd reach for my bag, sling it over my shoulder. I'm lost without it. Nervous, too. Gary could be going through all my things right now. For all I know, he could have tossed the whole bag out the window and run over it with his truck, book and all.

"Where are you headed to next?" Dion lowers his arms, then the raised leg. He wobbles slightly, then catches himself and switches, mirroring the pose on the other side. Where? If I had my way, nowhere; I'd stay right in this quiet spot with this rock under me and the water dancing in the light, slowly pulling up with the tide. Dion raises his arms. He looks more like an arrow than a tree, hands pointing straight up to the sky, ready to shoot himself into the blue. "Or you plan on staying here till the end of time?"

It's a life vest being tossed at me; I grab ahold. "Since y'all did my laundry, and you kinda gave me a ride and let me use the phone, maybe I should help out or something."

Dion lowers his leg. "Joe ain big on people wandering around here, though."

"The bathrooms are still pretty dirty." Wouldn't take more than half an hour. Then I could sneak back to this rock. Hide out. Forget everything else.

"Let me get this straight. You volunteering to clean our bathrooms. For free?"

I can't explain that right now, this peace—even with the risk of Joe popping out, yelling like an angry-drunk Chihuahua—is more than payment enough. "Unless you'd rather do it yourself."

He holds his hands up. "Fine. Just don't take or break anything. And try not to let Joe see you."

"Dion!" As if on cue, Joe's voice cuts through the calm from a short distance away.

"Duty calls. See you . . ." He trails off, his eyebrows raised, waiting for me to fill in my name. I hesitate, but his face is expectant and open, and if I'm here, he might as well know who I am.

"Indy."

"Nice to meet you, Indy."

"If anybody else ask what I'm doing here?"

He climbs over the wall. "If anybody catch you scrubbing the toilets and says anything other than praise the Lord and pass the patchouli, you send em to me."

"Where you keep the supplies?" I call after him, but he's already out of earshot. Behind me, the water faithfully laps, making sloshing sounds. I can't sit here, waiting for Joe to appear, for more memories to flood my mind. I pull myself back over the wall and make my way to the big pavilion, a large open-air dining hall with rows of benches and tables sheltered from rain or sun.

"Hello?" I call as I pass behind the empty buffet. No one. I step into the kitchen, a free-standing structure at the back. The windows here are proper—wide squares, screened off to keep flies out. A skylight above me welcomes in the sun, and an almond tree filters the light through, making it dance between the leaves. There's a second entrance, closed off with a screen door. The space smells of thyme and sautéed onions and garlic.

"Anybody here?" I call again. No one answers. The room has been tidied—obviously someone other than the newly fired cleaning lady and whirling dervish Joe is in charge back here. On metal shelves pushed up against one wall, I see huge jars of brown rice, bay leaves, tan and brown and red dried beans, creamy barley kernels, their dark eyes winking at me. Flour . . . sugar . . . aha. Baking soda. I grab the box. Empty glass jars are stacked on the top shelf, waiting to be put to work. Garlic hangs from the ceiling in an elaborately woven net bag, as if to keep vampires at bay. Bunches of herbs—

thyme, basil, rosemary, fevergrass, cerasee—hang upside down from the ceiling, too, drying, same way Grammy used to do. A massive plastic bottle of vinegar stands in a corner.

"Let me start this dinner," I hear someone say from outside. The voice is low and rich, a chocolate-sauce, extra-piece-of-pie voice. I'm betting it's Maya, the woman who brought the switcher last time I was here. I snatch up the vinegar, two jars, and a bunch of half-dried thyme, then dash out the back door, clinking glass and sprinkling aromatic leaves.

5

I ATTACK THE RETREAT'S bathroom the way Grammy taught me to clean: cussing and scouring my way through filth fast to get to the other side of boring. "I am halfway through *Pride and Prejudice,* and I want to reach the jokey part with that Mr. Collins coming to dinner before time for *our* dinner," she would say, barreling through the living room, rags in one hand, vinegar in the other. "Get up off that chair, come help me." Or, "If this old nasty stove keep me from my Psalms, it's gonna be Armageddon in here." Outside, the rest of the vinegar sits in the jar along with the still-green thyme, left together in the sun to infuse, the liquid gathering strength from the herb. I can't understand how Grammy let Mamma send me here, how she could give me that pregnancy book. Even so, I can't get her out of my head as the vinegar's scent fills the air. It's like that, with real family. Can't get away, no matter how hard you, or they, try.

I am small, so little that I still live with Grammy always. Above my head, Grammy has just set a jar full of vinegar up on the counter. The kitchen is flooded with midmorning light. She drops the squeezed-out lime halves from the switcher we just made into the jar, adds a big branch of thyme. The leaves have already been taken off and dance now in a pot of peas soup. The kitchen smells of onions and sweet pepper being sautéed, of tart citrus and earthy leaves. I pick up a stick of thyme off the floor and stretch up to put it into the jar.

"Now, be careful!" Grammy warns.

Then Mamma is stumbling in through the kitchen door, and I'm running to her. "Mamma!" and the jar wobbles. I stop. She's walking funny, a man following close behind her, his face hidden by a cap. "She ga be arl . . . awl right, mum." His words bump into each other. Mamma laughs strange and silly, clinging onto his arm.

"Indy, go in my room. Go." Grammy's voice is angry. What did I do? I didn't mean to make the vinegar jar wobble. But her back's already turned to me, reaching for Mamma. "Come in here, Sharice." Then lower. "Stand up straight, you want your daughter see you all mess up?"

Mamma's eyes find me peeking around the doorway. "Hi, bay . . . baybee!" What's wrong with her voice?

"Ain I tell you go in the room, girl? Git!" Grammy swats

at me, too distant to make contact. "G'on!" Gathering Mamma into her arms, even though Mamma is bigger, Grammy changes her direction easy. Mamma's limbs are sheets in a slow breeze, flapping everywhere and hard to catch. The back door hangs open; the man is gone.

"Let's dance, we could dance. Baby, come dance with ya mamma!" Holding her arms out to me as Grammy whispers to her, too low for me to hear. Mamma's arms sweep side to side, caught in a gust made just for her.

"Mind the vinegar!" Grammy warns, too late. Mamma's hand smacks into the jar and there is clattering and glass breaking and fumbling feet sliding and crying and cussing and the hard smell all through the air. The infusion's too young to have taken on the thyme's crispness, the lime's fresh tart. Grammy hollers one of the bad words I get a soapy mouth and two swats for saying. There's red leaking into the spilled vinegar now and I run to the back room and bury my face in Grammy's pillow and wait, but no one comes even though I must be in trouble cause I didn't go in the room like Grammy said, and then the jar fell and someone got hurt. I hear Grammy loud, rowing, and then hear water running, and then nothing. Finally I get up and tiptoe to the back room, Mamma's old room, my room now, except for when she comes and stays and the two of us curl in that one single bed and I pretend we are sisters. I peep in. Mamma's laid out on *my bed, in one of Grammy's old nighties, and Grammy's on the edge, sitting there, and she has the book she's been reading open.* The Old Man and the Sea. *Grammy's back is turned but I know from how Grammy's leaning in that she's reading to Mamma, reading aloud, but so soft only Mamma can hear the story. She's reading to her the same way she reads to me. I can see Mamma's feet are bandaged up. The smell of spilled vinegar is strong. Part of me wants to be there with them, to hear Grammy read and curl up beside Mamma, because she's quiet now. But part of me feels there's no room for me in there, feels this moment is a secret, Mamma's and Grammy's. In the end, the secret-believing part of me wins. In Grammy's room, I lie down alone and pretend to sleep. But I can still smell it, spilled vinegar, in the air.*

I pour more baking soda into the bathroom sink. It froths up, agitated. With a handful of that still-fresh thyme, I scrub it until it bleeds bitter green.

Dion's jeep is a hubbub of magazines, old newspapers, empty water bottles. When I look at it properly, it reminds me of a cavern inhabited by a particularly slovenly troll. *"Want a ride home?"* he'd asked a minute earlier. I wanted to say no; I've walked from the dock to the house many times before, and besides, I don't take rides from people. Now, though, all I want to do is lie down and sleep. I scrubbed the first bathroom within an inch of its life, then found the bigger bathroom, farther from the office and closer to those little cabins, and scoured two of the four filthy shower stalls. After, I poked around the retreat's footpaths, winding between the cottages and trees.

"You could get in," Dion calls from the back of the jeep. There's a clatter of metal tools. I see him drop the cutlass and a pair of shears into the back. He sees me staring and grins as he tosses in some kind of huge hammer with a wide, flat edge on one end of the head and a long point on the other. "Pickaxe," he says. "Found a young bay tree growing in the bush down the road. Gotta see if I can dig it out and bring it back. Maya's been nagging me to get one so she can have her own fresh bay leaves." He climbs into the driver's side, tossing an empty water bottle into the back. The air smells faintly of citrus, and I see why; he rummages around in the backseat and emerges victorious, holding up an orange.

"Want piece?"

I shake my head and he bites into the peel, then tears it off in fragrant chunks. Here goes nothing, I think. If he had something in mind, he'd have tried it by now. I climb into the passenger seat as he starts up the jeep. As we pull off, I keep my fingers close to the door handle, though. Just in case.

"So, what you think of the retreat?" He drives casually, swinging down the path several meters before he slams his door shut.

"It's nice. Except, your bathrooms are dirty."

Dion laughs. "You sure don't mince words, hey? So that mean you're coming back to finish the job?"

"Maybe. Who stays in those cottages?"

"Out-of-towners. In-towners who want someplace to get away for a bit."

"With Joe on the loose?"

He laughs again. "She ain all bad."

"Really? You two always arguing. I don't know why you work with her."

"You caught her on a couple bad days. She gets a little protective, is all. This her place, you know. And she stays here too, over on the far side, way behind the pavilion. Makes sure the guests all right in the night if any emergency comes up." Done with his orange, he tosses the peel out of his window. "Everywhere needs a Joe. Someone hard, but with a good heart."

I don't know about that, but I'm not going to fight with him in his own car. "I didn't think you would litter," I say instead.

"It's biodegradable. Turn here?"

I nod.

"So, you sure ain nobody ga come out with a gun when I drop you off?"

"You think I's cause that much excitement?" I laugh.

"What? A girl?" Dion grins back at me. "You know y'all mothers keep y'all locked up."

I snort.

"You know I right." He glances out of his window, his left elbow propped in the open space. "Most times a boy, he can come and go however he want. The girl? Lockdown. Curfew. 'Where you goin? Who you goin with? Who you meetin when you get there?'"

I can't help but laugh. "So you know my grammy."

"You live with her?"

"No, she's still in Mariner's Cay."

"Oh, that's where you from?"

I nod.

"You stay with your mummy, then?"

We're passing the dock. I look out, half expecting to see Gary's truck parked there, waiting. "Not anymore."

"I hope you don't live with that cousin."

I stare out the window. "Next left." I make my voice sound nonchalant, but I'm sure he can see through the calm I'm trying to squeeze into like a too-small shirt, see the belly pushing out, even in this skirt and loose top. "Seventh house on the right."

"No problem." If he minds me ignoring his statement, he doesn't show it, turning slowly down Aunt Patrice's street. "Well, hey, I saw the bathrooms after you cleaned, and they look great. You graduate this year?" He glances over at me, curious rather than judgmental.

The lie slides out unplanned. "Yeah."

"You know what you want to do?" As if it's the most natural question in the world. If I was Smiley, I'd have a thousand answers. *"Speaker of the House, so I could wear that sexy blond wig. A brain surgeon. Owner of my own beauty salon."* Her dreams are wide and light with room in them to breathe, and space to twirl. What I want? To have nobody touch me. Have people stop seeing Mamma all over again when they look at me. Beyond that, I can't think too far into the future. Can't think about where I'll be in five, six months. What I'll be. Can't think about what's inside me.

I slouch against the car door in answer.

"Your exams done?"

I shrug.

"You got a lot of secrets, girl. It's okay, we all have secrets," he adds quickly. "Me, my secrets don't go no deeper than that pickaxe in the back and a bay tree in the bush with my name on it."

We're here, pulling up outside the yard. As the jeep rolls to a stop, I see Gary in the driveway, polishing his truck, his bald head glistening in the sun. The hose is snaked around his ankles. "This you?" Dion looks past me at the truck, at Gary.

"Thanks." I reach for the handle. Time to get out. That's

what I'm supposed to do. Gary's turned, looking right at me. His expression hardens. My legs weaken, refusing. My stomach is a clenched fist. All my fears come flooding back; what will Gary do if his truck's got even one scratch? What might he do, even if it doesn't? Leaving the jeep, messy and orange-scented and safe, is impossible. "I forgot. I was supposed to get something from the store. Can you drop me out on the main road?" My voice is faraway, as though I'm hearing myself from the end of a tunnel. I see Dion's mouth move and I manage a nod before I close my eyes. The jeep's tires screech as he turns around, the sound nearly drowned out by the drumming in my chest. I can't go back there. I can't go back. What's Gary gonna do? What's he gonna tell my aunt? What if those girls told Ms. Wilson about the book they caught me with, and Ms. Wilson calls the house and tells somebody? What if I'm here by myself with him and he tries something? If not today, what about the next time? In that house, his house, there's always a next time.

When I open my eyes, we're almost at the main road. I fumble for the door.

"Here's fine."

"But you said—"

"Let me out!" I feel, more than hear, my voice. The jeep stops at the curb and I open the door, the ground surging up to meet my feet. The fresh air should feel good but my head doesn't seem to belong to the rest of me. I can hear children's voices, distant, as though they belong in another world. A layer of sweat on everything. Air isn't getting into me. I try to pull it in, fast and hard, through my mouth. My head spins. I close my eyes again.

"Indira?"

The voice, the touch on my shoulder, nearly sends me out of my skin. I jump, eyes fly open. Dion, his face inches away from mine. I try to shout "No!" but no sound comes out.

"Indira." He leans back a little, giving me space. "Listen to me. Indira. You gotta breathe. Deep breath in and out. Again, okay? Keep going. Focus on something. Focus on— the Super Save sign. See it there down the road? Look at that. You ain gotta think about anything else. Just look at that. And breathe. Close your mouth, breathe through your nose. Deep breath in through your nose. Deep breath out. Breathe slow. I'll do it too." Dion stands up straight. "This way, Indira. Look down at your feet. Feel how you standing on the ground? That ground ain goin nowhere. Bend—hey, hey, I ain ga touch you—bend your arms so your hands touching, press the palms together. Yeah, like when you having prayer time in primary school. Listen." I can barely hear him, let alone follow along—his voice is fading away, distant against the rushing in my ears, an ocean rising in me. Massive waves lift, crashing down, turning over, lifting again. "Come on, breathe in," his words an inflatable raft. I hang on, clinging to them. I pull air into my lungs. "Just look at that red sign, look at that red. Breathe out."

Slowly, slowly, the panic starts to drain away from me, a flood tide receding. Out of the corner of my eye, I see Dion's arms go up to the sky, before he changes direction, reaching down to his toes. Right there on the sidewalk, he goes into a lunge. Then into a push-up, and next, hands and feet flat on the ground, his bottom in the air. I'm watching him now as he carries out his routine, a slow rhythm, his breath steady and loud, through his nose. Fingers touching his toes again. Standing and reaching up. Last, hands back at his chest. And again. Third time, he looks at me, nods. I should follow along. I should start lifting my arms and stepping forward, back, stretching up and down. Here, in the middle of everything. It's so effortless for him, like walking, his breathing steady and deep the whole time. I want to join in, want to feel that ease and certainty, want to feel as though my body belongs to me.

I stand there and watch him, I don't know for how long, three minutes, five minutes, maybe. While I stand there, a throng of kids appears on the way back from the store, hands full of candy. They stop there, on the sidewalk, watching him. Dion slows his motions at last, coming into that funny position he did on the beach, standing on one leg, the other leg bent with his foot tucked into the top of the thigh. A little girl, wide-eyed, smooth-skinned, hair in a bunch of stumpy plaits, studies him intently, then copies him, lifting her stringy arms to the sky, a pink lollipop clasped between two fingers.

Dion brings his feet together again. Then he lowers his hands, holding them at his chest. *"Namaste,"* he says, and bows slightly to the girl. She bows seriously and runs off, her friends trailing behind her. "You still need to go to the store?" Dion asks, turning to me. I shake my head and he leaves it at that, just gets into the jeep, waiting for me to climb in. We drive back to the house in silence. When we pull up, the driveway is empty. The only trace of Gary is a trail of dirty water draining down into the street.

After Dion has pulled away, I sit outside in the backyard, under the scarlet plum tree, and wait for answers to fall from its branches. Soon, Smiley will be home. She'll have heard what happened at school. What if she tells Aunt Patrice? Now, in spite of myself, I long for Grammy's book, to see her words, to feel her presence. I'm afraid to go inside, afraid my straw bag won't be there, and even more afraid it will. Did he see the book? If so, what might he do?

In that enormous kitchen, Smiley and I peel veggies over the sink. Out of nowhere, a big black truck screeches up the driveway, stopping just short of Auntie Patrice's car bumper. I turn to Smiley, but before I can ask who it is, she lets out a shriek, carrot and knife clattering into the sink. Front door flung open and a

Smiley-shaped blur hurtles down the driveway, stopping at the truck's window, jumping up and down, beating the glass.

A man steps out. Not especially tall, not especially good-looking, but he walks with a swagger and he has a killer smile. I can see that, even through the window's screen and security bars. Quick and full, wide and white, a grin like Smiley's that makes scowls soften and cut eyes curl up, happy. It slaughters Aunt Patrice's fury; she comes striding down the driveway, hand on one hip, finger waving, gesturing at her car before she stops, felled by those teeth, and then he says something I can't hear, and it makes her cock her head to one side, then lunge forward, flinging her arms around him. The onion I was peeling falls slack in my hands as I watch the three of them come back up to the house. As they do, Aunt Patrice makes a strange sound, a kind of gasping and squawking and wheezing. Laughter. She can actually laugh. I glance up at the sky above them to see if goats are flying now too. The door opens again and in comes his voice, loud and delighted with itself, pausing every few words to check that people are still listening delightedly.

"And then I tell her, 'So what, you's take me for maid now, ay?'" this guy says, sending Aunt Patrice into another fit of cackles, and Smiley joins in. They're inside, in the front room, then closer, in the dining room. Their laughter is held together by the punch line to a story I haven't heard. I exist outside this joke.

Finally, they reach the kitchen, the air buzzing around them.

"*Mummy, what's this, you have a modeling agency now?
All these domestic divas you have stashed around the house,
with the head ties and the latest accessories—I see onions are
all the rage this year,*" the man says. Smiley giggles, strutting
through the doorway. Aunt Patrice's smile falls a little, but the
guy just laughs more, overjoyed with life, with himself. His
eyes crinkle up the way Smiley's do. "*I'm Gary,*" he says, and it
clicks, this is the big brother, the big-time hotel chef, the owner
of the room where I've just unpacked my one bag of belongings.

Before I can feel fear—*Is he moving back? Where will I
sleep?*—and that guilt you get when you've been in the space
of a person who seems to still half-live in a house, his hand is
extended and he's looking straight into my eyes. Not up and
down the length of me, quick and sneaky or open and slow,
the way a couple of Mamma's boyfriends used to. His eyes are
wide, a deep brown, framed with tightly curled lashes. His
skin is glowing, the faint outline of his shaved hair beginning
far back on his head. He's maybe twenty-five or twenty-six,
but he's surer of himself than most of Mamma's skulking boyfriends, and they were always much older. I reach out to shake
his hand and he flips it up at the last second. "*Too slow!*" he
shouts, and Smiley explodes into guffaws.

"*Smiley, go tell your daddy Gary's here,*" Aunt Patrice
breaks in, as though all this merriment needs balancing out
with a practical task. "*This is Indira.*" There's a touch of laugh

left in her voice, but saying my name quenches it. "Your cousin. Remember, from Mariner's?" she calls, following Smiley out of the kitchen. "Sharice's child?"

"Oh, yes, yes, I remember." Gary takes my hand, which I'm still holding out stupidly, and shakes it.

"I put Indira in your room," Aunt Patrice continues from the front room. "We thought you had left for good." Gary ignores her, holding on to my hand.

"Sharice's daughter. Then you's family. What we shaking hands for?" He pulls me in for a hug.

The hug is a breath longer than it needs to be. Or is that my imagination? Puff of air, as he exhales on my neck. Hand on my waist. Finds a handful of me and quick, so quick I almost could say it didn't happen, gives a squeeze.

"Stranger!" Uncle's voice booms from the doorway, and it's over. The two men jostle and joke as I shuffle myself off to the side, out of the way. Gary has his head in the fridge then, rummaging, and takes out the pitcher of water, filling up a glass. "Man, I thought we got rid of you," Uncle jokes. Thought you was all grown up, big man. What happen?"

"Didn't think I'd be back either, but my girl kick me out. You could believe that?" Gary eyes me over the rim of his glass. "Y'all women coldhearted, ya know?"

"Comes at a good time," Uncle says. "I'm out of town for two weeks. You'll be the man of the house."

"Yeah, stay here." Smiley comes back in, returning to the abandoned carrot in the sink. She wags it at him. "Indy won't mind. Then we get to share my room."

But later that night, Aunt Patrice hands me a pillow and two sheets, points to the living room sofa.

"I don't want you in with Cecile," she says, as though I'm a bad habit that might rub off on Smiley. "Gary's only here for a couple nights," she adds, turning away. Lying down, I try to relax. It's not so bad. Maybe better than sleeping in Gary's room would have been. I bring my hand up to the spot he touched. Try not to think of my things in his room. My underwear in the bottom of the straw bag. The book, tumbled into some corner of the closet, behind his clothes. I can hear him moving around in there, jostling things on the bureau, putting stuff away. Then he must turn off the light, because the bedsprings squeak a few times before silence settles all around. I lie there, but sleep won't come. Even in the quiet, with the rest of the house sleeping, the book haunts me. It's the same as those slightly-too-big bras, as the nickname Doubles. Made for someone else, but forced onto me.

I wake up to the sound of Aunt Patrice yelling for Smiley to hurry up before she gets left behind. I've slept through them coming home, probably slept through dinner, too. I stand up, straightening out my clothes, and tiptoe to the back door.

ide ne's left it open. The kitchen is empty, but
end? by the garbage bin. I grab it, relieved.
Mariner's ar the bottom, and everything else is
  I sling it over my shoulder and tip-
  d living rooms. Smiley's door is half
one away. there . . .
ent this to
I get word hind me. I try to put on a neutral
Don't mat- ound to face her.
ct."
all. Smash m?"
, I mutter, rd. I fell asleep."
e with me. what? And why you ain in your
ay where I
push open sound right, and the truth is out

ponytail. All

I ask. No her jacket pocket, taking out
  oves it under my nose. There's
her face. eep. Me inside. And Dion, a
  his?"
off my shoul- er it's not how it looks, in say-
and holds it already told her his version of

"You think you could just cut school and joy[...]
man? Listen. You know how I go. You want boyfri[...]
out. You don't go to your classes? You out. This ain [...]
My name ain Sharice."

"Neither is mine!"

Aunt Patrice holds my gaze as she puts her ph[...]
"Lucky for you Gary was the one who saw you and s[...]
me. If I had seen you myself, if I ever see you myself, if [...]
again you up to this behavior, you're out. Understand?
ter what your uncle say. I have my own child to prote[...]

I want to take that phone, smash it against the [...]
it against her head, knock sense into her. Instead
"Yes, ma'am." She is satisfied, or maybe just dor[...]
She turns away, heading for the front room. I s[...]
am until I hear the door close behind her. Then [...]
Smiley's bedroom door.

Smiley is in there, pulling her hair back in a [...]
showered and in a clean dress.

"You going to church with Aunt Patrice?[...]
answer. "Hey."

She straightens up, the usual grin gone from [...]

"What's your problem?" I ask.

Before I can stop her, she's snatched the bag [...]
der. In one quick motion, she pulls out the boo[...]
up accusingly.

"Gimme that back. If Aunt Patrice see—"

"So it's true." She drops the bag and the book like both are diseased. "And you couldn't tell me?"

"So what, you heard—"

"Everybody heard. Everybody know."

"Ms. Wilson—"

"Not her, dummy. I mean your whole class know. Karen told her sister in my class. I heard *after* all those people, even though you my cousin and me and you share a bed. I knew something was up." Angry as she sounds, her eyes are starting to tear up. "How come you didn't say nothing?"

"I—"

"You really pregnant?" Her interruption is welcome; I have no explanation. None I can say out loud. I nod.

"How far?"

"Five months."

"Indy." And then she's hugging me as the car horn toots outside. "I thought you was just getting fat."

"Thanks." I try to pull away. It's not the fat comment—I don't care about that, I know it's just Smiley, and besides, it's true—it's having someone pressed up to me. But Smiley refuses to let go.

"Mummy know?"

"You think I'd still be here if she did?"

"Don't worry, Indy." Her voice is muffled by the embrace.

"It'll be okay. I'll find a way to help you. Promise. I ga fix this for you. You watch."

"Oww, man, you hurting me," I lie, squirming away. "Get off me, your mummy ga know something's up."

There's another honk from outside. When I push Smiley away, her face is wet.

"You want me to stay home from choir practice?"

"For what?"

"Never mind. I'm gonna help you." She reaches for my bag again.

"What you doing?" I ask, pulling the bag away from her.

"Give me your phone."

"Why?"

"Just trust me." Smiley gives me that grin, wide and open and empty of harm. I reach into the bag and press the phone into her hand, giving her my passcode. I don't have anything to hide, at least not on the phone. Just a bunch of old texts to her, and the call to Mamma. She puts it into her pocket, then runs for the car. From inside, I watch them drive away and try to shake that feeling creeping up on me. That feeling of *Why me? Why it couldn't have been someone else?* And then, something else, something uglier I push down low. But it pops up again and again. *Why not her?*

6

IT'S JUST AFTER SIX the next morning when I march out to the garbage with a bag of hotel bread rolls in one hand, another one of those disgusting foil containers in the other. I'm midway through tossing it all in the trash when someone speaks.

"Hey."

Behind me. A male voice—not Gary. Still, I know better than to make any sudden moves. *Be slow,* I tell myself. *Be controlled. Show no fear.* I shove the foil tray deeper into the trash before I turn around. Long body, gangly limbs, light brown skin, low Afro patted down meticulously, white shirt carefully ironed and dark brown pants starched so stiff they could stand up on their own, knife-sharp crease pressed down the front. It takes a moment when you see something familiar out of place; a banana in the box of spinach, a red sock in the flower display. Then it clicks. Churchy. Of course.

"I-I-I I hope I ain scare you." He gunfires the words, spitting them out like broken teeth.

"What you doin here?"

"I-I-I c-c-came to see you." He nods, relieved it's come out so easy, his hairless chin bobbing up and down.

"What for?"

"You f-f-f-forget?"

I settle the wood cover over the garbage. He must be crazy. "Forget what?"

"L-l-last night. Remember?"

"Remember what?"

"You t-t-text me and say to come by early. R-r-remember?"

I look him straight in the eye. I remember Churchy knew me in Mariner's. He's the reason *Doubles* followed me here. I remember he knows, as much as anyone else back home, how Mamma is. I'd bet money I don't have that I know why he's really here. What he expects from me.

"So I guess you heard," I say.

"H-h-heard what?"

"And you thought you could come get your piece too." I move forward, hands on my hips, forcing him to take a step back; he bumbles into the bougainvillea.

"Wh-wh-wh-what piece you talkin bout?" He wears a wounded expression as he pulls a leaf out of his hair. "You

text me last night an-an-an tell me c-c-come by around six."
He takes a few steps toward his bicycle, leaning up against
the side of Aunt Patrice's red car.

"Churchy, don't play with me. You didn't hear what happened at school yesterday? You don't know what they sayin
about me?"

"I w-w-was s-sick, I ain b-b-been to school."

"We saw you at the restaurant, night before."

He shoots me a guilty look, and I get it. He probably had
to work at the restaurant during the day. I realize Churchy's
life might not be perfect either. He might not have wanted
to leave Mariner's himself, with his grammy, fat and cheerful
and loud, to go to school where the people who tease you
aren't even the people you know, have always known. Might
not want to work in that restaurant. That's the only reason
why I wait when he holds his hand up, pleading. He pulls
out his phone and shows me the screen. **Want to talk to you.
You could come by early before school. I get up at 6.** From my
number. I open my mouth to protest, I never sent that, then
remember Smiley clinging to me. *I'm gonna help you. Give
me your phone. Just trust me.* So maybe he's not a creep.
Doesn't matter. This still ain going nowhere. I pass his phone
back. "You better go. If my aunt catch you out here you ga
have to steer that bike home using your mouth."

He looks at me with the long, disappointed eyes of a

potcake that's been kicked one time too many. "Y-y-you ga be to school today?"

"I dunno," I say, turning to go. I feel a little bad for Churchy. He must have gotten up at four to be here by now, freshly pressed. But I don't have time to stand out here mourning for him. The smell of the garbage is already making me want to gag. "Hurry up. If my aunt see you—"

"Y-y-yeah. I kn-kn-know." He gives me a funny smile, and for a second he's not just that stuttering kid I've always known. "Sh-sh-she like your grammy? She ga come out and b-break off one switch to beat me with?" He swats at the air with his arm, mimicking the motion. I can't help but laugh, and there's a second where I'm a normal girl out in the front yard, sharing a joke. Then I glance over at the house and see the curtains fall back into place over the window. My heart skips. Aunt Patrice might be up. Might have seen us talking. If she did, there's no point delaying her wrath.

"Grammy would make you pick out your own switch," I tell Churchy, heading for the house.

When I open the door, Smiley jumps back from the front window guiltily. So damn nosey she couldn't even finish getting dressed before she came to peek out. Her skirt is hauled on but not zipped or hooked shut, and she's in her bra, blouse in one hand. Her problem's the opposite of mine; my bra can't even do its one job anymore, while hers is about as vital as a diaper on a cactus. "Who that was?"

I could slap her. "What you tell that boy come here for?" I ask, walking into the kitchen. I dig out a box of ginger biscuits and open it, nibbling on one. I'm not hungry, but if there's any chance Grammy's trick might help with this morning sickness, it'll be worthwhile. Smiley blinks at me stupidly, feigning innocence.

"What boy?" She drapes her blouse over her shoulder as she starts rummaging around in the cabinet, then retrieves the iron and ironing board.

"Don't play with me."

"I only tryin to help you, you know."

"Help me how?"

"Well, at least I had an idea. Oh, and I put some minutes on your phone."

I don't care about that right now. "What you think he could do for me?"

On the kitchen counter, my cell phone rings before she can answer. Smiley glances at it, then at me, as she starts to press the blouse. "You think that's him?"

"Him who?" Aunt Patrice says, surprising both of us. She's come into the kitchen quietly; how long has she been there, listening? "Who's calling you this kinda time?" she asks, looking over at me.

"I don't know," I say. I'm not lying; I don't recognize the

number, but if I don't answer now, I'll only be giving Aunt Patrice a reason to suspect me. I pick up the call. "Hello?"

"Hi. May I speak with Indira?"

A male voice. It can't be anyone from school, not using my real name. "Yeah. Yes." I can feel Aunt Patrice watching, straining to overhear.

"This is Dion. From the yoga retreat."

"Oh, right." I keep my voice neutral.

"I hope you don't mind me calling, I saw this is the number you dialed yesterday. Didn't think I'd really get you."

"Mmm-hmm."

"Listen, we really in a bind down here. We need some help all day tomorrow. Any chance you free?"

"Um—yeah."

"Can you come by this morning, too? It's a chance to make a little money." He sounds harried. "And I thought you might want to get out of the house. You done with exams now, right?"

I glance over at Aunt Patrice, who's starting across the kitchen toward me purposefully. "Sure," I say.

"Great!" Dion's enthusiastic voice is so loud Aunt Patrice has to have heard him.

"See you," I say, and hang up on Dion just as she reaches my side.

"And who was that?" she asks.

"It was a girl from school."

"And what's that you agreed to?"

"Helping her study."

Smiley snorts unhelpfully, her ironing abandoned.

Aunt Patrice gives me a long stare. "I hope that's the case, for your sake," she says.

"Morning, Mummy. Morning, Smiley." Gary shuffles past the kitchen doorway. No greeting for me; apparently I don't exist. Fine with me. He backsteps to glance at Smiley. "You ain goin to school dressed like that, ay?"

Aunt Patrice looks over. "Cecile Anne, if you don't put your blouse on!"

As she scolds Smiley, I retreat to the living room to get a fresh set of uniform. Hunched down by the sofa, I pick out a blouse and skirt from the stash of clean clothes I leave stacked in the corner so Aunt Patrice won't know I'm sneaking into Smiley's room to sleep at night.

"That's a nice little stunt you pull yesterday." Gary's voice, right behind me. I can hear Aunt Patrice in the other room, lecturing Smiley on modesty. They might as well be an ocean away.

"You don't walk around the house dressed that way," Aunt Patrice is saying. "You growing up now. You don't do them kinda things."

"You lucky I ain get no scratches on my truck." Gary is

bent down too, his mouth close to my neck. There is a heat that rises up out of him. I strain away but there's nowhere to go. "You could never pay for that. What your ma is go for again? Twenty? Forty? That can't fix no damage."

From the kitchen, Smiley's voice is a childish squeal. "So what, man? Daddy ain home, an we all family."

"Don't cross me again," Gary warns. A finger presses into my neck.

"Who cares?" Smiley's voice is defensive and shrill. "It's only *Gary*."

"I watchin you, ya know."

Feel his nail digging into my skin. I wish I could pull away, move even an inch, but everything in me is paralyzed, I can't so much as flinch. Everything except my mind. *Come in, I will* Smiley. *Come in, catch him, make him stop.*

"I see you with ya little friend. Your rescuer. Got a nice picture of y'all two. You lucky I ain tell my mummy you in trouble at school. You owe me." Voice drops. "How you wanna pay?"

I don't realize when Aunt Patrice finishes lecturing Smiley. Gary must not either. At the sound of a throat being cleared behind us, he springs away from me.

"Hey, Mummy." His voice is so normal, barely the slightest of shakes. "I gotta get going, they have me down for nine." He's gone quickly. I'm still frozen, crouched down, the school blouse in my hand clenched so tight it feels like part of my palm.

When I stand up, I see Aunt Patrice's lips pressed together in a line. Her eyes meet mine, and narrow. How much has she seen? But before I can read her, she's turned away.

At the retreat, the office is unlocked but empty, the paths deserted except for the potcake, who wags his tail lazily before settling back onto the grass.

"Dion?" I call, checking the kitchen, which is also empty. A huge pot, still sticky from breakfast grits, rests in the sink, half full of water. In the dining pavilion, a few guests sit with their plates. Out on the deck facing the ocean, a teacher calls out instructions to a class of a dozen or so people. I follow the path out past the bathrooms and call again.

"Over here." I see Dion waving from over by the beach, Maya standing near him.

"Hey," I call as I get closer. I come around to where they are, and there, off to the side, arms full of yoga mats, face screwed into a scowl, is Joe.

"Morning," Maya chirps. Dion greets me with a guilty nod.

"What you doing here?" Joe snaps, dropping the mats. "Dion? Why's she here?"

I shoot Dion a glare, hitching my bag up higher on my shoulder. "Leaving." Then I see his right arm, wrist and forearm wrapped in a brace. In his left arm, he clutches a plastic bag loaded down with something. "What happened to you?"

He grins sheepishly, holding the bag out. Inside, a pile of early scarlet plums, fat with juice. "I fell out of the tree. Gotta wear this thing for a few weeks now. Hey, you hung up before I could finish talking."

"Bad connection," I say. I can feel Joe glowering at me.

"Dion, why's this girl here on a school day? You getting kids to play hooky to cover your job now?"

"I'm finished school." I tell her. It's not a complete lie; I feel done right now. How can I go back, after what happened yesterday?

"Before ten?" Joe retorts. "And you're in school uniform?"

"I have graduation pictures." Now it's a lie. I turn to Dion. "What you called me for?" Beside him, Joe's scowl has deepened. She steps forward.

"I don't know what he told you, but we don't need you here." She sneers, a funny, lip-curling experience that makes her look like a disgruntled fish.

"Who you think's gonna fill in for me?" Dion reaches out, gently stopping Joe. "Who you think cleaned those bathrooms after you fired Steph?"

"Maya—" Joe starts.

"Uh-uh, don't look at me," Maya says as she starts down the path, excusing herself. "My job in the kitchen, that's what y'all hired me for."

"Why'd you call me here?" I ask Dion.

Dion looks from Joe to me. "We need you. Matter of fact, Joe needs you."

"Of all the idiotic times to go falling out of a tree," she complains. She looks like she might start walloping him with a rolled-up yoga mat.

I don't think I can handle Joe. She's just another Aunt Patrice, judgmental and angry. Right now, Aunt Patrice is mandatory; without her, I have no place to live. Joe is a choice. "Sorry, Dion," I say, starting to walk away.

"All right, then," he says, then turns to Joe. "I guess you might as well call the people on Mariner's Cay and tell them you can't make it. I hope they won't be too disappointed."

I turn back.

"Mariner's?"

"It's something new," Dion says, shooting a sideways look at Joe. "Something we wanted to start. Joe was going up there to teach yoga at a hotel and a few places in the community. But I guess that won't be happening now." Dion reaches for his bag of plums with his good hand. "The woman I talked to at the school told me she'd believe we were miracle workers if we could get her bad students to sit still and keep quiet for more than a minute."

I'd think he was bluffing if I didn't actually know Mrs. Whyms; she's sour-faced, fatter than, but not as cruel as, her sister, Mrs. Ellis, who made Churchy cry while he stood there under the casuarinas outside the white church, pants cold and stinking of pee, trying to stutter out the details of Adam and Eve's days in the Garden of Eden. This could be a ticket back to Mariner's. A ticket to Grammy. I would have to face her, with my secret that won't be a secret much longer. But either I face Grammy or I stay here, waiting for Aunt Patrice to throw me out. Or for the next time Gary corners me.

"That's a lot of mats to pack up by yourself," Dion says to Joe, cajoling.

Joe shakes her head. "What you know about this girl? She showed up from nowhere, twice now, middle of the day, not in school, acting funny, and I'm supposed to take her off the island with me? Who knows what kind of trouble she could get in? What if she goes off with somebody? And then what? I still don't have help, and on top of all that, her parents come looking for me."

While Dion reminds her how Mariner's is steep and rocky, how she'll have sixteen mats to tote, I try to decide what to do. Do I take this boat ride? Will this woman even let me?

"And you don't know nobody up there," Dion continues. "You think anybody want help you? Watch. You lucky if you don't break your neck trying to unload all them things at the dock." His usually mellow voice rises in frustration.

"Susan can't come?"

"Susan teaching tomorrow, but Indy could be there. Right, Indy?" Dion steps toward me, his face full of hope.

Joe makes an angry noise, throwing her arms up in disgust. "Look, you're the one who went and strained your arm doing foolishness. You figure it out. I'm loading up the car." She snatches up an armload of rolled-up yoga mats and storms out to the parking lot.

"Sorry about that," Dion says.

"I'm not trouble."

"I know, I know," he says. How do you know, I want to ask. How are you so sure, when everyone else takes a look at me and decides, right off the bat, I must be no good? "Look, we'll pay you for the day. A hundred dollars."

I don't think I've ever held a hundred dollars all at once.

"And I'll make sure she lets you have time to go see your family."

A hundred dollars. A hundred dollars closer to being free of Aunt Patrice.

"Free boat ride." His grin is convincing, but that's not what decides it. Neither is the money, even though that sounds sweet. This is my one shot to go home, to see Grammy. To be back on Mariner's Cay. What if I never came back to Nassau? I imagine walking up to Grammy's house, stepping onto the porch, my hand on the doorknob. Inside, bread will be baking. Shelves full of her books. Grammy will turn and see me and smile. I'll forget everything that's happened and just be Indy again. Light and empty.

Over Dion's shoulder, I see Joe in the distance, dropping two of the mats. She bends to pick them up and another falls, unrolling in the dirt. Man, this girl actually can teach yoga? That's what she looks like, I realize—a girl. She may be older than Mamma, but right now, she has no more idea how to handle life than I do. And no one's taught her how to fake it. She's never thought to duct-tape herself together.

"Man, come on." Dion looks back too. Joe gives the mats a kick—as solid a kick as you can give mats—and stomps away. She actually stomps. "Look at that. You don't feel kinda sorry for her?" He tries to sound serious, but a smile starts to take over his face.

"Nope. Matter of fact, I hope she does go to Mariner's by herself. Mrs. Ellis would cane her skinny behind if she start throwing tantrums over there. And Mrs. Whyms would have her mouth washed out with soap."

Dion laughs, totally erasing the somber expression of sympathy he's been trying to cultivate. "Please, Indira. All you gotta do, show up at the boat for six-thirty tomorrow. Help her load onto the boat, and back off at the end of the day. Maybe wipe down the mats."

We both look back at the jumble of yoga mats in the dust.

"And set up," Dion carries on, as if he hopes I won't

notice how arduous it's starting to sound. "She got about three classes lined up. You'd only have to be there for them; the rest of the day you could go see your people. You don't have to hang with her, just help her. Please. As a favor to me. I know your people raised you to help out someone in need."

I can feel it, the warm air in Grammy's kitchen, afternoon light heating the room. Her hands patting my back as she hugs me. *Look at you,* she would say.

She would look at me. She would see.

"A hundred and ten." Dion breaks into my thoughts. "One ten is the most we could do. Come on, man. Say yes. This a good thing for your hometown. She ain makin no money from this. None of us are."

"Then what you doin it for?" I don't expect him to answer, and sure enough, he twists the question back on me.

"I could ask you that too. What you come down here for if you didn't want to help?"

It's too much to explain, Aunt Patrice and Gary, school and everything. And anyway, this isn't about me. It's about Joe. "Her attitude so stink. Why you all here helping her? This *her* dream, right?"

Dion pauses, then sighs. "That's my mummy."

"Joe?" How is that even possible? I try to imagine a young Joe with a baby Dion. I picture her tossing a baby bottle against a wall, throwing a hissy fit over a dirty diaper. Well, I guess it's no more ludicrous than Mamma being my mother. It's still not a real answer, not for me. "So?"

"I here because I want to be here. This place feels right to me. I could stand out on that rock and enjoy the sea. I plant my little flowers here and grow my little veggies there, and Maya in the kitchen could cook her food in peace. Susan could teach the students here, right in the garden or facing that way." He looks out over the water, glinting in the morning light. "This place ain hers, this ours. I called you to ask you for help cause I thought you might want it to be yours too, a little bit. I thought that first day when you show up and fall right onto a mat . . . And when the next day, you jump in front of the jeep. And now today, time number three, you come all the way down here. Thought maybe this was your place too. But maybe I was wrong."

I want to say that something sympathetic in me poked through all the annoyance, the way a new shoot pushes up through rocks and soil. I want to say I heard Grammy's voice. *What I teach you? Do unto others, Indy May.* The truth is, this could be my only way home.

"I'll do it."

"Oh, thank you, Indy!" Before I can stop it, Dion crunches me in a hug. Then he's stepped back, almost bouncing from one foot to the other, babbling on about where Joe and I will be going, for how long, how much fun it will be. "You want to help load the jeep now?"

"I can't," I say. Missing school all day today won't help if I'm gone tomorrow, too. The longer I can at least half-pretend at school, the longer before Aunt Patrice finds out.

"Why not? I thought you done with school."

"I still have graduation pictures." It feels unnatural, lying to Dion, especially when he nods and wishes me luck.

"For what? The pictures, or tomorrow?"

He grins. "Take a little for both."

7

I WALK OUT TO the main road and wait at the bus stop by the clinic, keeping an eye out. It's dangerous, being outside school in your uniform during the day. Anyone who sees you knows you shouldn't be there. Of course, this time of year, grade twelves are done anyway. Question is whether I can pass for one of them. With this chest, chances are I can, but it never hurts to be careful. I go stand in the shade right under the clinic's awning. I figure if anyone sees me, I can say I wasn't feeling well. It's not a total lie. The walking, the sun, it all has me tired. Come to think of it, all I've eaten today is a couple of ginger biscuits. I wonder if Smiley packed enough lunch to share.

A hundred and ten dollars. I decide I'll save most of it, all of it, if I can. For later, that hazy time not far from now, when everybody knows and things really start to change, not just my body, but my whole life. I can't let Aunt Patrice find out I have a little money coming to me, no matter what. She'd find a way to get her hands on some of it, even if I was back in Mariner's Cay for good.

We're all in the living room watching TV, Smiley and Gary and even Aunt Patrice, when Uncle walks in the front door. Smiley springs up first, hurling herself at him like she's five, screaming, "Daddy! Daddy!" and hanging off his shoulders before he's even put his suitcase down. He laughs even though he's tired, and hugs her and swings her around.

"Hey, big man," Gary says, getting up.

They hug briefly, roughly, before Uncle stoops to give Aunt Patrice a kiss on the cheek. She stays in her chair.

"Indira," Uncle says. As always, he doesn't know what to say next. The way he looks away from me is different from Aunt Patrice. She always sees me as an unpleasant obligation, a plastic neon-green punch bowl with pink spots received as a gift, a thing she's required to keep but has no purpose for; he seems to recognize something in me that makes him feel ashamed. He nods his head now, aware that this is the point where most people would hug. "You all right?"

"Yes, thank you," I say, glad to leave it at that.

"How was Miami?" Gary asks, while Smiley prances around.

"Great. That black bag has the part you wanted for your truck," Uncle says.

"*You bring me anything, Daddy?*" Smiley's dance has reached ridiculous levels, arms flapping, feet kicking high. Must be different, feeling that way to see a man come home. Aunt Patrice frowns at the display, but Uncle only laughs.

"Go look in the outside pocket of my suitcase," he says, and she scampers away. "Here." He turns to Aunt Patrice. "I stopped for the mail." He hands her a stack of envelopes. Aunt Patrice sifts through them.

"Nothing from Sharice? Again?"

Uncle tries to lower his voice. "Probably late."

"This the third month she didn't send anything." Aunt Patrice gets up, heading for the kitchen. Her voice is extra loud; she wants to make sure I hear. "Where she think food and clothes come from? Thin air?"

I muffle a snort. Aunt Patrice might let me eat out of the fridge, but she's never bought me clothes, not even a pair of socks. The three or four times Mamma sent money, Aunt Patrice doled out a few dollars to me every week for the bus and pocketed the rest. Good thing I had a little put away from Grammy so I could buy pads when I needed them, though I haven't had to for a while now. And anyway, if Aunt Patrice knows Mamma so well, she shouldn't be surprised the money's stopped coming. I'm not.

Uncle picks up the envelopes without a word. He avoids looking at me.

"Indira, I know how you could earn some money." A grin spreads over Gary's face. "You want help me put this thing in my truck?"

As I get up, his laughter follows me all the way into Smiley's room, until I close the door and fling myself down on her bed. So what if Aunt Patrice doesn't want me in here? I have no place else to go. And what's wrong with my uncle? He can't hear what Gary said to me, right in front of him? They're out there talking about mechanics now, as if Gary's quip had anything to do with cars. I hate them all: Aunt Patrice crashing around in her big, sloppy kitchen as if not getting fifty dollars from Mamma is the worst possible thing in the world; Smiley, dancing around like a baby, worrying about if her daddy brought her presents, knowing that he always does, always will; Uncle, tripping over things he knows aren't right, dusting himself off, and pretending nothing is there. And Gary.

The door opens and I turn away. I'm not in the mood to listen to Smiley crow over some dress or shoes or nail polish.

"Here." Uncle's voice surprises me. I sit up. He's holding out a plastic bag. I peer into it while he stands there, shifting nervously. Three new toothbrushes, a pack of pens for school, three washcloths, a bar of chocolate, a fashion magazine. I reach in and bring out two bars of Pears soap. "I know your grammy buys that kind," he says. It's an odd collection.

It's been months since I got anything, since I unpacked my one bag of things from Grammy, that first day here. I didn't expect this.

"Something else in there," he says, reaching over and pulling out the magazine. I take it; something's nestled between the glossy pages. I bring out a white envelope. It has my name on it, in familiar handwriting.

"Grammy!" It's not that Uncle's never snuck me a letter from Mariner's before. He knows Aunt Patrice always keeps everything Mamma sends; since my first few weeks here he's been going through the mail before he gives it to her, carefully sliding me an envelope here and there with Grammy's cursive across the front. But Grammy's envelopes had stopped coming too. Getting this letter now is a promise. She still remembers me.

"Cecile!" Aunt Patrice calls from the front of the house. "Where your cousin is?"

"I don't know," she yells back, "but look what Daddy bring me!"

"She's outside, Pat," Uncle calls, stepping back out of the room. He nods at the envelope. "Don't let your auntie see."

Alone, I tear the envelope open. Inside, this time, there's no note. Only two ten-dollar bills, and a five. I tell myself not to be stupid. This is the first time she's sent something without writing, and I need this money. Even the biggest bra she sent me here with is starting to get tight already. I decide I'll get a new one this week. I hold the envelope to my chest, but without her words, it feels empty.

The clinic door opens and an older lady comes out, wig slightly askew, a straw hat perched on top. I say good morning; having manners is the fastest way to get adults to ignore you. Her hat wobbles as she nods her head at me. After she passes, I check that no one's watching, then discreetly dig at the back of the bra where the tape is itchy. I bought this bra with those last three bills Grammy sent me. If I'd known I would outgrow it so fast, I wouldn't have wasted the money. The door opens again.

"W-w-wait, Junior. D-don't go out there by yourself."

I'd know that stutter anywhere. A little boy, maybe three, dashes out into the parking lot, and sure enough, running after him is Churchy. Twice in one day and neither time at school.

"H-h-hold on, hold on," he says, catching hold of the kid. He hoists him onto his shoulders before he sees me. "D-D-Doubles. Wh-wh-what y-you doin outta school?"

"I could ask you the same thing. Who's this?"

"What y'all out here for, I tell you my ride comin for me, we might as well wait inside and stay cool," a girl's voice interrupts, following behind him. She appears, all sleek weave and overzealous face powder and bright red lipstick, in hot-pink pants. "Hey, don't put him up there, it ain safe." She reaches to lift the boy off Churchy's shoulder. The boy sets up an unholy wailing.

"L-leave him, he fine. Y-you know D-D-D-D-DD-D-D-D-D—"

"Indy," I interrupt.

"D-D-D-D-Doubles from home, right?" he continues stubbornly. The girl smiles faintly at me. "This my sister. You remember her?"

I do. Their mother sent for her from Nassau a few years ago. Mrs. Whyms would mention her in passing, mostly as a warning against going astray. And here is the reason for that, I guess, drumming enthusiastically on Churchy's head and jostling his glasses. I've never seen Churchy look anything less than pulpit-ready, pressed and neat, his jumpy speech the only thing out of place. The boy's doing his best to mess Churchy up. Churchy bears it with dignity.

"Hey, s-see your d-daddy comin," he says as a car swings into the parking lot.

"D-Daddy!" the boy parrots cheerfully.

"Look how you got my boy stuttering," Churchy's sister complains, sauntering up to the car.

He turns to me. "Y-y-you want a r-ride back to school?"

I look at the car as it pulls up alongside us. The tints on it are dark, heavy enough that no one can snap a picture of me and send it back to Aunt Patrice. I decide to make another exception to my No Rides rule. At least I know Churchy, and that's good enough, even if he was skulking around in the bushes this morning. Besides, I feel light-headed from the walk, and making an exception has to be better than passing out on the road. I get into the back and say good afternoon to the guy in the driver's seat, then buckle up beside Churchy and the little boy.

"So you always cut school?" I shout over the music. Churchy cups his hand over his ear like a deaf old man. I rummage around in my backpack until I find a school exercise book and a pen.

You always skip school? I write.

He reads my note, then reaches for the pen. *Jr. was sick and she thought she couldn't get off work.* He glances over. *What are you doing out?*

I pause, contemplating the consequences of honesty. *Someone asked me for some help.*

You ever missed before? he writes back, before shifting over so Junior can rest his head against him. I write *No, unless you count Burst Buttons Day,* but Churchy's so busy with the little boy he never reads it, and then the short drive is over. We part ways, me heading to the classrooms the long way, around behind the PE building and along the fence, him gliding up the driveway, controlled and upright, backpack clutched to his chest like a missionary clinging to a Bible as he walks into some war-torn country that never asked for salvation.

I get to math class a moment after the bell's rung. Everyone's shuffling books around and bumping their way to their desks. I take my seat and keep my head down, pretending to look for a pen in my bag and hoping no one will notice me. I hear whispers sliding around me. *It's not about you,* I tell myself. *It's not about you.*

"Look who showing her face," Samara says loudly.

"Ain her face I see showing," someone calls out from the other side of the room. I pull my exercise book out, focusing on the paper. *I can do this.* I scrawl today's date at the top of the page and flip the textbook open.

"All right, settle down," Mrs. Jones says from the front of the classroom. "Indira, it's nice you could join us today, but you may find a *math* book a little more useful." As the teacher turns to the blackboard, the class titters.

"You gotta excuse her, Mrs. Jones," I hear Tamika call out. "She got a lot goin on."

I shove the history textbook into my bag, slouching down in my chair. I don't belong here.

The minute class is over, I head for the door, rushing to be first out of the room. I bump into Tamika on the way. I don't mean to do it, but she elbows me hard, pushing past me.

"You in a hurry to go throw up, hey?" she tosses over her shoulder. "I don't know why you don't stay your pregnant self home."

Outside in the corridor, I head for the bathroom by the library.

"Indira!" Someone calls behind me. Ms. Wilson. I pretend not to hear her as I speed up, but a cluster of seventh graders spill out of a classroom, nearly tripping me.

"Indira, I need to speak with you," Ms. Wilson says, closer now. "Wait right there, please."

I turn around to face Ms. Wilson as she bustles toward me. "You made it in today."

"I have to pee."

"I think you can hold it while we discuss your situation here. Come to my office, please."

"I can't go to the bathroom first?" I plead.

Ms. Wilson tilts her head to one side. "You can go after," she says. "Come on."

By the time we get to her office, I'm out of breath. She closes the door behind me.

"Take a seat."

I perch uncomfortably on a chair. She knows. Somebody told her about the book, she can see I look different, she's already called Aunt Patrice, and when I get to the house, all my things will be out on the street. Ms. Wilson taps her pen on the desk, flipping through a file.

"You missed your first two classes this morning, Indira. This isn't characteristic of you."

"Sorry. I slept in."

She makes a note, then continues. "The other students manage to make it here on time. Including your cousin. You live in the same household, correct?" She pauses, looking up.

"Yes."

"All right." She nods. "Is there a problem at home?"

What am I going to say? Gary the charmer did something awful to me for weeks, for months, from the time I first reached Nassau, and I can't hide what happened anymore? Who would she believe—him or me? Her face is worried but I can't tell her the truth. "No, Ms. Wilson."

"Are you sure?" She sets her pen down, leaning forward. "How are you settling in here in Nassau? It's been almost a full school year, but it must have been a big change."

"Uh-huh." I can see she expects me to say more. "It's different."

"I see," she says, nodding thoughtfully. "Are you having trouble fitting in at school?"

"Um . . ." I weigh the odds. If I say yes, she might drag this conversation out even longer. If I say no, she might keep probing. "I guess."

She opens her drawer and produces a few printouts, sliding them across the desk as if she's giving me the secret to happiness. *Why do I feel this way?* is printed across the front of the first one, with a picture of a girl holding her head in her hands. Another is titled *Finding New Friends*. "You might find something helpful in these."

"Thanks." I shove them into my bag. Maybe we're almost done.

"Now, Indira, despite what you may have going on personally, you have to pull your socks up, okay? I'm concerned about your behavior. First, the hullabaloo in the bathroom yesterday—"

"I didn't hit her, it was an accident!" I interrupt.

"—okay, let me finish. I'm waiting for the letter you were to give to Samara. Do you have it today?"

Letter? That was the last thing on my mind. "No."

"I see. I also have a note here from Mr. McDonald saying you didn't even try to answer half the questions on your biology test. Now you're skipping classes. Is this how you want to go into your final year?"

"No, ma'am."

"Good. Now, I called and left two messages for your aunt yesterday," Ms. Wilson continues. "Please remind her to call me back, I need to discuss all this with her urgently."

My heart speeds up, but I fight to sound calm. "I'll let her know. I could go, please?"

Ms. Wilson leans across the desk. "One more thing. One

of the girls who witnessed the incident yesterday came to me and told me you had a certain book in your possession. Something to do with pregnancy?" She stares at me expectantly. My mind races, flipping through possible outcomes. I could say it wasn't mine, but what if Ms. Wilson finds it in my bag? Or I could say I just wanted to read about it. She still might ask why, and maybe notice how my blouse doesn't quite fit right. In the end, the truth comes out, or at least part of it.

"My grammy gave me that when I left Mariner's. It was hers," I say.

Ms. Wilson nods, but she doesn't look totally convinced. "Indira, I have to ask you—"

"I really need to go to the bathroom, please."

Ms. Wilson hesitates, but her phone rings, saving me. "Go ahead, then," she says, and I'm out the door before the words are fully out of her mouth. "Make sure your aunt gets ahold of me," I hear her call after me. "One more incident and I'll have to put a permanent mark on your record. We don't want that for you, Indira."

I make it to the bathroom, slam the stall door shut, and plop down, praying that none of the girls from class come in. For once, my prayer is answered. No one disturbs me. I stay in the stall until the bell rings for the next class. There's bustling in the hallway, and then quiet. I take my time; why rush to the classroom just to hear everyone talking about me? As

I walk through the empty hallways to history, I have to pass Ms. Wilson's office again. The door is closed; she's onto some other problem now. I wonder if Aunt Patrice really missed all those messages, if there's going to be trouble. Or if she just doesn't care.

"A yoga retreat?" Smiley screws up her face, picking at the last of her dinner. We're outside, the night quiet, the driveway empty except for Uncle's car. The TV's dull blare floats out on the air; Uncle's dozing in front of the news. "What you wanna go there for?"

I push my plate away. "Better than here."

"Oh. How you found this place?"

"I came across it by accident. It's not that far." I'm already telling her more than I'd planned. I'd thought, at first, to say nothing, to keep the retreat a secret. But she caught me emptying schoolbooks out of my bag, and when Smiley wants to know something, she can jump up and down on your patience until you practically want to bludgeon her with the answer. I'm not telling her I'm leaving Nassau for good, although I do wish I could say a real goodbye.

"The boat ride ain ga make you sick? I mean, you already havin"—she lowers her voice, leaning in—"morning sickness."

"How you know?"

"I have a nose, I can smell. I thought your stomach was

bothering you or something." She glances over at me. "Oh, don't worry, Mummy always stuffed up. She don't notice things."

Doesn't she? I think of that morning, Gary's finger pressing into my neck, the clearing of her throat. After the picture of me in Dion's jeep, I know she's watching me extra close. How long before she sees what I'm hiding? Even worse, what if she already suspects what's growing in me and is waiting for the right moment to throw me out? All the more reason to get on that boat tomorrow and never come back.

I've been quiet too long; Smiley's staring down at her feet, tapping her fingers on the step impatiently. She knows there's more. I wish I could tell her about getting rowed out for being in Dion's jeep, but it's all too tangled around other things. Why I was in the jeep, and why Gary would send the picture, and why he was mad, and the single biggest, ugliest why that can't be said out loud, not to anybody. Smiley would want to open her big mouth to Aunt Patrice and anybody with two ears and half a brain. I already know what people would say; in their eyes, if Gary messed with me, it's all my fault. "I like being by the water," I say, but the words are too few to fill up the holes in our conversation.

"So when are you gonna tell me whose baby it is?" Smiley turns to look at me.

I ignore the question, facing the street.

"Well, this must be the second Immaculate Conception,

cause you *always* here, and till these last couple days, I never knew you to miss school." Then, miraculously, she leaves it alone. "So what they's do out there?" she asks instead. "They's be standing on their heads?"

I try to hide the gratitude in my voice. "I ain seen that yet."

"So what you seen, then? You's be so secretive, man."

"Okay. I remember this one. Downward-facing dog." I step down onto the lawn, getting on my hands and knees. It's an invitation to be sick, moving around so soon after eating, but I don't care. I just want to be myself, even for a minute.

"An you supposed to do it barefoot?"

"You know so much, you do it," I say. She's right, though. The students at the retreat wander the paths with no shoes on, like the whole place is their very own backyard. I remember seeing a row of abandoned sneakers and sandals at the edge of the deck. I kick off my shoes, welcoming the cool grass under my toes. "Okay, downward dog, you get like this, then you lift your bongey in the air, straighten your arms and legs, and then you push back." I look between my legs and see her standing there laughing. I flop back down. "And you ask me to show you?"

"Sorry, but you look so funny." She must see my face, because she stops laughing. "Sorry. Sorry, man. Show me another one."

Be like Smiley, I tell myself. *Laugh it off.* I remember

Dion balancing on one leg, and imagine me trying to do that with an even bigger belly, in four months' time. It's not funny to me, but I force a smile anyway. "Okay, so they call this one upward-facing dog." I get on my hands and knees, do a shaky push-up, then lower myself back down. Then I rise up, legs down on the ground, arms straight, my back curved so my head is turned up to the sky. I try to mimic the shapes I remember seeing Dion make at the retreat. "And from this one you come up into downward dog again." I raise my butt in the air. "So what, you just ga watch me?" I peer through my legs again at upside-down Smiley. Her gaze is off toward the street, and a look of surprise lights up her face.

"Oh, hey! Churchy, what you doin here?"

I come down hard, back on my hands and knees, standing up so fast my head spins. There's no one here but me, the empty night, and Smiley. She guffaws like she's set up the best joke ever.

"Oh, I wish you coulda see yourself," she hoots. "What wrong with you?" she calls as I push past her. "I bet you he woulda enjoy that view. What, you can't take a joke?"

I shove the door open. She better not follow me. Uncle shifts slightly in his chair as I storm past him, heading to Smiley's room.

"So what, you think you could be with him?" Her voice trails behind me, a bad smell.

I whirl around. "Get out."

"This my room, you can't tell me to get out. I was only playing, Indy. What you so mad for?"

"Why you gotta keep bringing Churchy up?"

"What, you don't like him?"

Something about the way she says it, the sly sideways look, the secret-telling voice, gives me an uneasy feeling in my belly. It's as sickening as any tray of greasy leftovers. I don't think of Churchy that way. "No. I pregnant. You ain hear me before?" We both glance over at the open door, just in case.

"Look here, all you gotta do, go with Churchy one time. You know you ain got no boyfriend."

"How you know?"

"Oh, please. I know you. The only places you ever used to go was school and home, so I know you don't have nobody. And Churchy ain that bad."

I stare at her; she might as well be speaking a different language.

"You know what I mean. Only one time, and after that, he ga stay round. He's the type of guy who wouldn't go nowhere. He's exactly what you need. I ain know what you makin that face for," she says, barreling on. "What you plan on doin, then? Wait till after my mummy find out? She ga find out soon enough. I mean gee, you already so big."

"You think I'd set him up? I don't even know what you call that type of person." Yes, I do.

Mamma.

I go out into the living room, relieved that Smiley doesn't follow. I flop down on the sofa. Uncle stirs again in his armchair, then hikes himself to his feet, mumbling a good night. I turn off the TV, then the lamp. I can hear Smiley's nighttime sounds: brushing her teeth, the rustling of books, light switching off. And later, I hear Aunt Patrice come in from choir practice, see her look over at me, humph to herself quietly, and close her bedroom door. I don't care if I never speak to Smiley again. But sleep never comes for me, and when I hear the roar of a truck backing into the driveway sometime after one, I grab my pillow and sheet and fumble into Smiley's room. Lock the door, lean the chair up under the doorknob, even though he'd never come in here. Smiley is splayed out on the bed, but when I lie down on the edge, she shifts, whimpering in her sleep, to make space for me.

8

TEN MINUTES OUT OF Nassau Harbour, the air is fresh, the water transparent all the way down, no disguise for pockets of fish that dash and twist away from the ferry's hulk. Joe runs through our three stops for the day—the church on the hill, the all-age school, the hotel in the deep south—before cracking open a magazine, feet up on the bench beside her. "You don't have to stay here the whole time," she says. Her voice sounds softer out here on the water, the permanent scowl lightened into a furrow. "Meet me on the first level when we're getting ready to dock," she calls as I weave through the handful of couples and families spread around. The boat's not full, but I still head up to the top deck, where even the minor crowds give way to a few stray souls watching the last tip of Nassau disappear, sky and ocean unfolding all around.

"Hey, sweet girl." One of the crew hisses at me, liquid

slick. I ignore him, clinging to the railing as I go. Smiley was wrong; the motion doesn't make me feel sick. It feels good, this familiar sway. Reminds me of shorter boat rides with Grammy from Mariner's Cay over to Eleuthera, for her church's conventions, for the big school concerts, for the fair or a funeral or a wedding. *We could go up to the top?* I'd ask, and she would smile and follow behind me, her step as eager as mine, then plop down in a quiet spot, opening up whatever book she had on her that day, while I watched the boat bounce over the waves, or, on smoother waters, cut through the blue, scissors through silk. When we reached the shore, the crewmen, each sunned to his darkest tone, would jump the gap from dockside to deck, barefoot and easy, tugging and tying the boat up with fat ropes.

I take off my flip-flops, tuck them in my back pocket. Something about the boat makes you want to shed things. Next, I slide my hair elastic off; my scalp exhales as my hair poufs out. The wind fights hard to make its way through the thick, tight-curled mass, poking and pressing like a nosey neighbor rooting for gossip. It'll be a bush when I get to Mariner's, I don't care. I close my eyes. I'm going home. I can see Grammy in all her usual places: on the porch shelling peas; in the kitchen, the smell of onions browning for stew chicken; in the room, reading aloud. Reading Proverbs. Reading *Jane Eyre*. Reading the *Tribune*. Salt air and stories all through the house. I feel my way into my straw bag, fumbling past the toothbrush and underwear, the skirts and tops, until I find the book.

As I touch it, memories wash over me in waves. Grammy, straightening out my dress on the first day of school, scraping a brush against the tightly curled edges of my hair to get it neat and smooth. Her hands patting my shoulder over a test with a big *10/10* at the top of the page, circled in red. *You keep that up, now.* Grammy bending over the table to squint at homework, then waggling a finger. *You can't hand that mess in. Do it again. You know better.* And then after all that, *You gotta watch out for yourself.* If Grammy was so sure I'd end up pregnant, why would she have ever bothered? Why would she have acted like she believed in me? Why would she have whispered those words: *Don't let no one take advantage of you. You hear?* Like she thought I could stop certain things. Like advantage was something I could give willingly.

I turn my face to the wind, as if that will blow all these questions away, and the hurt, too. I get to see Grammy again today. I get to be with her. That's enough. That's everything. I pull the book out of the bag and let it fall open to wherever it wants. The pages rustle in the breeze, then stop past the middle, after the part about your belly button popping out like an extra nipple, but before it explains labor with explicit pictures and words like *forceps* and *tearing*. Grammy's writing isn't squeezed into the margins of those pages, but I flip forward a few and find something that brings her voice to life around me:

Those last few weeks can be murder. Let me tell you. When it was my time, skinny as I am, my ankles swelled up to almost the size of my calves, till one of my sisters came in and laughed at me, said it looked like I was trying to walk on tree trunks. I couldn't see my feet by then, but I could see my belly shift. Don't be scared if you see your belly do funny things. You might see an elbow or a knee poking out all of a sudden. That's the baby trying to find some more space. All you do is tap it right back in. If you think they hard to control when they inside, wait till they get out. But I wouldn't have missed that experience for anything. Big fat ankles and all.

I don't hear an angry voice, like Joe's, or one that's giddy and distant, the way Mamma's would be. It isn't the suspicious, hateful tone Aunt Patrice has. Instead, I hear the same old Grammy, full of stories and love. How could that Grammy ever think so little of me? I hold on to the book, remembering that day I pulled it out of the closet.

Early February. Two periods late, and the taste of dinner, puked up on the neighbor's hibiscuses, is bitter acid in my mouth. I'm in the kitchen washing dishes when I see Gary step out, walk across the yard. Fingers dripping soapy water, I run to his room, push the closed door open, dig through the closet, rummaging behind suits and neatly pressed jeans and cotton shirts, trying to hold my breath against the stink of his cologne. It hangs, always, in the air. My fingers touch the flimsy plastic of an old roach hotel, the dusty carpet in the back of the closet. Is it gone? I can hear voices out front, Uncle's low, sparing words, Smiley laughing. And more laughter, Gary's laughter—he must be back inside. Part of me wants to stand in the middle of the room, waiting for him. I want to confront him, to turn to the side, show him my waist getting wider, make him see what he's done. Instead, I push myself deeper into the closet, knocking over a tower of boxes, dress shoes and barely worn sneakers spilling, a toppled empire.

"You know how y'all women get," I hear him say as he steps into the room.

"And how us women get?" Smiley asks, her voice closer. She must be in the room too. My eyes are shut, body crammed into the smallest possible space. Get out of here, I want to tell her. Get out! But it's daylight, and it's Smiley, and nothing ever happens to her, and Uncle knows they're in here.

"Y'all always getting upset over some silly little thing," he says.

"Yeah, yeah, whatever." Smiley's voice grows fainter; she sounds bored. And now it's him and me in here, alone.

"Shit," he says. He sounds sad. The bedsprings groan, then squeak as he lies down. When I hear snoring, I start

to climb out of the closet. My toes touch something I missed before. Bend down and fingers find the softness of page edges. Pick up the book at my feet. I ease out of the closet and hurry out of the room, not daring to even look at him asleep on the bed. Once I'm in the hallway, I open the cover, see Grammy's steady, looped writing: To my girl. Something to help carry you through.

"Niceness. Niceness, how you doin?"

I open my eyes; a crew member has followed me up here, the same hisser, the same liquid voice as before. Smiley would think he looks good. Loose, curly hair that needs a cutting, skin the color of slightly burned peanut cakes. All I see, though, is the leer in his eyes, gaze pressed up against me like the weight of a body. I drop the book into my bag. I have nothing to say.

"You want give me your number?" He talks to my chest, staring at it like I'm carrying ripe mangoes for sale and he's eager to haggle on the price. That's the problem. I can pretend I'm something different. Pretend I'm not Mamma's daughter. Pretend I'm not pregnant. Pretend I'm a regular teenage girl going on a day job to help people learn to stand on their heads. Pretend I'm not me—until someone comes along and acts otherwise. Funny thing is, people really only see what they want. And all he wants is big breasts.

Deep breath in . . . in . . . in . . . He's looking at me. I close my eyes. Deep breath out. Nope, still feel like shoving him in the water. Either I'm doing it wrong or it's not fast-acting magic, this deep-breathing thing. Which would explain a lot about Joe.

"You look good, ya know. You ain wan let me check you, ay? I get off at six."

I let the breath out. I stand, yank my shirt up to just under my bra. His eyes widen: he can't believe his good luck.

"I *pregnant,* and this shirt ain goin no higher so don't even *dream* you seein any bubby from me. You wan like a pregnant girl? Or you wan leave me alone to catch my sweet breeze and enjoy the boat ride?"

He takes a step back, mouth gone slack.

"That's right, I pregnant. So you could go right back to doing your job. I'm sure they don't pay you to hit on pregnant *teenagers.*" I make sure to say it nice and loud. "I *sixteen.* I barely legal, and you a big grown-ass dusty man. Look like you got gray hair, and cobwebs in your teeth." He closes his mouth. I can tell it's over, he's not gonna hassle me anymore, but I can't stop. "What, you ain shame? That's what they's pay you for here? You see what somebody else do to me and you come to get your piece too? You disgusting. Your big goggle-eyed self. Look like a Muppet frog. What, they's call you Kermit, ay?" The couple standing by the rail turn around; the girl smirks. Whether it's at me or him, I don't know or care. A gaggle of tourists hold their heads rigidly the other way, trying too hard not to notice the commotion.

"Sorry, miss, I didn't mean no harm. Sorry. Sorry, I didn't know," he mutters, slinking away.

"Maybe try knowing next time before you come sniffing around people's daughters. I should be calling you Great-Granddaddy, you so damn old. Look like Methuselah and come tryin to chat me up." I finally let my hands fall from my hips as he hustles down the stairs. A couple of his crewmates caught the last of it; I can hear them hooting, calling him out as he vanishes from view. I yank my shirt back down, flop onto the bench. I feel the blood pulsing through me furiously. I pull the salt air into me, try to let it become part of my body. I'm pissed. And proud. More than anything, I wish I could talk this way to Gary, bold-faced, hard-voiced, and true. Where's this side of me, when it's him? I wish I could tell everybody who he is, what he is, when they're all fawning over his jokes. Wish I had courage then like I do now.

The yoga mats are stacked up on the dock, Joe standing off to one side, cell phone pressed up to her ear. The other passengers have already dispersed. Whatever Zen Joe soaked up on the boat is evaporating quickly.

"So what time are you going to be here?" she says, her on-the-phone voice so loud a pair of seagulls that were sidling up to us change their minds and take off. "I thought we agreed on nine-thirty. Yes, nine-thirty. A.m. Today. For Joe Morris. No, ten is too late. What kind of back-of-the-bush operation y'all running? Hello? Hello?"

An old woman who's settled against a post to wait for her own ride looks over at Joe, then at me. Joe stares at her phone, mystified by its betrayal. "You believe he actually hung up on me? Taxi driver told me he'd be here at nine-thirty and now he wanna have attitude when I call and tell him he's late. Man, these people don't know how to act."

The old woman purses her lips. She looks familiar; I'm sure she shushed me in church one time or swatted me for robbing her mango tree or pelted a grapefruit at me to chase me out of her yard. She reminds me of Grammy, no-nonsense and wiry. I'm not about to pitch a fit, but I'm eager to get going, too. The sooner these classes are done, the sooner I can go find Grammy. The thought gives me sparks of excitement, but it also chips away at a pit of fear in my belly. What will I say? What will she say? I want so badly to take off right away, leave Joe here shouting into her phone, and go straight to the house. No. That's not me. That's Mamma's way—do what you want, ditch people after you give your word. I said I'd help Joe and that's what I'll do. Even if biting my tongue nearly kills me. I glance over at her, shoulders hunched, scowling like a flock of gulls just decorated her head.

"He'll be here."

"Yeah, question is what time. First class is at ten, and now what? I gotta call these people and tell them I'm gonna be late?"

"Hmmmmph," the old woman says, shooting Joe a vile glare.

"Indira, these your people. What, they can't tell time?" She's got her phone out again, hammering into it. "Great. Now he isn't even answering his phone."

"Oh, sweet Lord, give me patience." The old woman shifts against her post.

"Call this number." Joe pushes the phone into my hands, with a scrap of paper. "Better yet, call somebody you know. Don't you have family over here? Do something, you ain gotta stand there like a lump." She starts walking up to the main road.

"Rudeness!" the old woman exclaims, loud enough that Joe turns around and stares before continuing toward the road. "That's your daddy's people, eh? She must be family, for her to talk to you like so."

I turn the phone over in my hand. I take a chance and dial Mamma's number. It's out of service.

"Hmph." The old woman glares at Joe's retreating figure. "No manners. She couldn't be from Mariner's. What y'all up here for, anyway?" The old woman reaches into her purse, coming out with a foil-wrapped package.

"*She* came to teach yoga. At the school, the church, and the hotel. No, thank you," I add as she holds out the package to me. Homemade bread, the layer of butter as thick as the slab of cheese between the two slices. "I came up here to help her, but—"

"Take piece," she insists, holding out the parcel until I reach in and take a square of the sandwich. "But you really come to see your people."

"Yes, ma'am."

"Yeah, I remember you. Miz Fergie granddaughter. Doubles, they call you." She bites into a square herself and chews slowly. "Almost quadruples now. Indira May Ferguson. And you was always the spitting image of that ma you got. Your ma is a no-good gal, you know, always running after man, always with a different one. I hope you don't follow after her."

"No." I see her give me a sideways glare.

"It's Mrs. Darville. You should remember me."

"No, Mrs. Darville," I say, but when she's not looking I cut my eye back at her.

"Mmm-hmm. I hope not. I see that boy on the boat you was tellin off."

I freeze. The last bite of sandwich turns into a wad of cardboard in my mouth. "You heard?"

"No, but I look up partway, see your hands on them big hips you got, and his head down while your tongue just waggin, waggin, waggin. I wish more young girls would tell these fresh boys where to go."

He wasn't a boy, I think. He was a man. I make myself swallow the last mouthful of sandwich, which lands in my belly like a rock. The old woman is still chattering. I nod along but my eyes are on Joe, who's reached the road and is peering down one side, then the other. A rickety car drives past and she waves her arms frantically, flapping even harder when it carries on without stopping.

"You hear me, girl?" the old woman says.

"Yes, ma'am," I lie.

"I say if you mean you goin to see your *mummy*. Can't go see Grammy."

The rock of bread and butter and cheese does a backflip in my stomach. Can't see Grammy? "Why not?"

A look crosses her face, the look of someone who thought they were discussing general knowledge and realizes they've blurted out a deep family secret. "Never mind, never mind. I can't get in that. Your mummy could explain it better."

"Something happened to my grammy?"

The woman gets to her feet. "No, no. She all right, baby. Look, this my son here. I suppose I should do the Christian thing and give y'all a ride to wherever y'all goin."

"Thank you." My voice feels as if it's coming from some-place outside my body. Grammy's all right. I try to believe that. She's all right. She has to be.

"Hey! Hey, rude lady!" Mrs. Darville calls after Joe, who glances over her shoulder, scowling.

"We have a ride," I add. That brings Joe scurrying. The middle-aged man who pulls up vacates the driver's seat and carefully sidesteps Joe's bustling frame, waving off her thanks and loading up the trunk with half the yoga mats, piling the rest into the backseat. "I guess y'all ga have to sit close," he says, gesturing at the narrow middle section and remaining passenger seat. Joe steps back.

"Go ahead, Indira."

The man chuckles as I get into the middle. I'm spilling out onto the passenger side, which Joe couldn't fill if she stretched out longways.

"Well, this was lucky," Joe says cheerfully. You'd think we'd tripped and accidentally fallen into Mrs. Darville's car. Thankfully, after that Joe manages to keep her mouth shut until they drop us off at the churchyard, the man dutifully unloading the mats and bags while Mrs. Darville hobbles inside to say hello to Pastor Michaels.

"Set up the mats quickly, Indira," Joe says, heading for the church door. "We're running late. I need to go find the woman in charge."

"Where should I put them?"

"Find a spot," she calls over her shoulder, still curt, but a little less bristly. "This is your stomping ground."

I stand at the top of the hill the church is built on,

looking all the way around. We're high enough to see over the trees. In the distance, the water stretches out forever. The island looks sleepy from here. Plenty of things go on under that canopy of foliage, though. Beside the church is the cemetery, there from at least a hundred years ago, old enough that the church couldn't foresee needing room to bury more than thirty or forty people. Next to that, the run-down basketball court and the trees where Mrs. Ellis used to line us up on the grass for Sunday school. From there, we could hear the music service bursting out of the sanctuary: raucous singing, tambourines, clapping, hollering, and the piano being beaten into submission. Grammy used to poke her head out the door halfway through, like I always begged her to do. She'd beckon me over as though there was an emergency; I'd steal a quick look at Mrs. Ellis and her switch, then make a run for it. Grammy's firm hands guided me back to the pew, tapping out the drum's rhythm on my shoulders as we went.

I decide on the grassy opening by the court. I start to lay out the mats, two rows of five, narrow edges facing forward, with Joe's mat at the head of the class, so everyone can see her. As I'm wiping off the mats, Mrs. Ellis appears from around the side of the building, her hair as gray as it's been for as long as I can remember, wearing the same shapeless skirt. Only difference, we're the same height now.

"Indira May Ferguson. What you doin up here? Your ma send for you, ay?"

"I came over with Joe."

"With who, now?"

"J—with Ms. Morris. For the yoga class."

"Mmmm." Mrs. Ellis presses her lips together as if guarding her mouth from a swarm of unpleasant bugs flying in. "Well, the pastor's daughter arranged that. I don't take part in them funny things." She tuts at the mats like they're rectangles of moral decay. "And your grammy wouldn't have neither. You better be glad she ain here to see you caught up in this."

"What you mean she ain here? Mrs. Ellis?" I call, but she's already walking away. I should run to the house right now. Forget how I feel, forget about the book. Just see that Grammy's there, see she's okay. Then Joe appears, and I have to put it out of my mind. Grammy's fine. Someone would have told me before if she wasn't. Didn't I just talk to Mamma? Wouldn't Uncle have known?

There's a young woman with Joe, in stretchy yoga pants and a sleeveless T-shirt. She smiles at me and I recognize her as the pastor's daughter. A handful of other people trickle out of the church after them, mostly other young women, also in tidy exercise clothes. I remember two of them from the boat ride over. Joe looks over the mats; I think I've done a good job. She doesn't praise me, but she doesn't complain, either, as she steps onto the one at the front. The others follow suit, getting comfortable on the grass. While they settle in, I sit under the cool of that familiar tree.

"Good morning, everyone. My assistant and I came over from Nassau early this morning, and we're both delighted to be here. I'm Joe, that's Indira over there." Joe speaks as if we go way back, her voice musical, lyrical. Delighted? I'd snort if it didn't, amazingly, seem true. Her quick introduction over, she begins the class with a sort of relaxing story. "Eyes closed, breathe in this good salt air. Imagine that with each inhale, you expand more, with each exhale, you let go of anything you're holding on to. The ocean is vast, large enough to cleanse our worries. Any thoughts that come up, simply let them float away on the gentle sea breeze." In spite of myself, I try it. I close my eyes. I breathe in. My breath feels short, but I exhale anyway and try to let go. Of fretting over Grammy. Of Mummy. Of Gary. Of the book weighing down the straw bag. Of the thing inside me. It's impossible. I open my eyes and glimpse Joe, her face disapproving as she looks at me sitting off to the side. Well, so what? I agreed to come here and help. Never said anything about class participation.

"Let's begin our asanas, our poses, by chanting 'Ohm' three times." She opens her mouth and sings out an unfamiliar but surprisingly melodious *"Ooooohhhhm."* The class takes a collective inhale right along with her and joins in. *"Ooooohhhhmmmmm."* They all look so serious and peaceful and the sound is so strong and shuddery that I'm breathing in myself. I'm almost ready to join in for the last one when a shriek tears through the air.

"Oh! Oh, Lord Jesus! Oh, expel this blasphemy from out of Your hallowed domain. Out! Expel it!" Mrs. Ellis's voice booms like it's outfitted with a subwoofer as she hurries out of the church. "Get out, get thee behind me."

"And slowly come up into a standing position," I hear Joe say, her voice quavering slightly. "Bring your hands to your chest, into prayer position—"

"See how they make a mockery of You? Hands together like they praying, and they out here exposing their bottom shape in these indecent clothings! Out, Jezebel! Out, Delilah! Out . . . out . . ." Mrs. Ellis trails off, fresh out of Biblical women of shame, but she's not stumped for long. "Temptresses!" she shouts, victorious. "Temptresses in the tight pants! Get out! Be expelled, demonesses, this is holy ground! Get out!" She's getting closer, carrying something smoking. She raises her hand, waving the smoke around in big, sweeping gestures. Familiar smell—sweet, choking. Like that homemade incense Grammy used to clear out the air. As she marches past me, I see a massive bundle of smoldering thyme, bay leaves, fevergrass, and casuarina needles all bound together. "Repent!" she shouts at me, wafting smoke into my face and leaving me spluttering as I escape to a safe part of the field.

It all goes downhill quickly from there. Literally. The pastor's daughter leaps off her mat, all her good vibes abandoned, and charges at Mrs. Ellis, who stops in her tracks, feet planted wide like she's doing yoga herself, about to swivel into some sort of deep lunge. Mrs. Ellis raises the burning leaves into the air, and a fortuitous gust of wind carries the smoke right into the students' faces. The class scatters, choking, gathering up shoes as they flee. Joe barrels toward Mrs. Ellis and the pastor's daughter, waving her arms, pointing and shouting, her words blown away by that same relaxing breeze she described. She loses her balance, tumbling into Mrs. Ellis and the pastor's daughter, and the three of them smack into the ground with so much force that they keep rolling down the hill. They pass me so fast I can't make out who's who, only see smoke and hear cries to heaven and less pious choices of words. I fling my head back, wicked laughter rising up out of me.

As the three of them start to untangle themselves, I head for the main road, leaving their raised voices behind. No way am I sticking around for the fallout. Knowing Joe, she'd find a way to blame it on me. Besides, I've waited around long enough; I have to see Grammy.

The first car passing slows down, and it's Mr. Abe's son,

who works for the electric company. I'd rather wait for a woman to give me a ride, but my ankles are starting to swell, so I take a chance and ask him to drop me off at Grammy's house. He keeps his hands on the wheel and his eyes on the road, doesn't say much and doesn't hassle me. Passing the familiar houses, the old stretch of coastline, makes this all the more real. I'm getting closer to her. I see her in everything we drive by: Grammy, swimming in her stretched-out undershirt and oversized panties shaped like a sail. Grammy, picking mangoes from that skinny young tree. Grammy, beating out the rug with a fury that only being distracted from her reading could produce. Grammy, pouring hot water over a handful of leaves harvested from the side of the road. I know she is waiting there, a thousand familiar Grammies crammed into and around that house, moving through the routines of a whole lifetime.

At the foot of the pathway, I look up at the house. Its open windows wait. The grass is overgrown. As I get closer, I see mint growing into the jasmine, rosemary kneeling from being left uncut so long. What used to be basil is flopped over and dried out in the sun, nothing but sticks now. My excitement evaporates, leaving behind fear. I'm scared to face Grammy. Scared for her to know. And scared for something else I can't name. Maybe I don't have to go in. Maybe Mr. Abe's son can drop me back to the church. I look behind me but it's too late;

he's already pulled away. I keep walking up.

Before I've stepped onto the porch, I see the broken window. Three, four empty rum bottles loll by the door. The remnants of cigarettes, stubbed out in bottle caps, and abandoned plastic cups are lined up on the wooden railing. One of the posts has been kicked out.

When I reach the door, I turn the handle and step into darkness. My foot finds a can, still half full. It tips over, sloshing brown liquid onto the wood floor. The smell is fetid; unwashed body, dirty laundry, old pee. In late May, it's boiling in here. The curtains are drawn. I sweep one of them open, and daylight shows me the ruined dining room. The old table's still there, but only one stained chair remains, mournful without its kin. "Grammy?" I call, even though I know she's not here. She would pass out in this place after less than a minute, never could stand stale air or close rooms, let alone a pigsty of a house, ankle-deep in garbage. The living room is worse; an upturned chair, abandoned dishes, huge scrape marks on the floor, smears and handprints on the walls. A roach, disrupted by the light, scuttles for cover. Grammy never let roaches set up shop in the middle of rooms, hunted the odd one that snuck under the door until it met the heel of her shoe. This place would kill her.

"Grammy?" No answer. I push the thought away, but it comes again. *Maybe it already has.* Down the hall, into my old room. The bed is stripped of sheets, exposing the bare mattress with the rusty stain from one of my earlier periods. There's a host of unfamiliar stains now, faded light brown. I turn back. "Grammy?"

The door to Grammy's room is open—no, it's missing. The curtains are drawn in here too, and there's a stirring, a faint, mewing sound. "Grammy?"

There, on the half-bare mattress, sheet flung to one side, legs sprawled off the other, eyes glazed with sleep and I don't know what else.

"Mamma." The word falls flat. She looks up at me, dazed.

"Indy? Babygirl, what you doin here? You call to say you was comin?" Her words slide one into the other. She tries to prop herself up and can't, flops back down. She smells rotten; I want out of here. "An you live in Nassau now?"

"What happen to Grammy?"

"How you get here?"

"Where Grammy?"

"Don't come back here, baby. Ain nothin here for you. You better off in Nassau." She finally sits up, moving like it's a struggle. "Oh, my head." She reaches for a cup on the night-stand, which wobbles in a new, ugly way. The bottom drawer is missing. "How you doin, babygirl? I was supposed to send some money down for you."

"Where she is?" I want to break up everything in this

place. Except it's already broken. "What you do to her? You kill her?"

"Indy, why you yellin?" She sounds whiny, a child's pathetic voice.

"Where Grammy?"

"In here cold. You feel cold?" She rubs her arms.

"Where Grammy is?" I'm shouting now, my anger rearing up, a snake ready to strike. "Where she is?" Yelling at her so close, so loud, the words reverberate off her, bounce back into me. "What you do to her? What you do to her? Tell me! She dead? You kill her? You kill her?" Mamma's stink is suffocating: alcohol and sweaty body, mold and pee, and some cheap, sweet thing she sprayed on yesterday or a week ago. It hangs like one of those tree-shaped car fresheners on a huge pile of cow dung. "Where she is? You better tell me!"

"She safe! She with good people, baby. The people had to come for her, I couldn't look after her alone, I couldn't, not no more, but she with family, she safe, she all right." Mamma's scrambling across the bed away from me, as if I'm the one who stinks, her eyes fearful and wide. She's backed against the wall; nowhere else to go. Memory flash: man's voice raised, Mamma against a wall, same eyes, me hiding behind a chair, Grammy snatching me, running outside. *Do what you gotta do.*

She doesn't look at me, keeping her head down. She thinks

I'm gonna strike out at her. I've never hit anyone. I wouldn't hit her now. Wouldn't even touch her. Feel like I'm gonna pick up scabies or something from standing this close. But I know she's lying. What family could Grammy be with? If she's not here, and she's not with Uncle, what safe place would she be?

I stand back, and Mamma crawls off the bed and struggles to Grammy's bathroom. She slams the door closed, but it can't shut out the sound of her bawling. I reach for the bathroom doorknob and push it open, easy. She's too out of it to have even bothered with the lock.

"Don't hurt me." She's cowering in the bathtub, old wrappers of I don't want to know what laying in there, a rim of dirt and rust stains around the sides. "Babygirl, don't hurt me. You ain even know how it was, the money was running out, and things didn't work out with Chris, and she tell me move in here, and then the house, it wasn't safe no more after the last storm, the roof was leaky and all, and I couldn't watch her, I couldn't keep her, I couldn't—" She looks up into my face, a child begging. "Babygirl, I couldn't let her stay here."

My chest aches, my head starting to spin. The heat, the anger, the urge to take something and smash it. *Breathe,* Dion would say. *Breathe in deep, hold, breathe out.* How do you breathe in when the air is a wall of ugly and disease and dirt and you have to carve yourself a door just to get out? I feel the square of butter sandwich rising. No, not here, not here—and I vomit right into the tub. She whimpers, moving out of the way and slipping.

I try to straighten up. The room is beginning to close in, pinprick dots dancing before my eyes. "I have to get out." Barely know if I say it out loud or only in my head.

"You see this? And that ain even the worst thing I seen this week," Mamma says. She's laughing, now. *Laughing*. I straighten up, making my legs work. "This what I livin in, Indy. Ain only you who think this all I am. Everybody know. Even your grammy know it. You see how I livin. I couldn't let her stay here with me. It woulda kill her, baby."

Spit it out with the last of the bad taste. "I wish it kill *you*."

Don't watch, don't wait for her face to catch it, register it, and start to unfold. Don't care. Only run out, through the dank living room to the open door. Mamma's long, low wail follows me. Outside, down the pathway, onto the road. I shouldn't, but I turn back and look at the house. I see it for what it is. A husk of a life I can't ever go back to. Windows broken, stained curtains tugged by the wind into the hard air outside. Inside, her, rotting. Wallowing in puke. And me? I'm her Double. The thing, the person, everyone expects me to become.

9

IN TOOTE'S GENERAL STORE, I pick up a bottle of home-made ginger beer and a pack of crackers.

"Ms. Ferguson granddaughter?" Old Mr. Toote peers at me from cataract-glazed eyes.

"Yes, sir."

"Hmph." He shakes his head. "The way your ma treat her is a shame."

I push my items across the counter, glancing over my shoulder in spite of myself. The store is quiet, but I still have to check.

"Nobody else in here. Although everybody know anyway." He leans back in his chair. "The people from Social Services come for your grammy. I don't know who call them. They say she in a home in Nassau someplace." He glances at the drink, then at me, his brows raised. "Now, that ginger beer is the grown folks' brew. That one have alcohol in it."

I count out some change and push it across the counter. "I know."

He looks at the money, then back up at me. "Think you business drinkin that?"

"I do today."

Mr. Toote reaches across the counter and tosses down three plastic-wrapped coconut tarts. "Keep ya lil money," he growls. "If Ms. Ferguson find out I sell you that, she'll have my head."

I sit out on the front steps, watching the odd person stroll in and out of the bank or the post office and library. It must be past noon. Joe's probably at the school now, if she's not still in the churchyard duking it out with Mrs. Ellis. I crack open the ginger beer. It fizzes, the yeasty scent of alcohol hitting me right away. I'm thirsty, but the smell reminds me of Mamma. She probably drank when she was pregnant with me. "And I wind up just fine," I say to nobody. Still, I pour out the beer, the liquid snaking down the steaming-hot road. Behind me, I hear the store's door chime open.

"Don't waste this one," I hear Mr. Toote say as he plunks something down. When I turn around, he's disappeared, a bottle of regular old ginger ale soda beside me.

I start walking to the school, my bag dragging my shoulder down. The possibility of Grammy leaving Mariner's never occurred to me. Grammy's always been here, her house the anchor keeping me in place. Mamma, too. Even when Mamma sent me away, I always knew Grammy was there in her kitchen, on her porch, waiting for me. Now that's gone. I try to twist this mess into a new pathway: Grammy is in Nassau somewhere. I could find the home she's living in. Someone will know where she is. I could move in with her—no, it's a home for old people. She could move in with me, protect me from Gary. Except if living in that house was a real possibility, she'd already be there. Uncle probably wants her there, but Aunt Patrice wouldn't take another outsider under her roof. We could live in our own place. Except I don't have any money, and Grammy's too old to work. I try to find that new road to Grammy, but every detour I take is a dead end; everywhere I turn, there's no way out.

I try to get out of my head, focusing on walking down Mariner's familiar streets. I should feel at home. Instead, everything is strange, reality wrenched to one side. It's a dream, being here, the kind where scenes change without warning, where dead people live and breathe and your teeth all fall out, where cats talk and dolphins fly. When I wake up, I will be in Aunt Patrice's house, and Gary will be standing over me. That's the only reality I can see. A car pulls up behind me, honking.

"Indira May Ferguson, gal, if you keep walking and don't

turn your head like your grammy raised you right, I'll get out this car and slap you silly." It's a woman's voice, and the cussing is so familiar it could almost be Grammy talking. I turn around, and there's one of Grammy's friends, leaning out the window of an old van. Mrs. Robinson, Churchy's grandmother. She flings the passenger door open and waves me around. I get in.

"Good afternoon."

"Don't you 'good afternoon' me, I ain seen you in all this time, and now you here you ain tell nobody you was comin up." Mrs. Robinson gives me a sideways hug and a pat on the arm as she pulls back onto the road.

"I—"

"Oh, that's a shame bout your grammy. I ain even know where they take her. Nobody hear nothing from her, I made couple calls and she ain at Merciful Twilight, nor at Jones Roberts Home for the Aged."

"She—"

"Oh, my. And how bout my Churchy? I hear he at the same school as you. See, if I'da known you was comin, I'da sent you back with something. Where you goin now? An today is a school day? How you get outta classes? And ain even got on no uniform. Boy, you lucky your grammy ain here, if she was to see that. You ain drop out, ay?"

"No—"

"Talk up, girl. You put on weight? Watch those extra pounds, now. You ain tell me yet where you goin. Which way? What, you lost your tongue, ay?"

Her constant stream of questions makes me smile. No wonder Churchy stutters. Probably from having to start a sentence eighteen times until his grandmother left enough of a pause for him to get a word out. "Up to the school."

"And you here because why? You need a transcript? But you could get that from Nassau. You goin off to college or something?" She turns into the school yard. "And I guess you saw that good-for-nothing granddaughter I got there. Already start pumpin the babies out. Don't you walk in her footsteps, now, Indy. Nor in your ma own. Don't mind how they's call you Doubles. You your own person."

If only that was true, I think as she parks, dust pluming around the car.

"And you still ain give me an answer. You here till what time?"

Out the window I see Joe, standing beside her pile of mats. "I go back on the four o'clock boat."

"So don't go nowhere, I comin by to let you carry something to my grandson. And that good-for-nothing girl."

I climb out, and the van spins around, raising even more dust. When it settles, I start walking toward Joe. She's got her cell phone out and she's poking at it, her face dejected. I better start sucking up now, for bailing on her. "Sorry."

"No signal." She holds it out to me. "Supposed to go to the hotel after this, and no signal. Can't even call a cab."

"Shouldn't we set up for the class here?"

"The teacher said she changed her mind. I guess her sister is the woman at the church. She called her and told her what happened. And now I'm stuck here. With all this." She sits down on the mats, defeated. I know I can fix this. And, strangely, I want to. Not because I feel sorry for her or because I want to help. But because I said I would come today and work. Because I need that hundred and ten dollars, more than ever now. Because I need to keep busy, keep moving, keep my mind off what I've seen. Because I'm not Mamma.

"Hold on." I jog after Mrs. Robinson's van, waving one arm while I try to hold my chest in place with the other. This stupid bra isn't made for running, and neither am I. Churchy's grandmother isn't driving fast, but she doesn't see me as I chase her down the driveway and out onto the street, panting and wheezing and waving through the dust. A knife of pain shoots through my side. She's about to vanish behind a curve when the brake lights flash on and her hand sticks out the window. She reverses her way back to me.

"What happened? That smart-mouth Nassau woman givin you problems? Oh, everybody heard about what happen with her and Mrs. Ellis and the hill and the smoke and—"

I'm too out of breath to try to cut in when I hear Joe beside me. She sounds almost polite when she says, "Good afternoon, ma'am. Could you give us a ride out to the hotel?"

Churchy's grandmother agrees to come back for us at three-thirty and take us to the boat. Joe disappears into the hotel while I start hauling the mats up to a deck raised over the water on solid wooden poles, like a giraffe's legs. A roof topped with still-green palm leaves provides shade, and there's a mild breeze. I give the deck a quick sweep, then set up. It's circular, so the mats look funny when I try to lay them out in rows. I try them going one way, then the next. Finally, I stick Joe's mat dead center, then fan the others out, like sun rays. Everyone can see, and there's just enough room to fit in all fifteen mats we've brought. I break off a casuarina branch and dust off the mats. Rubbing the needles between my hands releases a woodsy smell, familiar and sweet. Grammy.

"It isn't terrible. It might actually work." Joe inspects the setup before she makes her way to her own mat. *Thought you'd like being the center of the universe,* I think.

"Sorry about what happened at the church," I say instead. She gives me a small, businesslike nod before rising into downward dog, a single graceful motion, her back flat as a sliding board, heels against the ground, arms and legs straight and strong. Sure, when she does it, it's a graceful athletic feat. When I do it, it looks obscene.

Students start to file in, a mixture of staff and hotel guests. They already know what to do, even as Joe goes through her own warm-up. Most settle themselves sitting down cross-legged, the way we did in primary school for assembly. A few sit back on their heels, one or two lie on their backs, arms relaxing at their sides. Finally, Joe sits too, simple and upright. She glances over at me, then at the last mat, raising her eyebrows. I shake my head. No way am I about to publicly try to tie my big self into knots.

"Go ahead and come into a comfortable seated position," Joe says. "Spine straight, shoulders down and back, lower belly slightly engaged."

"Hi!" a young voice calls up at us from down on the sand.

Joe's forehead creases briefly before it smooths out again. "We'll begin our meditation—"

"Hi, hi, people!"

"Hi, lady!"

"Y'all playin? What y'all doin?"

"Y'all from Nassau? Y'all from Miami?"

"We'll begin our meditation—" Joe tries again and is interrupted as a big wad of dry seaweed sails through the air and thumps onto the deck. Before she can move, I get up and hurry down to the sand, where there's a collection of three little boys, old enough to know better and young enough not to care.

"Hey!" I put on my best Grammy voice. "Hey, y'all stop that."

"Y'all stop that," the oldest one mimics, tossing another bit of seaweed up toward the deck. I know better than to try to start chasing them. I recognize their faces, but can't remember who exactly they belong to. Then a name comes to mind.

"Ms. Ellis!" I call.

The smallest one pauses, dropping the clump of fresh seagrass in his hand.

"Ms. Ellis ain here," the oldest one says, but a look of concern crosses his face.

"No, but wait till I tell her what y'all been doing. And that y'all ain in school." I catch myself using one of Mamma's old tricks: the hollow warning spoken seriously. "And I bet she'll have something to say to your parents."

"I ain scared of Ms. Ellis," the oldest one says, but he motions to the others.

"If y'all go play way down on that end of the beach," I say in a confidential whisper, "maybe I won't have to tell her."

They take off on their bony legs, jogging down the beach. I dust the sand off my feet in the grass, then step back onto the deck, hoping to quietly make my way back to my place. Instead, I meet the whole class on pause, everyone staring at me.

"And that, everybody, is my assistant and lifesaver, Indira," Joe says. "Indira, I think you have to join us on this last mat here. We'll wait for you."

Our eyes meet, and it's different. Something's changed; now, Joe actually wants me here. I step onto the mat and sit down.

Joe goes into her meditation spiel again. I close my eyes, following along, but the air barely gets into my chest. I breathe out, a stunted little puff. Again, I breathe in, but the breath snags on something rough inside me. I open my eyes. All around me, people sit, perfectly serene. Joe's voice washes over them, water against sand, then reaches me, bouncing off like I'm the one rock sticking up on a peaceful shore, rebellious and wrong.

The students begin, hands and knees on the ground, arching their backs, then curving down, then standing, bending forward, and reaching up. Joe continues demonstrating poses, sometimes stepping off her mat to walk around and offer adjustments, talking all the time in this calm, lyrical voice. "Keep breathing, constantly, deep breaths in, deep breaths out, always through the nose." Is this the same Joe? But there's no time to stop and wonder. I follow along as much as I can, always a step or two behind the others, it seems. Warrior pose now, legs wide apart, left leg bent, right leg straight, arms slicing through the air. "And smile, don't look so serious. Look at this beautiful place we're in, the air, the water. This earth is a true blessing, and these bodies we've been given, and these poses that strengthen our bodies."

Partway through the class, my mind gives in, gives up, and I'm working so hard I can't think about anything but *when is it gonna end?* Lunges, side stretches, then a sideways push-up. I follow the remedial poses—*modifications,* Joe calls them, but I know what she's getting at, it's yoga for dummies and fatties—except when I look around, I notice I'm not the only one taking the easy route. An older guy puts his knees down in the push-up pose Joe called *chataranga*. One of the young women rests, forehead on the floor, body curved like a comma, when Joe takes the more advanced students up into a headstand. I do the same. Resting, I make a mental note to report back to Smiley: yes, they do headstands and stuff.

We end lying on our backs, eyes closed. "*Shavasana,*" Joe explains, "final relaxation." I don't know how long we lie there, or even realize I've dozed off, until I hear people moving around me. I sit up slowly.

"It was a great class, wasn't it?" One of the women gives me a smile as she puts her shoes back on. I look around for Joe and see her chatting with a few other students. I get up, taking my time. I feel cleared out, and strangely still.

"We sure hope you'll be back," the last man calls as he heads down the walkway. I should wipe off the mats. I pry myself away from my spot and go to the side where I tucked a clean cloth and a spray bottle of herbs and vinegar.

"You must have needed that *shavasana*," Joe observes.

"Guess I'm tired." I spritz down the first mat.

"Leave it," Joe says. I look up at her, surprised, and see she's holding out a small roll of bills. I take the money, a hundred and two fives.

"Thanks." I stoop down to tuck it into the straw bag. I fold the cash carefully into a pocket. The glimpse of purple should feel special; I've never had a hundred-dollar bill before. Instead, it feels hollow. When I stand up, Joe's looking at me funny, her head tilted to one side.

"You all right?"

"Yes."

"Did you get to see your people today?"

A lump forms in my throat, almost too sudden for me to swallow it down. I can't speak. I nod, looking away. She keeps going.

"It's your mother who lives here? Your grandmother?"

"Yeah," I say. "I have to go to the restroom."

"Okay." Joe turns back to the yoga mats and I hurry off. I feel like my head is about to explode. I can't hold myself together, can't pretend. "Wait!" I hear behind me. When I turn around, trying to arrange my face into some type of half-normal, Joe's holding out another ten.

"Dion said a hundred and ten," I protest.

She waggles the money at me. "Little bonus. You did a good job. Go get something to eat."

In the hotel's gift shop, I get a bottle of water, then sneak through the lobby and back onto the beach, nibbling at one of Mr. Toote's coconut tarts and tucking my change away. Now that Joe's paid me, I'm holding on to more money than I've ever had at one time, by far, but the magic of Joe's class has already drained away, the threat of the boat ride closing in on me. I know what's coming, what waits for me on the other side. Scouring Nassau to find Grammy, with no real answer to the question of what to do next. Knowing that my old home here doesn't exist anymore. Worst of all, Gary and that house, and the swell of my body, and I wish I could hold on to *now*, the way Joe said. Be in this moment. Push myself into some weird pose and breathe, deep and even, like life's upside-downs and knots are as easy to fix as sitting still.

Back in Nassau, I help Joe load up the jeep. From the bus stop near the dock, I watch her pull away. *You need a ride?* she asked on the boat coming back, but I said no. Now that

I'm stuck in Nassau, no way can I afford to be caught in the jeep again, even with a lady.

"You ga be waitin awhile, they had a big accident downtown, traffic tied up," a woman calls as she strolls past. "Faster to walk."

It'll take close to two hours to walk the whole length of Main Street to the house. I'm tired, the straw bag is cutting into my shoulder, my feet are sore and puffy, and my legs are weary from the day. I wish I'd eaten properly at the hotel, like Joe told me to. I reach for my phone. I hate wasting data on something that isn't essential, isn't finding Grammy. Text Smiley. Just got back. Stuck down by the dock.

She texts back. If only you knew someone who could help. Maybe someone with a bike. Hmm. I wonder who.

I reach into my bag. Next to the book is the parcel Churchy's grammy gave me. A whole loaf of banana bread, peanut cakes, and a container of curried chicken. I scroll through texts sent. Squinting at the screen in the late-afternoon light, I find his number. I have to get this stuff to him anyway. I press Call.

10

I THOUGHT MAYBE HE would have got his sister's boyfriend to come, when he said *I-I-I ga be there s-soon,* but instead Churchy appears perched on his bike, back ramrod straight, a beanpole backlit by the low sun. He slows as he approaches me. He doesn't smile, exactly, but he gives me a polite nod that would be accompanied by the tip of a hat, if he was wearing one.

"You ga give me a ride on that?"

He takes my bag, depositing it in the crate he's got nailed to the back. "Y-you behind me."

"You serious?"

He's already on the seat, his face expectant. I wait for him to make a crack about whether I could manage to get up there, or what good cushioning I'll make if we fall, but he waits quietly, loosely gripping the handlebars.

I hoist myself up. My feet dangle awkwardly; luckily his bike is tall too, so there's no danger of them dragging on the ground.

"Wh-wh-where you need to go?"

I manage one deep breath before a jitney pulls past us, blaring gospel music. A puff of exhaust leaves me choking. I fan the air around my face. "Anywhere." I need to find Grammy, but I don't know where to start. "Anywhere but home."

We bob and weave through traffic, cutting slightly west, then more south, across the island. Finally, Churchy stops the bike by the ramshackle building that houses his family's restaurant. "Y-y-you hungry?"

I almost laugh with relief. "I could eat one of everything on the menu right now." That reminds me. I climb off the bike, energized by my close proximity to food. I reach into my bag and hand him the parcels from his grandmother. He goes through them, a slow smile spreading across his face. He disappears upstairs with the curry, then comes back down with two bowls heaped high, freshly reheated. He clutches the dishes like treasure and holds one out to me. We sit on the steps at the side of the building and eat. The chicken is tender around the shards of bone; Mrs. Robinson must have butchered it herself. The food seasoned just enough, bits of orange goat pepper warning of extra heat. Hunks of creamy potato and sweet carrot offset the spice. We don't speak until our plates are empty.

"H-h-how my g-granny d-doin?"

"Fine. She said you have to share the bread with your sister, and the peanut cakes for your nephew."

He looks up at me with a flash of defiance as he tears open a bag of peanut cakes and crams a whole one into his mouth. He holds the bag out to me. I take one, biting through the roasted nuts and sugar brittle, caramelly and sweet. He settles on the stairs, savoring the treat. "What you b-been back for today?"

"For work."

"You see your g-grammy?"

So he doesn't know. "She ain there no more."

"What, M-Ms. Ferguson? Wh-where she is?"

"Nobody know. Mamma couldn't tell me, your granny couldn't find her. For all I know, she dead."

"Sh-sh-she ain dead. You would know if she was."

I'm not so sure. We sit in silence.

"L-let's go someplace."

I want to go anyplace that gets me out of my head. "Where?"

"You pick. Y-y-you remember how to ride?"

This time I sit on the seat while he balances on top of the crate, my bag tucked over his shoulder. Churchy looms over me, a thin, spindly tree. He is close, close enough to smell (Irish Spring soap and peanut cake breath), and his knees keep bumping me. I ride, careful, then reckless, down the middle of the empty road, ringing the bell. I can reach the pedals by pushing myself up to almost standing. We hurtle down the street, nothing to lose. *This how Smiley must feel,* I think. I ride us down to the rickety dock by the retreat, then turn up to the beach, which is empty of cars, too dark for swimmers. Hoisting myself off, I lean the bicycle against a casuarina and sit on the sand. Churchy sits too, a little ways from me. The water spreads out before us, the tide low and shallow, sand exposed.

"The place I was the other day, it's right down from here," I say. He looks at me expectantly, waiting to hear more. "I kind of work there. It's a yoga thing. You go there, some people stay overnight, they have classes—"

"Y-y-you mean the retreat."

"What, you been there?"

"I ain dumb, ya know," he says, tired and disappointed, and I'm ashamed. "Y-you could show me how you's do it?" I look at him, quick, to see if he's asking in that creepy, let-me-watch way. Churchy looks back at me, his eyes on my face, waiting quietly. I remember Smiley, laughing in the backyard. *You look so funny.* Can I trust him?

"I ain showin you a damn thing. You could do some *with*

me, though." I walk him through what I liked best from class today: sitting in meditation, opposite each other. "Your eyes closed?"

"L-l-look an-an-an see."

"Keep your eyes closed. We supposed to be breathing deeply."

He lets out a deep puff of air, and we both dissipate into giggles that stretch up into the sky. Grammy's under the same sky, somewhere. Maybe not that far from us right now. I push the thought away. I'm not ready to tackle that yet.

"Be serious," I say, struggling to remember shapes my body's only made once or twice.

In the sand, feet sinking down, I show him warrior one and two, tree pose and triangle. We fall over, getting grains of sand everywhere. Finally, we sit back down, watching the moon rise out of the water.

"This n-nice, I-I-Indy."

Something shifts in the air, something subtle. *Breathe,* I tell myself. *Just breathe.* I close my eyes, but I still can't make myself step into relaxed.

When Churchy leans over and kisses me, it's gentle, barely a brush. My first kiss ever. It is light and slow, and surprisingly soft. Mouths always seem so hard, lips stretching wide to laugh or shout, or puckering in irritation. Who would have thought. My mind is empty, and I let it happen. One kiss. And another, and another, and then his hands are on my waist and—

Hands on my wrists, drunk breath. Turning away, look-ing away, and still catching everything in the TV's reflection. Clothes nothing but rumpled fabric, don't look too close. His form blurred, don't look at what it's doing. My own eyes crys-tal clear. In them, that same look Mamma used to have, not sad or angry or scared. Blank, accepting. Trying to focus on something outside what's happening right now, and instead seeing my future as her past, on repeat.

"No!" I jump up, feet in my shoes in one second, bag on my shoulder in two. Hurry through the brush. I hear him behind me.

"D-D-D-D-! W-w-wait! W-w-w-w-wait! D-D-Doubles! I-I-I- s-s-s-s-orry!"

His voice fades away as I hop onto the bike, pushing off, wheels whirring as I whip down the road. Pedal faster, faster, away from his voice, his hands. Faster, until the *thumpthumpthump* in my chest drowns out everything. Drowns out the memory of Gary.

The next day, I stumble from Smiley's room to the kitchen and grab a ginger biscuit that barely agrees to stay down. I crawl onto the sofa, pulling a sheet over me. When Aunt Patrice asks me why I'm not ready at seven-thirty, I mutter something about a bellyache.

"I hope for your sake that's true," Aunt Patrice says as she slams the front door behind her and Smiley. Once I'm alone, I snatch the yellow pages from the living room and call two, three, four, five old folks' homes, one after the other. They all say the same thing. *No one here by that name. No, sweetie, we don't have no Eunice Ferguson here.*

I shower and put on an elastic-waisted skirt the color of a wet lawn in May. I stare at the busted bra and the roll of duct tape waiting for me. I wince as I press the tape against my skin, then pull on a T-shirt. In my bag, I feel for the money Joe gave me. I don't know what to do next about Grammy, about school, about Aunt Patrice. But as I head toward Main Street, I'm sure of one thing. This bra has to go.

In the underwear store, I pick up something bigger than my old size and head for the fitting room. I try it on, pulling the new bra, wide shoulder strap and heavy line of hooks and all, right over the taped-on one. Good enough. Better than what I have now. At the front, when the woman asks if I'm sure it's my size, I nod and hand her the money. I see the cashier sneaking a look at my belly as she bags the bra. I can't get out of the store fast enough.

It's a relief to reach the retreat. All I can think of is getting to the bathroom, taking this old thing off, and putting the new bra on. As I walk by the jeep, in a shady patch of the parking lot, I glimpse a note taped to the back window. *Indira: unload the jeep properly. Wipe off the mats and put everything away. Then clean the bathrooms.* So much for on-the-mat Joe from yesterday.

"Sure, you're welcome," I say to the trees. I'd still rather be here than at school, dealing with Ms. Wilson and those girls, having to face Churchy. In the bathroom, I carefully peel off the tape and trade in the old for the new. The stiff fabric stings a little against my skin, but it's worlds better. I stash my bag in the office, then scrub the mats and stack them up neatly.

"How you doin?" Dion calls as I come around a curve in the path. He's digging a hole with his good arm, the injured one curled close to his body. "How was Mariner's yesterday? You got to see your family?"

"You could say that."

"You don't sound too happy about it. Everything okay?"

I don't answer. "Where's Joe?" I ask instead.

"Oh, she's teaching a partner yoga class with Susan. But she must really like you now."

"Yeah, she left her marching orders on the jeep."

Dion rams the shovel into the soil so it stands up on its own, then leans on the handle. "She wants to hire you part-time."

"Really?"

"Mmm-hmm." He slides a young tree out of its pot, grasping

it gently by its trunk, then easing its roots and the soil clustered around them into the earth. "She said you weren't too bad."

"Flattering."

"That's high praise from her. You know the last compliment she gave me?" He pats the dirt down around the tree's base and straightens up. "'The entryway to this place looks ugly. When are you gonna fix it up?'"

"That's a compliment?"

"Yeah, cause the rest don't look ugly, only the entrance. And I could change that. Anyway, pay ain much, but once the cleaning's done, you got unlimited rock-sitting time. You could even do a class. Couple hours, three-thirty-ish until you done. In case you got more exams or anything."

"I tell you I'm done with school."

He gives me a quick sideways look, and I wonder if he knows more than he's letting on. Probably not, I tell myself as he asks, "So, think you want that job?"

I'm quiet for a moment, thinking it through. Could I make it on my own? How long before they notice I'm pregnant here? What will Joe say? And how long can I keep skipping school before Aunt Patrice finds out? Could this job give me enough money to leave? Could it be a way out?

I have to take the chance. It's something. It's a start. I nod at Dion before I head back to the jeep. "I do."

• • •

In the afternoon, Dion offers me another ride home, but the memory of last night is still too much, and I pass, walking instead. As I get close to the house, I see Churchy and Smiley sitting out front. Great.

"Ahh, there she is, the bike bandit," Smiley calls as Churchy gets to his feet. He gives me a nod and an embarrassed little grin.

"Hey," I say. "I left it in the back."

"Why you ga take the boy's wheels, Indy? How he suppose to get around? He tell me all about last night."

"N-n-not all about it," he interrupts quickly.

I scowl at him, hoping he'll get the message, but it's too late. Smiley looks from him to me as she gets up, heading for the door. "Oh, please. I know y'all two been up to something. Get a room." The door slams behind her.

I head for the back gate. "You wanna get your bike?"

He points to the lawn, at a purple bicycle sprawled across the grass. "Th-that's for you. U-used to be my sister own." I try to imagine him riding that thing over here, legs jacked up like mountain peaks, knees nearly grazing his chin.

"You didn't have to do that." I drag his bicycle into the front yard.

"S-sorry. About last night. I j-j-just thought—"

"Thought what? Thought I must want it? Thought you could do whatever you wanna do?"

His hands are raised, backing up. I shove his bike at him and it lands against the croton bush, one wheel spinning around, handle twisted up into the air.

"N-n-no, n-n-no way, I ain th-th-that type, I ain l-l-like that. I-I-I-I-I—"

"What? Spit it out!"

"I th-th-thought we could g-g-g-g-go for a ride sometime," he says, not meeting my gaze. He looks like I felt in that classroom full of kids stuttering *D-D-D-D-D* at my popped-open blouse. I remember his words from last night. *I ain dumb, ya know.* Before I can open my mouth to say sorry, Gary's black truck roars up to the house; he slams on the brakes and starts to reverse into the driveway.

I grab the purple bike, straightening it out. I jump on, ignoring Churchy's gaping expression. "Let's go now."

"N-n-now?"

"Now." I ride over the bumpy lawn, between bougainvillea and garbage cans, then onto the road. "Now!" I yell back. "Now!" I hear the *click-click-click* of Churchy's bike behind me. I keep looking back, but no one's following us. He lets me lead the way again, through the neighborhood streets, until darkness gathers in the sky.

Monday morning. I hear Smiley's alarm, roll over, and reach to turn it off.

"You ain getting up again today?" she asks, switching the light on.

"I feel bad," I mutter, pulling the cover up over my head. My legs are cramped and sore from riding the bike, my head swirling, my back aching.

"All right, lazybones," she sings, prancing out of the room. "Indy say she sick today," I hear her tell Aunt Patrice.

"Fine. If she want miss all her classes and flunk out of school, that's her business," Aunt Patrice says, so loudly I know she wants me to hear. A minute later, Aunt Patrice thumps into the bedroom, yanking the sheet off me. "Get out this bed."

"I don't feel good," I whimper.

"Make up the sheets and let Smiley get ready. You want lie up in the house all day, do it on the couch."

Smiley comes in quietly as Aunt Patrice leaves. She shoots me a sympathetic look as I head out, curling up on the living room sofa. I listen to the sounds of the household around me; I might as well not exist. I must drift off again because when I wake up, there's nothing but silence. The clock says 8:50. I'm ravenous.

I get up, listening carefully. Nothing, no one. The kitchen is empty, no cars in the driveway, Gary's truck gone. I finish the cold grits left in the pot, then head for the bathroom with clean underwear, my new bra, and a fresh shirt and skirt. The door shut and locked, I peel off my nightclothes and dump them into the hamper. It reeks of sweat and cologne. The smell makes me gag. I shut the hamper fast and step into the shower. The spray of water catches the early light spilling through the window, making rainbows as the two collide. My skin is still irritated where the duct tape was. It stings as the water touches it. I grit my teeth and soap up. When I'm done, I turn the water off and reach for my towel.

It's not there.

I push back the shower curtain. The spot on the rail where my towel always hangs is empty. Smiley's pink towel is nowhere in sight either. Nothing but the old, worn one Aunt Patrice wants us to dry out the tub with when we're done. Someone's left it on the floor, behind the toilet. Dirty clothes would be better, except that I've dropped my pajamas into the hamper with that disgusting, sweaty stuff. I step out carefully, then shake out the floor towel and stretch it across myself. Ugh. It barely even covers my chest on one side, my behind on the other. I creak the bathroom door open and step out.

"Hello, sunshine."

I cling to the scrappy towel, step back with one foot, and lose balance, nearly falling on the wet bathroom tiles.

"Nice wrap." Gary eyes me up and down.

"Your truck—"

"Oh, I let my friend take it. Hope no silly girl cause him

scratch up the paint." The fleck of a threat in his voice.

If I run for the bedroom, he could grab me. If I stay here, I'm trapped. He knows it, too. I can feel the grits fighting their way back up. *Not now. Please, not now.*

"Get out my way."

"Ain nobody stopping you. Would be nice to get in there so I could shower too, you know."

"Where you put my towel?"

"Maybe Mummy took it to wash." He eyes me again. "Come on, I ain got all day." He steps forward and I bolt for Smiley's room. I barely make it past him before I trip, falling and landing on my hands and knees, yellow vomit bursting from my mouth. Scramble for the towel, slipping, bawling, puking, running for the room. Before I get there, I hear him mutter, "Disgusting." The bathroom door closes with a click. I lock Smiley's bedroom door behind me, start hammering on it with my fists, yelling *"Leave me, leave me alone, leave me alone, don't touch me, don't touch me, don't touch me, leave me alone!"* Wish it was Gary I was beating. Wish it wasn't my puke smeared all over the floor. Wish, instead, it was his head.

When I wake up, the house is quiet. I listen for several minutes. Nothing. My mouth tastes sour. I'm sweaty, the shirt and skirt I pulled on stale and damp. I open the door. In the hallway, the tiles have been cleaned. I check every room to make sure I'm alone. When I open the washing machine, my towel is inside, balled up with Smiley's. I wash everything together in extra-hot water and take a fresh towel from the laundry basket. I have to get out of here today. I shower a second time, so fast I almost fall again. Something keeps me upright. I dress right in the bathroom, hooking on the bra. Suddenly, it seems as old and broken as I feel. I can put on a new bra, but it won't make a difference; underneath, I'm still falling apart.

In the afternoon, I bike toward the shore, turning off onto the retreat's dirt road, past the blur of trees. At the entrance, a new collection of flowers is planted around the gate, droopy in the heat. Inside, the parking lot is empty; for once, even the jeep is gone. I lean my bike against the closed office door. Just start walking, my feet taking me to the same path I went down that second time here, to the water, to the large rock I saw Dion balancing on. I'm not in the mood to swim, but I lie back on the rock, feeling the bumpy surface under me. The salty breeze and the slap of the waves start to relax me. My stomach is still knotted, though. *Just let it go, don't let this thing kill you,* I think. My eyes are open, it's not proper yoga, not the way Joe did it on Mariner's Cay. I sit up, deciding to try it the right way, on my own. I let my limbs dance through the poses, I don't know how many times. When the light finally begins fading, I stop.

Stepping onto the path, I welcome the evening. Out here, away from streetlights, night is complete, in a way that makes me feel at home. As my eyes adjust, I can make out the roof of the dining pavilion, the murmur of conversation ornamented with laughter. I head the other way, into the part of the retreat I'm most curious about: the smattering of guest cottages hidden in the trees. Most are darkened now, the odd square of light peeping through thin curtains. As I approach the buildings, a woman emerges from one of them, into the night.

"Hi there," she calls, seeing me.

"Hi." I've stopped walking, without meaning to. I shouldn't be here, shouldn't be at the retreat at all, not at night, and definitely not skulking around where the guests stay.

"It's beautiful here, isn't it?" She comes toward me on the path. "I just got in this morning and I can't get over how serene it is. Must be a nice place to work." She unties the shawl around her shoulders, then takes it off. "I don't even need this, do I?" Turning back to the cottage, she runs in, opening the unlocked door. When she switches on the light, I catch a glimpse of a bare, simple room. Bed, old bureau, one bulb hanging from the ceiling. She's got a suitcase open, clothes strewn around it on the floor. "Just smell that ocean air," she says when she comes back out, not surprised, it seems, to see me still there. "So close. I bet if I leave the door open tonight I'll hear the water when I'm going to sleep." She waves as she leaves.

The walkway goes on a bit farther, then curls around to one last cottage. It's a little thing, half the size of the others, and more run-down. I turn the light on and peer in. The bed is bare and it's missing a bureau, but the bedside table stands, ready. It's like looking into another world. Everything a person could need, all there, all private. A bed you don't have to share. A door that can lock. Bathrooms nearby, and a place to eat. The water is close enough to hear through the open windows. Nobody on the other side of the door. Compact, but so much room. Turning the light off, I step in and sit down on the floor, the wooden boards squeaking and groaning beneath me before they settle, agreeing to let me stay.

It's long past dinnertime when I find the bike and pedal away, leaving the quietness behind me. I can't bring myself to go back to Aunt Patrice's house—not yet. I circle the neighborhood a few times before I let myself cycle down Churchy's street. I don't know why I do it. Maybe I want to believe that he's not such a bad guy. Maybe I just don't want to be alone. I park the bike and go up the stairs, gently rapping on his apartment's window. He opens the door, still in his school uniform, neat as ever.

"You busy?"

"N-not really." He steps aside, letting me in.

I glance around this part of Churchy's world for the first time. I don't know how he could share it with his aunt and uncle; barely looks like there's enough room for one. It's got a table, three chairs pushed in neatly around it, and a TV on the opposite side of the room. There's a tired beige sofa and a coffee table, scratched but cleared off except for a tidy stack of newspapers. A single mattress and box spring is tucked against the wall; on top is a pile of freshly washed and ironed school shirts. The door to the bathroom stands open, taking up even more space.

"You mind that I came?"

"I just s-s-surprised."

"Oh." I can imagine Smiley's voice. *What, you don't know how to flirt?* I'm not sure I do, or that I'd ever want to, but I know I want to be here, near Churchy. Right now he's my closest thing to home. "This is a nice place."

"Y-you hungry?"

"Kind of."

"Y-y-you could sit anywhere," Churchy says. I pick a spot at the table. The pot on the stove chatters and Churchy reaches over for a spoon. He's deft in the kitchen, snatching up utensils, tasting this, sniffing that.

"You sure I ain interrupting?"

"N-n-no. You ain interrupting." After a few minutes of clinking and clanking, Churchy sets down two plates for us, piled high with food.

"What is it?"

He rests a fork on the edge of each plate. "Roasted pumpkin. I p-put ginger and anise on it. Chicken in s-s-sweet lime sauce. Rice and garlic black beans. S-salad greens."

"You make all this when you could eat right downstairs?" I dig my fork in, then look over to see his head bowed over his food. I stop guiltily, dipping my head too, glancing over until his lips stop moving.

"S-sometimes I want something d-d-different."

We eat in silence for a few minutes. The food is amazing, the pumpkin steamy inside, the outside sticky and sweet, the chicken crisp, the sauce drizzled over it tangy, the rice seasoned just right. I wish I could shake this guilty feeling. I wish there was some better reason I'm here, something normal. He thinks I'm visiting, just because. What would he say if I told him I can't go home? That I don't have a real home to go to? What's waiting for me at Aunt Patrice's house? What's growing inside me?

"H-h-how it t-taste?"

"Better than what me and Smiley got from downstairs. Almost as good as Grammy's food."

"Ain only Mariner's w-woman who could cook," he says,

smiling shyly before taking another bite of rice. I wait for him to ask me why I came. Instead, he turns on the TV, finds a movie that's starting. After we've eaten, we sit awkwardly on the couch, the TV's light a gentle flicker on our faces. The movie gives us both a break, him from his stuttering, me from real life. While we sit, I can pretend. Pretend there's no reason to avoid Aunt Patrice's house, pretend everything's good with Grammy. Pretend I could go home anytime and be happy to be there, pretend I know what home means now. Pretend I'm like everyone else who's sixteen, hanging out at a friend's house. Pretend I'm normal. Halfway through the movie, the front door opens. Churchy's aunt glances at us as she disappears into the bedroom, wishing him good night. Later, his uncle comes in and ignores us both, closing the bedroom door behind him.

When the movie ends, Churchy shifts, stretching out on the couch. He isn't touching me, but I can feel his warmth, the brush of his shirt against my arm. I lean back, lean into normal like it's a pillow. Like it's mine.

"Y-y-you better get home, Indy," I hear Churchy say. It's the last thing I remember that night.

11

SOFT BREEZE ON MY arms, warm light on my skin. A woman's voice far away. A lower, less frantic tone than normal. It's not Aunt Patrice. *It's not Aunt Patrice.*

I sit up so fast my head spins, and blink against the morning sun. I take in my surroundings; the sofa, Churchy—still in yesterday's school uniform—curled up at one end. I stayed out. I can't believe I stayed out. Churchy's aunt speaks again, and I realize it's coming from the bedroom. I should go right now, but before I can gather everything together, footsteps approach. I run to the bathroom, closing the door after me. I hear someone go out into the living room.

"Hey. Get up," Churchy's aunt says sharply. "Whose bag this is?"

Why didn't I bring it in with me? Why didn't I just run out the front door? *Please don't let her look through my bag,* I pray.

"Th-th-that ain n-n-nobody own, Auntie," I hear Churchy protest, and I just know she's going through my things. The book. What if she finds the book? What if she tells Aunt Patrice? I'm dead. Either way, I'm dead.

"What foolishness you got goin on in my house? Why the bathroom door close? Don't you lie to me, boy."

"Th-th-that's just my f-f-friend," Churchy says, keeping his voice low.

"Friend? Since when do friends stay all night?"

"W-w-we miss and f-fall sleep—"

"Ain no miss an fall sleep." Churchy's aunt sounds annoyed, but it's nothing compared to what Aunt Patrice is gonna unleash on me when I get home.

"D-d-don't tell Uncle! Sh-sh-she goin right now."

"That's right," his aunt says.

Maybe Aunt Patrice didn't notice I was gone last night, same way Churchy's aunt didn't know, until now. I can't worry about Aunt Patrice yet; there's a brisk knock on the bathroom door. I open it. Churchy's aunt stands outside, as tall as he is. She holds my bag out silently. I take it and dash outside.

Smiley hurries out the front door to meet me as I ride up to the house.

"Indy!" she squeals, then catches herself and whispers, "Where you been last night?"

"Aunt Patrice home?" I ask, tucking the bike around the side of the house, out of sight.

"She in her bathroom. Go round back." She leads the way, looking at me with a funny expression. Surprise. Even . . . awe.

"Anybody else home?"

"Uh-uh. Daddy already left for work, and I ain know where Gary is. She bathin, you better try sneak in now." Smiley pushes the kitchen door open, peering around the room before she scampers into the depths of the house, through the dining and living rooms and down the hallway. "Hurry up, go in my bathroom." She comes in with me, closing the door behind her.

"I thought you said she was in the tub," I whisper.

"Yeah, but you can't be too safe."

My sentiments exactly. "You don't think she'll be suspicious if she come out and the two of us in here?"

"Uh-uh. I wan know exactly what happen."

"Shhhh." I reach for my toothbrush. "Happen where?"

"Don't play dumb with me. You was by him? You follow my advice or what?"

"Him who?"

"You know who I mean, man. Churchy!"

"Yeah, okay? I was by him."

"All night?" Her eyebrows are raised so high her hairline threatens to swallow them.

"I didn't mean to." I reach over and turn on the tap, running water to drown out our voices. "I fell asleep by mistake."

"In his bed?"

I glare at her. "On the sofa. With my clothes on," I add.

"Hey, y'all been together the night, that's enough for Churchy. You know he ain too bright. Sweet, but ain too bright. I bet you he think you's get baby just from sitting by a girl."

"Sometimes, Smiley, I think you're the one that ain too bright. You better get outta here before your mummy come and hear us two whispering in here." I push her toward the door.

"You better tell me everything later," she warns.

I intentionally take a long, long shower, killing time until everyone should be gone. I listen for Gary, but the house is silent, the door to his room open. I dash to Smiley's bedroom, locking the door anyway. I dress in a black shirt and a long skirt, deep red folds flapping around my legs in a warning. I leave the bike and walk to the bus stop instead. Part of me wonders what would happen if Aunt Patrice saw me, out of uniform, in the middle of the day. I sit down in the back, reach into the bag. I bring out Grammy's book. Today, it opens up to chapter four: "The Second Trimester." Over the chapter number, Grammy's words are crammed together; she has plenty to tell me.

Now don't mind what the books say. There's no rule on

*what you can do. Just listen to what you feel. I was on my
hands and knees, scrubbing the wood floor, straight through
my middle months, and my mother worked in the field with
all of us. Mind, my oldest sister didn't do a lick with her last
one. Just sat up in bed drinking herb tea and eating oatmeal
cookies and rainbow cake, and when the baby came, it was a
month early and we didn't think it would live, though it did. I
don't tell you that to scare you. Her baby was fine in the end,
big Defence Force officer in Nassau now, six foot three and
have to get his uniform specially made. Point is, every woman
is different, believe me.*

I don't know about working no field, but helping out at
the retreat? That I could do, at least for now. The question of
Aunt Patrice still hangs over my head. If she throws me out,
even the little bit of money I can earn at the retreat won't save
me. I read over Grammy's words again and again, looking for
the answer I need, but every time, I only get more confused.
The words in the book always sound like they're meant to
help, but that doesn't make sense. If she knew I'd need this
book, why did she let Mamma send me here? If she ever
even half-loved me, why would she think I'd end up this way?
What would Grammy really say if she saw me? Probably not
every woman is different. Would she ask why? Or would she
point over to the book, as proof of fulfilled fate?

• • •

The 10 a.m. yoga class is twenty minutes in when I steal up the path to the deck. A massive silk cotton tree stretches its branches overhead, its bulky trunk hiding me. Susan, the tall teacher whose class I stepped right into that first day, is leading again. The students seem at ease with her; they smile as she smiles, even while they're moving through the poses. Comfortable as they are, I can't imagine myself ever being one of them up there. Not me. It was one thing in Mariner's, with just a few people, but here, I belong on the pathways, between those cottages, on the wall looking over the water, on the rocks, with my feet in the sea. Even in the pavilion, with all those mysterious foods being dished up, I know what to do. Eating is simple. But that deck full of lean bodies in clingy pants and snug shirts, all moving in unison, somehow anticipating where Susan's going, gliding into positions before she's even said what comes next? That's no place for me. They are too perfect. None of them has to fend off some freak, none has a secret growing beneath those Lycra clothes.

From down on the grass, peeping around the tree, I can follow the class just as well. This isn't lurking, not exactly. Besides, from this angle I'm sort of in line with Susan instead of facing her. Hopefully she won't see. Won't think to look. I watch as Susan raises her arms above her head, bends at the waist, and brings her hands down to the floor. Then she's stepping back on one side, then the other, following the same routine Dion did that day on the street. I look around, making sure no one's watching me. When Susan and her flock of students begin the next round of moves, I join in.

When Dion did the postures that day, his breathing was even. The same thing with Joe. Here, I can't stop huffing and puffing. When I bend forward, I feel dizzy. When I straighten up, my back is sore. Hands at my chest, I can't get my thumbs in the right place. Either they're too high up, or I feel like they're fighting to reach my breastbone. Now they're in some sort of push-up position. By the time I get there, everyone else has moved on to downward dog. I manage the lunge on time, at least, before they've swooped back up, arms raised.

"When we getting to the sitting still part?" I mutter, hauling my arms up, then stopping short, as the bottom edge of the new bra nips into the irritated skin. I've barely caught my breath before they're off again. *And you're supposed to feel calm through all this too?* I think, sinking down to the grass. Sitting still, closing my eyes, I breathe. That much I can do. It's rough and choppy at first, but then it slows, growing deeper. I breathe and I imagine. What if I was one of them? Dancing my way, graceful, through what I should do.

I hear footsteps coming closer and turn around to see Joe. She's moving purposefully, and I hope she doesn't see me, but sure enough, she steps off the path, heading my way. I brace myself for a tirade.

"Susan's our best teacher," she says instead. "She's a good person to learn from."

"Oh."

"Dion told me you're going to be around here more often."

"Yes."

She gives me a brusque, almost curt pat on the shoulder. "Don't let us down."

I'm under the tree outside school, waiting for Smiley to appear after her volleyball practice. **Meet me at 4:30. We have to talk!!** her text said. Now I'm stuck hovering around the last place I want to be. It's ten to five; they must be running late. I fiddle with the bike's handlebars, praying no one I know will see me. What's taking so long?

"Hey, Doubles!"

I look up to see Raisin Legs and Raquel, prim in their tucked-in uniforms, each with a few books in their hands.

"You're waiting for Smiley?" Raisin Legs casually glances at my midsection. I wish I hadn't been cleaning all day. A bead of sweat drips down the small of my back.

"How come you keep missing school?" Raquel says.

"Is it true, what everybody sayin?" Raisin Legs blurts out before I can reply. Raquel elbows her in the ribs, but she waits just as expectantly, eager for an answer. They remind me of Gary. Interested in me only for themselves. Hovering, like I'm something to eat. Like I'm exactly the meal they expected. I close my eyes, breathe in deep. Breathe out.

"She zonin out, ay?" Raisin Legs asks.

I breathe in, open my eyes. "What everybody sayin?"

"You know." Raquel shifts uncomfortably, reluctant to say the words.

"I do?"

"That you pregnant, man," Raisin Legs says, impatient.

"Why you wanna know?"

Raisin Legs glances at Raquel. "Well, everybody say— and then that book—"

"Yeah, but why do *you* want to know? Why you care if I am or not?"

"We was only—"

"We're not friends." I take my time with the words. "You never used to talk to me before. Now you want to know all the details of my life. Why does it matter to *you*?"

"Hey!" Smiley calls, jogging up to us, rescuing me. They sidle away, heads together, whispering already.

"I been here twenty minutes."

"Yeah, volleyball ran overtime. We gotta hurry before Mummy come for me. I told her five-fifteen."

"What's the emergency?"

"What you think? I wanna hear all the dirt from last night. Away from the house, so we could talk."

Good choice, Smiley. No eavesdropping's ever happened in a school yard. "Ain no dirt. I went by, he cooked, and after we ate we was watching TV and I fell asleep, didn't wake up till this morning. The end."

"So did y'all do anything? Y'all at least kiss?"

I grip the handlebars. This is what she had me come here for, what I left the retreat early for? "I gotta go."

"I only tryin to help you. You better hurry up and sleep with that boy, or too much time ga pass."

"I probably five months along, dummy. I think he could at least count that far."

"Yeah, but you ain got that much time. And especially since you skipping school now. Everybody talking, and Ms. Wilson really on the warpath for you—"

I plop down on the seat of my bike and start pedaling away. I'm mad she wasted my time. But I'm madder she keeps thinking I'm going to set up Churchy. Mad she thinks that's who I am. I might be pregnant. I might not know what to do. But I'm not a liar and I'm not going to be with a guy to get something out of him. Not money, not safety, not some illusion that things are all right. That's not who I am. Right?

Watching Churchy cook is both familiar and weird. It reminds me of being with Grammy in her kitchen; his gangliness is transformed into a kind of fluid purpose. He glances over at me as he shakes rice into boiling water. There's something so comforting, so simple about that motion.

"I have to tell you something."

He salts the rice, then stirs it, not missing a beat. Nods, as though it's part of the cooking process.

"And you sure your parents ain home?"

Churchy shakes his head. "Uncle downstairs. M-M-My aunt gone to the store. You all right."

I take a breath in, then spit it out. "I'm pregnant."

He sets the spoon down on the stove, slow, so methodical I don't know if he heard me, or if he's about to go all psycho. He turns around, looking at me with clear, wide eyes. Nothing in between us, no distraction of cutlery or stirring. "P-p-pregnant? H-h-how?" The words sputter out. "W-w-we only kiss—"

"No, no, not you. Not from you. I'm five months, at least."

"W-w-w-w-w-wow. W-wow."

"You really didn't know?"

"Wh-wh-who? Wh-wh-who's the daddy?"

I swallow. "It doesn't have a daddy."

He turns around to look out the window. From here, it looks like he's staring at the tops of the lampposts, like they might dislodge themselves and start tracing out answers in the sky. "Y-y-y-you think I st-st-stupid? Every baby have a d-d-daddy."

"Some don't even have a mummy."

"Wh-wh-who it is?" His voice grows louder with every syllable. "Wh-wh-who?"

"Nobody."

"You don't know?"

Gary's grip on my leg. Easy laugh. Nail pressing into my skin. *Don't cross me.*

"Y-y-you still care bout him?"

"I never did."

Churchy turns around again, his gaze holding mine. His voice is lower again when he speaks. "You care bout me?"

"What kind of question that is, Churchy?"

"I s-say, d-d-do you care bout me?"

"I like you as a person—"

"Y-y-you tryin to trick me? Y-you take me for a dummy? Just cause I's st-st-st-st." The stammer stops him cruelly. "Cause I can't talk so good? You think I st-st-stupid? Just cause I st-st-st-st-stutter?" He stands there, briefly victorious over the word.

"I tellin you now, right?" I sink down onto the sofa, wishing the cushions would swallow me.

He picks up the spatula, twirling it like a baton. He turns back to the stove. A pot sizzles. He begins again to stir. To lift lids. To reach for seasonings in the back. I wonder, did anything just happen? Did I imagine it all?

"Give me some t-t-time. I got an idea," Churchy finally says. "I c-c-could help you."

• • •

Later, I let him drop me off at Aunt Patrice's house. At the edge of the yard, he leans in and plants a quick kiss on my cheek. "Night, D-D-D. Night, Dee." His eyes glisten, catching the streetlight's glow. Dee. The syllable, standing alone, is soft and melodious. No one's called me this before. Dee. The promise of something better. Short and sweet. It feels clean. Feels new.

Inside, the house is quiet, except for the blare of the TV. I lock the front door and head for the bedroom.

"Gary?" my aunt calls out as I tiptoe past her door. For this, she has the hearing of a bat. "Your shift finish early, ay?" I keep going, hurrying for Smiley's door. "Indira." Her voice is right behind me now. I turn around to face her. She's wearing her housecoat, her wig off for the night, exposing the low-cut hair underneath. Her feet are pushed into beat-up pink slippers, despite the heat. "Where have you been?"

"Out."

She shifts her hand to her hip. "With who?"

"A friend."

"The same friend who you slept by last night?" Her voice is too loud for the hallway, for this conversation. If Smiley is sleeping, she won't be for long. "Listen," Aunt Patrice says in the way that tells you the rowing is just getting started, "I've allowed you to stay here, but I told your mother and your grandmother the same thing I told you. No slackness. No problems. No staying out. I know how your mother is. You and me both know. If you plan on following behind her, you can head for the door and leave your key when you go."

"I'm not like her." I want to spit the words at her, but they come out mumbled.

"Sleeping out. Coming in after ten. Ain even showing up to school. You want to be woman when it comes to man, but you don't work, you don't pay bills, who knows what you do all day long. You just like she was when she was your age. All you need now is to go get yourself pregnant and you could be her clone." She looks me over like I'm something she didn't buy, festering in the fridge. "Why you goin in Cecile's room? She already asleep."

"I have to get my stuff."

"What stuff? You ain business having any stuff in there, you have a spot in the living room. You think I'd let you come from who knows what man bed, ten-thirty in the night, ain been to school, ain been home last night, then turn around and prance in my girl child's room?" She's right up in my face now, just a few inches away. I need to be someplace else, anyplace else. I want to fly at her, want to attack her, want to show her my belly stretching out, shout at her *It's your fault, your son did this! If you hadn't made me sleep out there in the living room, with no door, no privacy—I'm a girl, what you think would hap-*

pen with him lurking round? I'm sure you could hear him, you know so much about the world, about Mamma, and you couldn't even stop to think what might happen in your own house? You couldn't even see? But I can't. Breathe, have to breathe through it. I need this place. For now, I have nowhere else to go. *Do what you gotta do.* I have to hold back. I need to be here.

"I was out working."

"Working where?"

"Tasty Spot." It comes out too fast for it to sound convincing, even to me. It's the first thing, the only thing, I can think of to say. "I got a job there. For a little extra cash," I add. Maybe that'll make her feel bad about those times she took the money Mamma sent me.

"That's a lie right there," Aunt Patrice says. "I want know how you sick one minute and then working at a restaurant the next. And can't be bothered to show up to school? Explain that. What? You lost your tongue now, ay?"

I stare at the floor, swallowing back the words that threaten to burst out of me.

"One time. I ga let this coming in late business slide one time. If you want drop out of school, that ain my problem. But I got my good child in this house, and you ain ga corrupt her, not on my watch. First you in man car, and now this? I catch you staying out again, and that's it. Don't care what your uncle say. You understand?"

She glares at me, expectant, like she's waiting for me to gush with gratitude for her letting me stay here, on the living room sofa. For letting me be under the same roof with Gary. I don't have any choice but to be here right now, but I can't be grateful for it. I can't even say I understand, because I don't. I don't know how she can look me in the face, all hauled up and righteous. Maybe she really doesn't know, though she never seems to miss anything else. Could she really be blind to this? I'm afraid to find out; I squeeze past her into the living room without a word.

"And stay out there," she calls after me. "I'm watching you."

I fumble through my bag, blinking back my rage. Draw the book out; hold it to my chest, like I'm holding on to Grammy.

After a while, once my heartbeat has settled, mostly, the hallway light flicks off and the house is stone-silent. I lie there on the sofa until I hear Gary's truck pull in, hear the keys in the doorway. I grab the book and run past Aunt Patrice's room, to Smiley's door. Turn the handle. She's fast asleep on her side, doesn't even stir as I come in. I close the door but stay with my ear pressed up against it, listening as Gary comes down the hall, humming to himself. I hear his bedroom door open, then shut. Any minute, Aunt Patrice could come check on me, come thundering in and order me out of

Smiley's room, maybe even out of the house. I can't stay in here all night, not this time. I listen, but there's no motion, not even a bedspring creak. I take a chance, step out into the hall. Tiptoe in the dark, toward the bathroom.

I feel, rather than see, Gary step into my path. I press up against the wall, willing him not to touch me.

"Thought I missed my friend in the living room," he says. His bedroom door is closed; he's been waiting out here this whole time, trying to set me up, to catch me. He reaches out and I twist away just in time, running for the bathroom, slamming the door louder than I should. Locking it behind me isn't enough, I lean my whole weight against it. Quiet settles again; even with the noise, no one stirs. It might as well be just me and him in this big, empty house.

"Night, Sharice," he whispers through the door, laughter in his voice. His door opens and closes, and this time I hear him lie down on the bed. I curl up on the bathroom floor and wait. Only when I finally hear him snore do I go back to the living room and let sleep come.

12

IT'S LUNCHTIME AT THE retreat. I'm ravenous, my stomach complaining. I step into the pavilion, glancing around, but I don't seem to stick out; no one seems to notice me as I walk up to the buffet. I hang back, looking at the unfamiliar dishes.

"What can I get you?" Maya asks, smiling.

"What do you have?"

"No macaroni or peas and rice, I could tell you that." She lowers her voice. "Joe doesn't go for anything with white rice or white flour." Maya sighs under the burden of these restrictions. "Anyway, we got some spiced lentils here, quinoa-corn salad, roasted eggplant, and broccoli."

Despite her disapproval, it all smells delicious. My stomach growls. "I don't know. What's good?"

"I would kill for some fried chicken right now," she says,

dishing up a plate with a little of everything. She hands it to me. "See what you think of that."

I take it back out onto the beach, sitting down in the shade. It's seasoned right, and not overly peppery like Aunt Patrice's cooking, or oily like the stuff from Churchy's aunt and uncle's place; it reminds me of Churchy's food, brighter, lighter, and prepared with care. Farther down the beach, I hear someone coming and look over to see Susan carrying her own plate. She waves at me as she approaches.

"Mind if I join you?"

"Sure." I finish off the last of the eggplant and get down to the quinoa-corn salad, tangy and sweet.

"Dion tells me you're working here now."

I nod, digging into the broccoli. There's a nutty sauce drizzled over it; I wish I'd asked for more.

"So when are you going to come to one of my classes instead of lurking behind the trees?"

"Oh." I put my fork down. "I didn't think you saw me."

She smiles. "I'm sure anyone who's paying attention sees you."

What does she mean by that? I carefully pull my shirt away from my belly.

"You don't have to be shy about it. You do yoga?"

Maybe she doesn't suspect me of anything more than a fondness for stretching behind shrubs. "I guess I tried couple times."

"How was it?"

"It's okay. Relaxing."

"It can be. It can be really hard work, too."

"How come you do it?"

Susan takes a bite of her lunch and chews pensively. "It helps me manage certain things. If I can control my breathing, I can control my thoughts. If I can control my thoughts, my mind isn't wandering and I can keep focused, and it's easier to control my body."

That's where we're different; my body's going down a path that I can't seem to stop. "Sounds like you can do anything."

She laughs, setting her plate down on the sand. "Well, I can't fly."

"Do you ever breathe and close your eyes and pretend something's not happening?"

"You mean when I'm in a hard pose?"

"Not really."

"Like a boring class in school?"

"Sort of, yeah."

"Well, the idea is to not be in a bad situation to start with. Not taking the boring class in the first place."

"Okay, but what if you have to take the class? What if you don't have a choice? What if someone's making you—" I stop. I can only imagine what she'll think if I keep going with this. I wonder about Susan again. How much does she know about me, without me having told her? How much is it okay for her to know? "What if it's something you didn't choose but it's happening and you still have to figure out what to do?" I notice her frown and add, "Like if a parent makes you do something."

She looks more comfortable with that. "I guess you could try to pretend something's not happening. But you know what the idea of yoga is? I mean, the whole reason? To be able to sit still in meditation, without moving. All that breathing, all those poses, all that practicing, they're all to get you ready to sit still, in peace. It's about being where you are, not zoning out."

I lean back, looking out at the water. Sitting still. It all sounds a bit pointless to me. "I thought it was to stand on your head."

Susan laughs. "No, although that's a benefit too. But choose carefully where it is you're sitting still. If something's that bad, don't breathe to pretend you're not there. Breathe to make the right moves to get out."

Later in the afternoon, as I'm walking from the dining pavilion to the bathrooms, Susan's words play in my head. *Breathe to make the right moves to get out.* As though it's that simple. I pause on the path, in that not-so-hidden spot behind the silk cotton tree. I can hear Joe up on the deck now, her voice musical and soothing, the way it was in the classes on Mariner's Cay.

"And inhale, reaching your arms overhead, fingertips reaching for the sky," she says. Even *put your hands up* sounds magical here. I take a few steps back, then feel my mouth stretch into a smile. My arms lift, the spray bottle of vinegar and thyme lifting with them. "And now exhale, bringing your hands down to the earth. Inhale looking up, and exhale, big step back with the right foot, into a lunge." I heave my foot back, and the spray bottle, still in one hand, sends a shoot of vinegar arcing into the air. I strain to see what they're doing up there and find them already halfway through lowering from a push-up position straight down to the ground. No way I'm doing that. I pause, in that awkward straddle, waiting for them to get somewhere I can join in again. Then, suddenly, there are hands on my shoulders.

"Gotcha!"

I let out a yelp and jump about a mile high— it's a miracle I don't pee myself. The spray bottle goes sailing and lands with a thud, a few feet away from the deck's steps.

"Sorry, sorry!" Through laughter, Dion shushes me, although Joe's already glaring in our direction while she leads the class into a balance pose. His chuckling is barely suppressed.

"What wrong with you?" I scurry over to retrieve the bottle, not daring to look at Joe, and beat a hasty retreat down the path. Dion jogs to keep up.

"Sorry, Indy. I was only playin. Why you didn't go up on the deck and join the class?"

I look down the length of myself—lumpy under my loose shirt and long, uneven skirt—then back up at him. "I look like I belong up there?" I hold his gaze. I dare him to laugh, to come up with some sunshiny retort. *Everybody belongs in yoga. Why not?* For a scary second, I almost want him to know. Want him to see, to really see. I realize, right then, that my time here is going to end soon. I'm going to get too big to hide it. No one wants a pregnant teenager around, don't matter how she got that way. I'll be out, same as Mamma. Moving homes every few months, every boyfriend. A new thought pops into my head: maybe Mamma didn't want those men, only needed them. *No.* I push the thought out.

When Dion doesn't joke, doesn't smile, just says, "You want to do some yoga with me, then?" I nod. We pass by the office, each taking a mat, then spread them out under a sapodilly tree by the parking lot. I'm thankful for its shade, for the breeze coming in off the ocean and between the buildings, finding its way to me.

"I don't think I'm made for this," I say as he kicks his shoes off.

"Oh, what, because of those sun salutations? They're only the beginning. Only the warm-up. You know how many fun poses there are?"

"My balance is horrible. And I can't even touch my toes."

"Keep practicing, it'll get easier with time."

I snort. "I don't think so. Not in my case."

"What case that is?" His gaze is honest, patient, clear. If only I could tell him.

"Nothing."

"Okay, then. Let me show you something easy. And here's the trick, if you can't balance on your own, you just gotta hold on to something to help you out."

Dion starts to walk me through tree pose, since I've seen it and tried it before. Last time, I bobbed and swayed, a palm in stormy winds. Now, when I start to teeter, Dion reaches out a hand.

I hesitate. "I don't want to make you fall."

"It's okay, I'm stable."

I take his arm, wobbling.

"Now you pick a point of focus for your *drishti, your gaze.* Pick something straight ahead, something that'll stay put."

I stare out at the strip of ocean, my leg still shaking.

"And now breathe. Focus on that, deep breath in, deep breath out."

While I cling to him with my right arm, my left arm flails, trying to keep me upright.

"Bring that left hand to your chest." He demonstrates, lifting his own right hand, tucked into its brace, to his heart in half a prayer. I bring my left hand up, thumb resting on my breastbone, my fingers pointing to the sky.

"Don't forget to breathe. You focusing?"

I give the tiniest nod. My leg is wobbling less, less. Dion's words fall away until all I can hear is his deep breathing, steady and easy. He pulls his arm away and I am upright on my own for one second, two, three, then tilting, tilting, and I'm down on the ground, laughing. Dion laughs too.

"Good try. Let me stand on the other side of you, and we'll try again."

The next side is just as tricky, slowly getting up, the one foot tucked up against the other thigh. I feel like a confused flamingo, but I keep going. Hand to chest, other hand holding on to him.

"Okay, and now, don't tense. You gotta relax into it. Breathe, remember? You ain fightin. You ain gotta hold your breath."

Ocean before me. Breathe in, breathe out, breathe in. Gentle hand pulling away, my left hand finding the right, touch and touch. Breathing, standing steady, staying strong. It's like being perfectly anchored and, at the same time, flying free.

The sudden sound of fast wheels on gravel jolts me, making me plop my foot down, spinning around to face the parking lot. Someone whizzes through the entrance on a bicycle, kicking up a cloud of dust. Dion jogs off to investigate. I lean up against the tree and realize I'm breathing hard, a few droplets of sweat forming. Was I working that much? Didn't feel like it. I'm letting my face catch the sun when I hear two sets of footsteps coming back.

"She's right here," Dion says. It's Churchy with him, looking even taller than usual. He could almost rest his chin on the top of Dion's head. "He say there's an emergency," Dion adds, gathering up our mats. "You go ahead, I'll wipe these down."

"I could t-t-tell her m-myself." Churchy glares at him.

Dion smiles, oblivious. "See you tomorrow, Indy."

"What happened?" I ask as Dion disappears down the pathway.

"This your w-w-work?" Churchy's still scowling.

"I finished my work for the day."

"And this what you's do?"

"What you mean?"

He shakes his head. "I got n-n-news for you. L-let's go." He hops back on his bicycle.

"What's your problem?"

"An you was lookin for your grammy?"

"You found her?"

He doesn't answer. "Wh-wh-where your bike?" His voice is hard. Who is this different Churchy? I turn away toward the office and come back pushing the purple bicycle, my bag hooked over the bars. When I wave bye to Dion, Churchy rolls his eyes, turning away. As we ride down the drive and onto the main road, I can't shake a sick feeling that has nothing to do with his sulkiness. I'm about to find out what happened to Grammy. I imagine the worst.

"We goin to the graveyard?" I try to swallow down the fear collecting in my throat, thick as phlegm.

"N-no." He laughs, at what I don't know. "If it was that, I'd t-t-tell you straight."

Something lies under those sarcastic words, but I can't worry about that now. After everything, I'm going to see Grammy. She's alive, and I'm going to see her. It's been nine months since that day we said goodbye, standing on her porch while Mamma blew the car horn.

We ride for a long time, west, as if we're heading for the airport. Churchy finally turns down a quiet road with a smattering of houses, then stops opposite a wide, run-down place. A fence runs around it, scraggly crabgrass scuttling up to the edge of the road.

"She in there."

An old folks' home. I'd never have found this place; there's not even a sign, but there's a collection of ancient men and women in beaten-down chairs scattered across the lawn. I peer at the building as I slide off the bike. Its white paint is peeling, the roof missing more than a few shingles. "In here? How you know?" He can't have gone knocking door to door until someone answered and admitted they had an old Mariner's Cay woman stored inside with a stack of books tall enough to build an extra wall and enough herbs to open a back-door shop.

"I kn-kn-know." Churchy leans his bike against a tree, then joins it, making it clear he's not coming in.

I take my bag with me, walking up to the gate. Unlatch it and try not to notice the squat woman blinking out at me through sun-squinted eyes, calling *Daughter, you got dollar?* in a strong, clear voice, or the three old men in the cool of the house's shadow. The door is open, a screen letting breeze in and keeping flies out. It's still stuffy as I step inside.

"Can I help you?" a younger woman asks. She pauses in the hallway, a pack of adult diapers under one arm. She's big and frowning; she must work here, though she only looks a few years younger than some of the residents.

"I lookin for my grammy." I can barely choke the words out. I'm not going to cry.

The worker frowns more, her lips pressed together like I'm being silly. "Grammy have a name?"

"Ms. Ferguson."

"Eunice? She's right in there. Down the hall."

Eunice. People don't call her *Eunice.* Even her friends— Ms. Munroe down the street who would come by with fresh eggs, Mr. Toote down at the store, Churchy's grandmother—

call her Ms. Ferguson, Ferguson, Miz Fergie. I've never heard anyone use her first name. The worker's voice is inappropriately cheerful. "Miss Darlene, you see your niece dropped off some more Depends for you," she sings out, like Miss Darlene might dance with joy that someone whose bottom she probably used to wipe is dropping off diapers for her, now. I tiptoe down the hallway, slow. Now that I'm here, something's holding me back from going toward that room. Part of me doesn't believe Grammy could be in this place with the daylight only half filtering through dusty screens and the windows that can't open enough to air out the reek of Dettol and bleach and pee, of clothes that haven't really been washed clean. As I force myself to keep going, I try not to look in the other rooms, try not to see the frail woman lying in bed, face turned to the wall, or the two men sitting beside a radio, leaning forward and listening to the obituaries as if hoping to hear their own names called.

Finally, I step into the doorway of that room. *God, let her at least be out of bed. Let her not be crazy, let her remember who she is. Let her know who I am.* "Who's there?" I hear my grammy say, her voice croaky and fearful. What if she's here because she's sick? What if she can't see? What if her mind's slipping away?

She's alone in a room with three beds pushed up against the walls. She sits on the edge of a plastic chair facing the window, her back turned. She's in a pink housecoat that can't be hers; she hates pink. *Insipid color. Only a ninny would wear pink.* Slippers on her feet and the sun not down yet, her body tense, hair twisted into childish braids.

"It's me."

"Who's me?" She clears her throat, and when she speaks again, her voice is the Grammy I know. "Hold on, let me get my glasses." Pushes herself up, fumbling for the nightstand. "That sound like—" She turns around. Grammy, same two deep wrinkles in her forehead, her eyes knowing behind her glasses. Wiry and built to last through the apocalypse. "Indira May Ferguson." She gives a little puff of air through her nostrils. "Bring your tail here." She opens her arms up and I step carefully into her embrace. I want to hurl myself against my grammy, to hug her close enough to make up for these long months, but I have to keep a space between us. She can't feel my belly. She can't. "Oh, Indy," she says, hanging on, and she draws me in so tight the space disappears and she has to feel it, has to know, but I can't bear to let go. She's so right, so unchanged, so strong in that thin, stooped old woman way. "Let me feel you, make sure you real." Her hands are firm as she slaps my back. "My baby girl. My Indy." Even in here she smells of home: herbs and vinegar and Pears soap. "What a thing this is, ay?" she says, and I pull away. "Sit down, sit down." She pats one of the beds and lowers herself back into the chair. "Look at me in here."

The worn sheet and cheap blanket have been tucked to near perfection, but the Grammy I always knew would have put a good bedspread on top. I stay standing and look around the bare room. On the closest nightstand, I recognize the ceramic angel that used to sit on her bureau, and, faithfully, a pile of books: her Bible on the bottom, a romance novel above that, a dog-eared copy of *Emma,* an anthology of poetry. What happened to her other six dozen favorites? "Sit!" she orders again. The bed sags under me, squeaking miserably. I hold my bag on my lap, feel the weight of that one book I've been carrying around. But here, face-to-face, I'm not angry anymore. It's Grammy.

"I would have come sooner. I only found out you were here today."

"How you found me?" She mashes her lips together. "You think I want you to see where I am? Pushed way in the back of Nassau, here, and no good to nobody."

"It ain your fault, Grammy. Mamma did it to you. I know."

"And how you know that, now?" She tilts her head to the side, bracing for a long story laced with half-truths. "You's woman now, ay?"

"No, but—"

"Matter of fact, I called the house for you several times. Bout three or four weeks ago, but I kept getting your aunt Patrice's boy. Garvey or something."

"Gary."

"That's it."

"You could call my cell, Grammy. Mamma gave her old one to me. Uncle know you here?"

"I told him not to say. I wanted to tell you myself. I thought that woman might have said something to you anyway. Patrice. Never had any sense in her head. I could only imagine how her children turned out."

"Aunt Patrice know too?"

She leans close, looking me over. "Look here, it don't matter. You tracked me down, Indira. Come here, let me look at you."

It does matter, though. "Churchy found you for me."

"Churchy?"

"Remember, from home? Mrs. Robinson's grandson?"

"Oh, *him*. That little soft boy?" She chuckles. I don't. He doesn't seem any kind of soft to me right now. Grammy pats my face, my hair, her hands and fingers bent with arthritis. The flat parts of her fingernails are cool on my face, but gentle. Her frown lines deepen. "You different. You grown up since you been here. Stand up again, let me see."

"Grammy, what happen?" I lean away, trying to redirect the conversation. "I saw Mamma, I saw the house . . ."

"*Happened.* What, you forgot how to speak your proper English? You got bigger. How tall you is now?"

"Five three. But—"

"You filling out, too." She rubs my arm. "Gettin ya granny's big bubbies." She's always been flat-chested, but I can't laugh at the joke. Her hand moves up my arm, her fingers passing over the bottom edge of the new bra; the skin is still sore underneath, and I flinch. "What wrong with you?"

"Grammy—" I pull back.

She frowns. "What you pullin from me for?" Her hands at my stomach. I'm frozen. Her familiar hands, patting down, stop. "Indira? What is this?"

I stand up fast, backing toward the door.

"Don't you yank back from me, child. You forget I bring you up, ay?" She stands up too, reaches out to pull my shirt taut against my belly. "No, no, no. No, Indira. No, no, no." It's like Churchy's stuttering, trying to get the word out enough times to make it true. "No, no." She slowly lifts my shirt. I look up; the ceiling seems too low, too close. I lower my eyes and meet my gaze, my own reflection in the dusty mirror over the bureau. Me, standing there. The shirt hoisted up to just under my chest. The edge of the new bra riding up over raw skin. Underneath, the belly. My stomach's never been flat. But it's firmer, my waist curved out. And I see what she's staring at. Something I hadn't noticed. Guess I hadn't looked, guess I've been trying not to. A vertical line runs down the center of my stomach, from below my chest through my navel, disappearing into the waistband of the skirt. Dark and straight, like someone's taken a crayon and divided me. Grammy lets my shirt go, steps back. "How far?"

I cover myself again. I look away from the mirror. I've been inspected and failed. I feel filthy.

"Let me ask you one more time. How you get this belly? You come over here and get yourself a little boyfriend? You been lettin somebody fool with you? It ain that Churchy boy, is it?"

"I don't have no boyfriend. I never had any boyfriend." I make my voice as hard as I can. *Stop it, don't ask me nothing more. I should go. I shouldn't have come here.*

"How you get that, then?" She points, looking me over. "Things don't just happen. Even weed has to have a seed drop for it to grow."

The room is getting smaller, the walls boxing me in. I have to get out.

"Who been droppin you?"

"Everything okay in here?" The same worker from before stops in the doorway, a gloved hand carrying a tied-up garbage bag.

"Miss Johnson, this my grandbaby," Grammy says. "Indira."

The woman extends a gloved hand. I stay where I am, staring out the doorway, beyond her. Past this woman who packages up used adult diapers, who helps these people in and out of the bath, who brings them to the table to eat, who's been seeing and talking to Grammy all this time. Past Grammy's disappointment, past her patting-down hands.

"She's about to take me outside for some air." Grammy slides the slippers off her feet and steps into a pair of worn-out loafers. "Pass me my cane." The worker reaches beside the bed and pulls out a shabby brown cane I've never seen before. "Thank you," Grammy says as the woman leaves, then turns to me, her voice low. "Come. All kind of ears in this place."

She takes my arm, but her grip is strong, holding me up. I want to run out the way I came in and never look back, but Grammy pulls me past a few rooms and out a back door onto a tired lawn. A few chairs are scattered over a covered concrete area. A man dozes in a rocker. "Get two of those chairs they have," she orders. "Set them down here." Once we're both settled, she leans in close. "Now. Tell me how you got this baby."

"I have to go."

She holds on to my wrist. "Wait." Pulls me down till my face is level with hers. "Look at me, girl. *Look* at me."

I look into Grammy's face. I've always feared seeing disappointment in her eyes, and sadness. What I see now is even worse, something I never imagined I'd see: Grammy's ashamed of me.

"Indy . . ."

A band of tightness starts to grip my chest. I want to close my eyes, to make this all fade away. But her eyes hold mine; she won't let me escape.

"What happened? Somebody bothered with you?"

Breathe, breathe. Out here, I can suck in an inhale, though it feels like dragging a whole bedsheet through a buttonhole. A little breath out. Again. Again.

"Is it your uncle?" Her face close, eyes searching for an answer.

I want to tell her and I want to be running away, want the air moving around me as I fly on the bike, far from here.

"Not one of your teachers? Come. You could tell me."

I try to pull in a deep breath, but it stops. My body won't let the air in.

"Indy." Hand on my face, gripping my chin. "Who do this to you? A neighbor? Somebody in the house with you?"

I yank my head back, away from her.

"Not Patrice's boy. What's his name? Garvey? Gary?"

Something in my expression must shift at hearing his name. "It's him, isn't it?" she says, and I pull my wrist out of her grasp. Grammy leans back in the chair, turning her head away. I look across the scrappy yard. No flowers are planted here, only patchy grass petering out over the concrete slab covering the cesspit.

"How long this been going on? Since you came? Your uncle tell me it was only him, Patrice, and their girl." Grammy runs a hand over her forehead. "Lord, forgive me for this. If I woulda known . . . I thought you woulda been safe here. Living in the house with your uncle, I thought you would be in good hands. Your uncle keep to himself and he travel a lot, don't hardly talk to me, don't have the time of day for your ma, but I thought you woulda been safe."

"It's Mamma who sent me here."

Grammy sighs. She says something, but her voice is so soft when she speaks, I almost think I don't hear her right. And before her words have fully sunk in, the worker comes out, rousing the sleeping man and waving at Grammy.

"Okay, Miss Eunice, we'll have your dinner soon. Time for your granddaughter to go."

My mouth is too dry for words. I get up and reach into my bag, my fingers closing around the book. I pull it out and toss it onto the chair beside Grammy. It lands with an accusing flop.

In the silence that follows, I start walking. I don't look back.

"You have a couple minutes, you could tell her bye," the worker says, but I keep moving, around the house and straight through the front gate, keep breathing, in, out, but I can't breathe past Grammy's whispered words just like I can't breathe past the feeling of having to throw up, past the memory of Grammy's house, my old home, past Gary. Churchy calls out to me from across the street—I forgot he was even waiting there. I step out into the road. A car honks, slams on its brakes, the driver shouting as I cross a foot or two from its front bumper. On the other side, Churchy stutters out something; I see his lips moving but register no sound. I stand there, trying to breathe past those words. Let him help me onto the purple bike. The weight of my bag is lifted from my shoulders, but I still feel like I'm covered in wet sand.

"You w-w-want go home?" I hear him ask, and his voice is impatient and concerned as if he's asked again and again, and I shake my head no. Balanced on the seat, trying to catch myself, trying to breathe. "Or you r-r-rather go by your boyfriend?"

Now he's got my attention. "What boyfriend?"

"You know who I mean. At the retreat."

"What you talkin about?" I get off the bicycle.

"I s-s-see him and you. With his hands on you. I s-s-see y'all when I ride in. I see y'all two in the back there alone. That's what you get paid to do?"

"You serious?" I snatch my bag from him. "Hands all over me? For money? That's what you think?"

"That's h-him? That's the daddy?"

Dion? It's gotta be a sick joke. Looking at Churchy's face, though, I see he's serious. And angry. Furious. His jaw is clenched. The twig he's fiddling with snaps.

"Go where you wanna go." I shove the bicycle at him, walking away, fast.

"W-w-wait." He comes riding up alongside me, his gangly frame upright as always. "L-l-let me follow you home."

"Leave me alone. And take your bike." I glance back at it, lying in the grass like a left-behind teddy bear. "I'll catch the bus."

"D-d-d-don't b-be mad."

"You think I do that? You think he actually touch me that way? You think I let people do stuff to me for money?"

"I s-s-see y'all holding h-hands—"

"You see him helping me learn to balance for yoga. You know what? Don't matter. You ain no different from everybody else. If you even knew. You—" I can't say anything more. The beginning of tears stings my eyes. I feel a wave of nausea threatening to surge. No, oh no, I am *not* doing that. I walk faster.

"I bring you here. I f-f-find your grammy for you." His voice is pleading now. My feet hurt and I'm tired. I look around for a bus stop, if buses even run out here.

"Come on." He's stopped. The sun, hanging lower, bronzes him, warming his eyes. "I t-tryin to help. Y-y-you wouldn't even tell me who is the daddy." His face is calmer, anger gone as quickly as it appeared. "Y-y-you could forgive me?"

I don't answer him, but I retrieve the abandoned purple

bike and force myself to start pedaling. I feel every jostle and jolt; my chest hurts every time I go over a bump in the road. I wish it would shake everything that's inside me loose until it falls out. I stop only once to let another wave of nausea pass, then keep going. I follow Churchy down the side streets and eventually onto Aunt Patrice's road. The driveway is empty again. I lean the bike against the fence.

"Thanks," I say. "For Grammy."

"D-d-don't worry, Indy." He reaches for my hand. The feel of his fingers around mine is foreign and cool; I want to pull away but I can't seem to find the right muscles. Just like I couldn't find them to pull away while Grammy hauled my shirt up. Just like I couldn't pull away, couldn't even scream when Gary—

"I-I-I got a way to fix this."

Fix it how? Someplace for me to stay? A job that pays even more? A magic wand? A time machine? "How?"

"Th-there's a place that could t-t-take care of this. My sister b-been one time. She help me make an appointment for you."

His face is so open, so eager. Churchy isn't stupid. He isn't slow. But I don't think he really understands what he's saying to me. I don't know if this is the fix I want. I don't know what I want to do.

"W-w-we could go from school," he carries on, like we're

making plans for a party. "W-we gotta be there t-t-tomorrow at t-two. Y-y-you could trust me."

I watch him spin around and ride away, the ding of his bike's bell a tinny promise of hope, a thread of sunshine filtering through clouds. But when he disappears around the bend, I'm alone again. Alone with the heft of my body, the weight of carrying all this. Alone with this new decision he's already made for me. Alone with what Grammy said, her voice low and her head ducked down, unable to look at me. *"Wasn't her, Indy. I told your mamma to send you here. I told her to let you go."*

13

"TRUST ME." IT'S THE fourth time Churchy's said that today, three words that are like someone asking you to love them. You either do or you don't; the request can't change things. "M-m-my sister say this place is real good," Churchy adds, as though he knows *trust me* isn't enough, glancing over from behind the wheel of his sister's boyfriend's car. I wonder what kind of bribe he had to come up with to borrow it, especially since he doesn't have a learner's permit, much less a license.

Outside, ahead of us, a tall woman is crossing the road with her daughter, who looks five or six. The girl stops, crouched down by the sidewalk, transfixed by something. The mother beckons for the girl to catch up, but the child ignores her and reaches down, comes up with a spray of something green. We pass them by and I see a speck of a flower in the girl's hand. "Hurry up, man, I ain got all day," the mother drawls, and the girl runs to her. The mother cuffs her in the back of the head. In the rearview mirror, I see her shaking her finger at the girl. When I look at the mother's face, she's barely older than me.

"D-don't worry." Churchy reaches over, resting his hand on mine.

"Let go." My voice is a shadow of its usual self. I close my eyes and breathe deep, the way Susan said to. *Breathe to make the right moves to get out.* I can't be Mamma. I can't be that woman. Can't be Grammy. When I open my eyes, his hand is gone.

The car stops outside a green building off Collins Avenue. I thought it would look different, run-down or dark, inconspicuous behind a bunch of trees. *Grammy told me they were illegal,* I said to Churchy. He shrugged. *B-b-better you go to a real doctor who ga d-d-do it for you right than you go to some back-of-the-bush person who don't know what they doing.* Well, this place isn't in the back of the bush. A large sign proclaims the practice of Dr. A. Palmer, Dr. C. Adderley, and Dr. S. Johnson. Above the sign, the sky is a painful blue. I get out of the car, but my feet feel rooted to the pavement.

Churchy says something, coming over to my side of the car. He puts an arm around my shoulders, walking me, walking us, up the four steps to the door, and I wince as his arm bumps the sore skin under the bra strap. Catch our reflection in the glass, me hobbling along, the purple of my skirt too rich, too bright for the day. Then the door is opened and we disappear. Inside, an air conditioner hums; it's a freezer in here. At the counter, the receptionist hands me a clipboard.

Name.

I stare at the paper for what feels like years before I write in Mamma's name. Sharice Ferguson.

Age.

"Put nineteen," Churchy whispers once we are sitting, and when my hand won't write, he writes for me. He carries my papers back up to the desk. I reach into my pocket and feel for the wad of money Churchy's taken from the cash register at the restaurant. *I-I-I could always pay that back*, he'd said when he gave it to me.

"You can pay after," the woman at the desk says, taking the clipboard without looking up. I sit back down again.

There's another girl sitting against the wall, maybe a year older than me. The woman beside her, probably her mother, glances over at me, frowns, and picks up her phone. I can't look away from the girl. Even with her mother scowling beside her, the girl seems so peaceful, so sure. I bet that same mother will still drive her home after this, a home where she's wanted, to a home that's safe.

"They're good here," the girl says, smiling, unperturbed by my stare. "This my first baby, and they're good. Set your mind at ease. Look like me and you are almost the same place. How far are you?"

I can't fathom the excitement in her voice. "I'm not too sure."

"I'm five months. This your first visit?"

I nod, fraudulently. First visit, and last.

The girl struggles to her feet and shuffles over a few seats so we're closer. "Don't worry," she says, leaning in. "It isn't bad. They ask you questions, weigh you, check if everything is normal. You'll feel better after. Ain nothing to be scared of."

The girl's mother glances over at us, her lips pursed. I can imagine what any mother worth having would think of two pregnant teenage girls swapping stories. The mother gets up, phone pressed to her ear. "I'll come back in half an hour," she says, heading for the door. The girl is unbothered; she leans back in her chair, chattering about baby clothes and a due date in September.

"My back-to-school baby," she says, like it's an accessory. Maybe she's joking. Beside me, Churchy shifts nervously.

"Marcy Dean," the nurse calls.

"Oh, that's me," the girl says, looking over.

"Dr. Johnson is in surgery today, so you'll be seeing Dr. Palmer," the nurse tells her. "You can go through to room two; it'll be about ten minutes, okay?"

"Coming now," Marcy answers. "You'll be all right," she

says to me, giving me a smile as she gets up. "I need to use the bathroom first," she calls after the nurse, following her down the hallway.

"Sharice Ferguson?" another nurse calls.

Hearing Mamma's name out loud is jarring; maybe we really are the same. Churchy looks over, waiting for me to answer. *Do what you gotta do.* I force myself up out of the chair and follow the nurse. At the end of the hall, I see Marcy waiting in line for the bathroom behind two other women. The door to the ladies' room opens and a huge woman waddles out, one hand on her belly, the other on her back. As she passes me, she rolls her eyes and smiles as if we belong to the same special club.

My nurse shows me into the third room and leaves, closing the door behind her. I change into the cotton gown that's been left for me, then sit on the examination table alone. The room begins to close in. My head feels light enough to drift away. My chest threatens to collapse in on itself. *This is happening.* I have to keep my mind occupied, but all I can think about is what will come after I leave. I don't have any hope of living with Grammy ever again; no one at the home will let her leave to go stay with a teenager, even if I'm her granddaughter, and I certainly can't move into that place with her. Even if we had someplace where we could be together, everything's different, now that I've seen that shame in her face, now that I know what she did. Nothing can erase that. I'll have to go back to Aunt Patrice's house. Another thought crosses my mind. Maybe if Gary knew what he's done to me, he'd stop. Maybe he'd leave me alone if he saw my belly. Maybe this thing that's happened could have protected me. What will protect me now?

I hear footsteps approaching the door—no, don't come in. I need to think. Why didn't I think about this last night? The footsteps pass, but the panic still comes in waves. Air. I need air. I get off the table and scramble toward the window on wobbly legs, cranking it open. Not enough. I crank it farther, leaning on the screen. Still not enough air. All I want is to be able to breathe. Press my face up against the screen and pull, pull, pull that air in. Close my eyes. Imagine sand under my toes, not cold tiles. My chest rises, ocean sweeping up the shore, warm water lapping at my feet. I can feel my shoulders falling, the tide slipping away. Space opens up around me—a seagull calls. I am not here, in this office, in this room, with this thing in my belly, getting ready to do what I'm about to do, then going back to that house, with him, with nothing to stand between me and what he wants. A little more of that good air. I can almost see the outline of a ship bobbing on the horizon. A little more . . . little bit more . . . and then there's the pop of something coming loose in the window. Sweet fresh air on my face.

Baaam! Baaam! Baaam! An alarm bursts to life, slapping me back to reality. Cold tiles under my feet, my fingers on the window's lever, a security system wire dangling out of place. I jump back from the window—what if they come in and see it was me?—and I open the door, stepping into the hallway as nurses bustle past.

"Look out!" one calls, nearly bumping into me. "Just wait in the room, someone will be in."

Then I am alone in the hallway again. Across from me, room two's door is still open. Down the hall, the bathroom door is closed. I don't know if Marcy's in there, but I take a chance. I step into her room.

It's empty. I close the door behind me, leaning against it. The alarm's clang keeps sounding, sounding, then abruptly stops. I can hear voices from the reception area; someone laughs with relief, worlds away. I hear a knock, then the door starts to open against me. I step away as a woman peers in. She must be a doctor; she has on a long white coat over her dark jeans and loose, flowery top. She's short and plump, her skin a rich brown, her hair pulled up in a bun.

"Marcy? You okay in there?"

My voice swells in my throat. I want it to be true. Want Marcy's happy, her excitement, her certainty. I want her life. "Yes."

"I'm Dr. Palmer." She holds out a hand to shake mine.

"Looks like someone opened the window in room three." She rolls her eyes. "Set off the whole security system in here. Trying to make all these pregnant women have their babies early." She closes the door behind her. "All right, let's get you comfortable on the examination table. Come on." She takes hold of my arm, helping me up, then turns to the sink to wash her hands. "I'm filling in for your regular doctor today. So when you see him, don't tell him we tried to give you a heart attack with the alarm." She gives me a warm smile I don't deserve and picks up a folder that's laid on the counter, scanning the pages inside. "How have you been feeling since your last visit, Marcy?"

"I'm not—" The words almost tumble out. *I'm not Marcy, I'm Indy, except you think I'm Sharice. I came for the abortion, and I pulled the alarm, and Marcy could come in here any minute, and I wanted to feel what she feels, even just for a little while.*

"Hmm." Dr. Palmer frowns. "The nurse hasn't taken your vitals yet today, so you aren't quite ready to see me. All this excitement must have thrown things off. Wait here for a minute, I'll send her in to check you." She smiles as she steps back out into the hallway. As she closes the door, I hear her say, "No, someone's in there. You are? Okay, come out to the waiting area and have a seat, we'll get you sorted. We got two Marcys today. Busy busy."

Any minute now they'll figure out what I've done; I have to get out. When the hallway sounds clear, I crack the door open. No one's in sight. I sneak back over to room three and quickly change into my clothes. When I come out, a man in a doctor's coat is striding toward me.

"Sharice? We've been looking for you—"

I hurry away from him, down the hall, then through the waiting room, past Marcy, who sits patiently, still waiting to be seen.

"Wh-wh-wh-wh-what happened?" Churchy calls, spring-ing up as I approach him. "Y-y-you finish already? Th-th-they ain charge you nothin?"

I keep going, pushing the door open. I can't get outside fast enough. I almost run out of the parking lot, but despite my fears, every time I glance back, no doctors are chasing me. It's only Churchy.

"D-D-Dee?" he stutters.

I couldn't do it, I imagine myself saying, calm and sure. *I couldn't breathe, I couldn't even stay in the right room.* Except I can't turn around, can't even face Churchy. Part of me is mad at him; he brought me here, he made me lie, he didn't even let me decide. And part of me feels I've let him down. He arranged *everything,* called his sister, got the number for the doctor, made the appointment, borrowed a car. He texted me last night and again this morning to make sure I knew where to be and when. If Smiley was here, she'd tell me not to be stupid. Tell me to talk to Churchy sweet so he'll stay. Right now, though, all I want is to get as far as I can from this office.

I reach into my pocket, pull out the money, and give it back to him. I want to tell him about Gary, want him to believe me, to care, to have an answer, a way out for me. There's so much Churchy doesn't understand that I don't know where to begin. "Sorry" is all I can choke out before I start walking away. He walks beside me for a minute or two on those long legs before he falls back, giving up. I keep going, hear the roar of the car's engine, then a honk. Through the open window I see Churchy's face, hurt, confused. Then he speeds up and pulls away.

The house is empty when I come in. Lock the door, drop my bag in the front room. In the kitchen, dishes are piled up in the sink, more waiting on the counter. *Leave those things out, you might as well send a handwritten invitation to the roaches,* Grammy would say. I turn the hot water on and reach for the soap. Dishes. Like scrubbing scum off tiles. Like stuffing thyme into vinegar, baking soda on anything. Reliable. A problem so simple to fix. Pick them up, wash them off, rinse them, fill up the drainer. If only everything was so easy. If only anything was. I'm so caught up I don't hear the key turn, only hear the door slamming shut. I glance at the clock. Almost five. Must be Smiley home from school.

"Hey, practice run late again?" I ask, half turning, a plate still in my hand. Gary stands there in his chef's pants and shirt, holding a long pan covered over with foil.

A half-smile on his lips. He opens the fridge, shoving the pan in. "You home by yourself?"

Aunt Patrice's car isn't in the driveway. Uncle is out of town for his work. Smiley has practice this afternoon. He knows all this. The plate slips out of my hand, clattering into the sink. My eyes dart to the back door, then to the doorway leading to the dining room and beyond. I have to get out of here; which way to run?

I make a dash for the back door but he's faster, blocking my way out. Before I can try to get to the dining room, he moves toward me. I back up until I feel the counter's edge pressing against my behind.

"You miss me?" He plants his hands on the countertop so his arms wall me in on either side, caging me. He towers over me, so close I can smell the lemon starch on his uniform, the food he's cooked today. Boiled fish, sautéed onions, sickly-sweet icing.

"Let me go."

"I talkin to you."

"Stop it, don't touch me!"

"Ain nobody touchin you."

Garlic, too, and burnt oil. No one's coming to help me—

no one ever does. But maybe if he knew, he'd leave me alone this time. I pull my shirt against my stomach. "You can't."

He stays where he is. His expression hardly changes. He barely moves, nothing more than a flicker of his eyes, down, then back up. "You getting fat," he says, but the slight shake in his voice tells me he understands. This is my chance, he's off balance; I try pushing past him but he's expecting it, now, arms rigid, locked into place. He throws his body forward, pinning me against the counter, knocking the breath out of me.

"Where you think you goin? You just like ya ma, you know." His voice is steady now. "Always getting in problems. Y'all too slack for ya own good. I know you sleepin around. How was he? Your friend in the jeep? And that little boy you got comin round here with the bike? You got plenty friends. Hey, Sharice?"

"Stop! You did this to me!" I've never yelled so loud. Now, when it's daytime and there's nobody to wake up, to hear me.

"What you yellin for? Quiet, man. You ain gotta carry on. You ain gotta get all feisty like you did in the truck. You still owe me something, from then, ya know." He takes a step back, but his arms don't move. "Turn around. Turn. I know you don't want hurt that little thing in there."

I struggle against him one last time, pounding my fists against his chest and arms, but I can't break free. He's too strong for me. He grabs my arms, forcing them down to my sides.

"Turn around."

I can't run. I can't fight. I can't even move.

He wrenches my body around so my back is to him.

Out the window, the bougainvillea rustles in a slight breeze. And then his whole weight slams against me. Pressed into the counter until I am it, it is me. This isn't happening. The *ssshk ssshk* of coarse polyester pants rubbing up against old cotton skirt. "Look at you, big up an ain even seventeen yet. Just like ya ma."

I close my eyes. Not happening. I am not here. I am by myself, I am on the beach. Sand. And—I can't. Can't feel sand, can't feel sun, can't hear water, only *ssshk ssshk ssshk ssshk ssshk*. This is nothing, I tell myself. I am nothing.

"I gotta be careful. Can't touch a little slut like you." He gasps. "I ain know where all you been," and then nothing but hard counter edge cutting into my belly. His whole body shakes and he collapses against me.

I am hollowed out.

He steps back, breathless. Pants being unzipped. *No, not that. Please, no.*

"Look what you make me do." His words stilted. He steps out of the pants, tossing them down by my feet. There's a wet spot near my hip, growing cold. "That's nasty."

That sour salt in the air, that ugly, animal smell.

"Clean that shit up." Footsteps going away. And then

coming back. Purple bills flutter, dead moths, one, two, three, four, land on top of the pants. Four hundred dollars. "Deal with that. Don't bring no mess in this house. And don't go lyin bout it bein mine. Ain nobody ga believe you anyway."

The back door flies open. I didn't hear a car pull up. Neither did he. He swears as Cecile barrels in. The smile on her face belongs to a different world. She's in her gray-and-red volleyball uniform, shirt untucked, socks half up, half down, hair messy.

"Hey, guess what?" And she stops, sees him in his boxers and socks, the chef's coat and pants on the floor, the money. "What happened?"

"Ain nothin, Indy offer to take these to get dry-cleaned for me. You know how she always keep things clean," I hear him say. "I goin in the shower, I hot from work."

"Wait!" She's still by the door. Why won't she come farther in? "Our team win today. We goin to the finals on Saturday!"

Gary pauses. "That's great, Smiley." He gives an awkward smirk as he turns and heads to the back of the house.

I bend down, my arms sore from where he held them, and gather up the wad of white fabric, the money. On the pants, the tiniest smudge of purple. I look down at my skirt. Dye rubbed off. Smiley's head is deep in the fridge. ". . . in the last minute of the game, you shoulda seen it," she says, emerging, nibbling on whatever was in that foil pan. Can't she smell it, the thing that he's done?

"You okay, Indy?" She gives me a funny look, confused.

"Yeah." The word comes out heavy, but she doesn't seem to notice.

"Okay, well, you wanna come?"

"Where?"

She frowns, impatience reshaping her face. "You don't even listen to anything. The whole volleyball team goin out for pizza and they say parents and family could come."

"Where's Aunt Patrice?"

"I told you, she's waiting in the car."

They couldn't have been here ten minutes before?

"See her coming now?"

I shove the clothes and money in a plastic bag, tie them up before the back door opens again. Aunt Patrice scans the room as she comes in. "This kitchen a mess. You couldn't clean up?"

"She getting ready to do laundry," Smiley says helpfully. "I ask if she wanted to come and she say no," she says, making the decision for me. "You want us bring you anything back?"

I shake my head. Aunt Patrice sniffs, then frowns. "In here smell funny." Her eyes catch mine as she reaches to crank the window open all the way. "Who been in here?"

"Gary." I hold her gaze, anger bubbling up in me. I want

her to know. I want to tell her, want her to see it, acknowledge it. Even if it means she'll kick me out.

She stares at me, her lips pressed together, then looks away. "Spray some Glade or something."

The back door slams shut, then the car doors. I wait to feel something, anything, as I watch them pull away, but I'm numb; even my anger's gone. I don't have time to waste—Gary could come back in here any minute. At the kitchen sink, I wash the skin under that awful wet spot, scrubbing until it stings. Hurrying down the hallway, I can hear the shower on. I lock myself in Smiley's room and pull on a different skirt. In the living room, I push my clothes into the straw bag. One last quick look around before I head back to the kitchen. I take the bag with the pants, with the money. I don't know why, my head's not clear, but I'm not leaving it here, no way. I put the ruined skirt in its own plastic bag and put all these dirty things in one big garbage bag together. They can't touch anything else. I see the old roll of duct tape on the counter and stuff it into my bag. I hear the shower still running as I leave through the front door.

I don't realize how hard I'm hammering on Churchy's door till he opens it and I stumble forward into his apartment. He catches me, keeping me upright.

"D-D-D-Dee? What happen to you? Y-you okay?"

I hear him, but I can't speak for the longest time. I let him lead me in, sit me down on the sofa. I hear him pour out something to drink, then set a glass on the table near me. He sits beside me and takes my hands in his. I know I've come here, but I want so badly to pull my hands away. He's holding me closer to him. It's meant to be an embrace but it feels like suffocation.

"Indy?" He leans back, giving me space. "Somebody hurt you?"

I wish I'd said the words out loud to Aunt Patrice. All the words. *Gary did this to me. You don't know? Really?* I don't want to carry these things in me anymore. Churchy's eyes are fixed on my face and I want somebody, anybody, to see me and know, really know me. To hear what's happened to me. And to understand the difference.

"I know you might think I just like my mummy. But before you, I never had a boyfriend. Nobody ever even kiss me."

Churchy frowns. "How you could get baby and—"

"Somebody made me." The words tumble out, but in parts. Gary's name a hard thing I can't quite choke out.

"M-m-made you? What you mean somebody m-made you?" He looks at me, confused. Then less confused. "Somebody at school?"

Shake my head.

"Your uncle? He—"

I open my mouth again, and let it come out. "Gary." I wait for it to feel better, to feel lighter, having his name out of me.

"Wh-wh-what?" He leans back on the sofa, jerky with shock. Runs a hand over his forehead, trying to unscramble my words. "Y-y-your cousin Gary? Smiley's big brother?" His hands forming fists so clenched they might implode. "Wh-wh-when?"

"From last year. September." The lightness isn't coming; why do I still feel heavy?

"Wh-what? Wh-wh-why you didn't tell me? Wh-when was the l-last time he touch you?" He looks straight at me, straight into me. It's too much. I look away, focusing on his hands, the smooth brown skin, the bony knuckles, the pink tinge of his palms.

"Now."

His fists open and close. "J-j-just n-n-now?"

"Just now."

He walks to the fridge, opens it. A clink as he reaches for something. The fridge door slams shut, every bottle in it rattling. Then a crash, and smashed pepper sauce dripping down the wall by the microwave, orange-red guts and glass everywhere. "I goin by your auntie. I gone kill him." At the knife drawer. "He l-l-like woman so much, I could make him into one right now."

A half dozen images flash through my mind as I spring

up. Churchy, Gary, blood, siren lights flashing, handcuffs, those hands slack and sorry, sliding bars. Churchy in prison. An impossible thought. I get up and press my back against the door to block his way out. I can't let him go like this. He really *will* kill Gary.

Churchy opens the drawer again, puts the knife back in. The air smells of goat peppers, eye-stinging hot. Through searing tears, I watch his hands drop.

"S-s-s. S-s-s." His fists clench. "Sorry." He spits the word out, a bullet.

Did I make Churchy this way? Balled fists, knife inches away, broken glass, and pure hate? I search his face for the Churchy I know—not the awkward boy stiffly stuttering, but the one perched on his bike, flying through the streets of Nassau. Sitting cross-legged in the sand. Holding out a dish of food. Making the rounds to unmarked nursing homes, asking for my grammy, asking and asking until he found her. There's no trace of that Churchy now.

"Don't get mix up in this."

"I ain know what wrong with you. Y-y-you think I c-can't do it? Y-you think I ain m-m-man enough?"

"Churchy—"

"Wh-wh-why? Y-you tryin to protect him?"

"I don't want you getting in trouble. I leaving, I got it handled, I—"

He chops into my words. "What, y-you like it?"

I stare into his hard, angry eyes, watching them turn sorry, sad, full. He opens his mouth and I know what has to come next. *I didn't mean it. I sorry. Don't take it that way. I was only.* Words Mamma's boyfriends would use on her. *I didn't mean to hurt you, baby. I love you. I was mad, you know how my temper get.* And later she would say *He's a good man, ya know. You could see he's a good man, he only need patience, and I could give it to him. He's a good man, he only need someone to give him a chance. He's a good man, he only like too much woman, he only, he only.* I won't be her. I turn away from Churchy and walk out of the apartment. For once, he knows better than to follow me.

I lean his sister's purple bicycle up against the wall outside the restaurant. I walk to the bus stop, and thankfully, there's the number 18 pulling into view. I get on, hold out five dollars to the driver.

"I don't give change," the driver warns. I drop the money in the jar and sit down. I don't care. It doesn't matter anymore.

The bus stops at the end of the road to the retreat. I walk all the way down. In the dark, I open the gate by feel. The trees stand silent and upright, dropping shadows.

I use my phone to see as best I can. The jeep is gone, but a light's on in the office. I glimpse Maya moving around in there as I follow the path through the trees and around to where I can smell the sea. I head toward the cabins, hoping I won't meet people on the way. The walkways are empty, my only company the chorus of frogs and crickets that fall silent at my footsteps, then pick up behind me as I pass by.

I stop at the last cabin. My cabin—the one I found the other day. No light is on. I turn the door handle. It opens; the place is empty. It's been waiting for me. Yank the curtains shut so no one can look in. Everything is still there; bed, nightstand, closet. The wood floor hasn't been swept. The door doesn't lock, but there's a hook. I latch it closed. Then I lie down. Sleep should come, I'm exhausted. Except every crackling twig is Gary, moving through the living room. I maneuver carefully in the dark, wedge the nightstand up against the door, and lie down again. The cabin starts to shrink. I can't stay in here right now. So what if someone sees me? They can't do anything worse. I push the nightstand out of the way and open the door.

The night is growing cooler, like tea coming to room temperature. In the distance, two women laugh. A bell sounds. I step out into the grass. Every sound makes me spin around but every time, no one's there. I pick up my pace. Moving faster, path growing wider until it spills out onto the beach, sand giving way under my feet. I gasp for air, backing toward the water.

I hear more laughter. Farther down the beach, surrounded by torches staked into the ground, I see a group of women standing. As their laughter settles, one begins moving into a more serious stance. Upright, back a royal palm. *Tadasana. Correct standing pose,* Joe said that day on Mariner's. *Big toes touching, heels slightly apart, legs straight, back straight, belly in, shoulders back and down.* How Joe-like to call it *correct.* The others fall in line, following, each in her own space. I watch their movements, illuminated by the orange glow from the torches. Arms up, then down. Bending at the waist. Legs lifting, torsos twisting, strong yet light. Each woman glides along at her own pace, mirroring the others, but on her own time, in her own way. Each herself. I bring my hand down to my stomach, firm and curved out. A flicker of envy.

My feet shift, almost without my thinking. *Why not me?* Big toes together in the dry sand. Heels seashell width apart. Shoulders relax, chest rises and falls. Bring hands together, palm to palm. Thumbs at the center of chest. *My chest.* Inhale, bringing in air. Scent of the sea, salty, alive. I lift my own hands, then bend down. This time I'm not dizzy, though I feel the belly pressing against the tops of my legs. More tonight than a week ago. *My belly. Mine.* I keep moving on the beach, at first copying poses from the glittery figures a ways off, then transitioning into ones I remember from Joe's class, from Dion, from glimpsing Susan's instructions through the leaves that shield the deck, and finally, moving in the ways I want to. Holding one foot, the other planted on the ground, my leg shaking. Lying on my back, then raising my hips into the night, my feet firm on the sand. I stand in a lunge, and when I bring my arms up, the new bra chafes me. Reach back and unhook it. Pull the whole bra loose and out from under the shirt. I slip it off and drop it on the sand. I raise my arms again.

And when I am tired, my body warm, my arms and legs aching, I sit, crossing my legs. Eyes closed—no need to stay open, looking for the unsafe—and my breathing slows, grows deep. The night is nothing but quiet now, waves lifting, falling, the sea shifting in sleep. My eyes start to make water. I sit there and breathe as the tears fall onto my collarbones, my hands, my legs, my belly.

And then I feel it. A flutter. Sudden, quick, a moth scuttling for light. Inside me.

I bring my hands to my belly; another flutter, this time harder.

I bring my knees up, wrap my arms around my legs, and rest my head, sitting together with this thing. This thing in me. Another flutter, then it shifts away, retreating to a place so deep I can't feel.

The last of the fire from down the beach goes out. A half-moon hangs in the sky, painting my skin with a milky sheen. I get up from the sand, dusting the grains off my backside, my legs, my skirt, and shaking out the abandoned bra. Walking back to the cabin, my hands around my belly, I don't know what's going to happen next. But I do know who I am. Not Mamma. Not Grammy. Not Doubles, the girl who Churchy, Gary, Aunt Patrice, and Smiley think I am. I'm Indy, and I choose to be different. I'm doing this my way.

14

BACK AT THE CABIN, I still can't sleep. I check my phone. Twenty missed calls, and a bunch of messages I don't read. I leave it on silent and use it as a flashlight as I step out onto the front porch. I sit down on the wooden floor, leaning my back against the wall. Thoughts swirl in my mind. Grammy. *I told your mamma to send you here. I told her to let you go.* Aunt Patrice. *I have my own child to protect.* The pants in that garbage bag. *Don't bring no mess in this house,* Gary said, money tossed at me like he was paying for what he did. As though a handful of purple bills could cover this, could cover me. The bills are still crumpled up with those pants. I'll never use that money. Why did I even keep that bag full of nightmare memories? Showing Gary didn't make any difference, but maybe the pants and that dirty money will. *Do what you gotta do.*

Beside me on the porch, my phone lights up. Incoming

call from the house. Twenty missed calls. I can't hide forever.

"Hello?" I keep my voice hushed.

"About time!" Smiley screeches back at me. I want to cry with relief. "Where the hell you been? Everybody lookin for you. Mummy ready to have your head on a stick. She been callin your mummy and all. She even called your grammy. You never told me she came to Nassau!"

"How come you callin me on the house phone?"

"You know how much trouble you in? Mummy check my cell phone an all to see if you send me any messages. She watchin me like a hawk."

"You call to tell me that?"

"Don't play with me." We always joke, a mix of teasing and toughness, but it's different this time. I'm not joking, and there's no smile in her voice either, now. "Where you gone?"

"Where you think?" I expect her to say something crude about Churchy, but she surprises me.

"You at that retreat place, right?"

"Aunt Patrice know?"

"She don't know you's go there."

"An you ain tell her nothin?"

"You ain hear me? She don't know where you is."

"I mean bout anything. Churchy or—" I can't get the words out. "Or anything. I'll never talk to you again if you tell her. I mean it."

"Why you think I would tell her?" Smiley's voice squeaks in defense. "When you comin back?" she asks, softer.

"You could have the whole bed to yourself. Aunt Patrice should be happy."

She makes a dismissive noise.

"What happen, you lonely? You need friends, ay?"

"I only called to check on your behind." Her voice is breezy, now, trying to sound casual. "So how come you gone, man? And the teachers at school wanna know where you gone. Ms. Wilson won't stop bugging me. Everybody askin questions."

I look out into the darkness. "Don't worry about it." What would I tell her, anyway? Your brother is a monster and I think your mummy know what he does to me? Today I almost had an abortion and then got out of it by pretending to be somebody else?

"Hey," I say, because the line's been quiet for too long. It's not like my cousin to let any kind of hush fall. I picture her crouched down somewhere quiet, trying to talk without being caught.

"Yeah?"

"What Gary say?"

"Nothin. He say last time he see you was in the kitchen, when we stopped by the house after the game. He went in the shower, and when he came out, you was gone."

There's a pause—the perfect time to tell her about Gary. Except I don't have the perfect words. I think of what happened when I told Churchy.

"Indy, what you ga do? Mummy past mad. This a whole mess. Daddy away, and you know how she is. She ga go to the police if you don't come back soon."

There's a click on the line. Someone else has picked up.

"Hey. I want use the phone." Gary's voice. I pull the phone away from my ear to escape the sound of him, but I can still hear.

"Well, wait," Smiley snips, faraway but still audible.

"I'll wait right here," he says.

"You ain got nothing better to do?" she protests.

"Guess not."

I can imagine him, the phone pressed to his ear, looming over Smiley on the sofa. Be careful, I want to tell her. Run like hell from him. He's her brother, though; he's not gonna do anything to her. I put the phone back up to my ear.

"Who you talkin to anyway?" Gary says on the other line.

Don't tell him, I think as hard as I can. *Don't tell him anything, Smiley, don't say a word.*

"None of your business."

"You talkin to man, ay? Or you found our runaway? Let me talk to her."

"Leave me, man, your head ain no good," Smiley

complains. "Five minutes, then you could have the phone."

"Wait till Mummy get home." He speaks like I'm not even on the line. "I ga tell her you talkin to her, an you ga be sleepin out too, before she know it."

"Five minutes."

"Hurry up," he says, annoyed. There's the click of the phone as he hangs up.

"Gary and his big head!" Smiley shouts after him, more for my benefit than for his. She continues talking, something about school, someone she thinks is cute. Every few words drift in, and the rest pass me by. Her voice makes me sad. I can never tell her about him, what he did. We're so different, and the words from my world don't translate anymore. Maybe they never did. "Hey?" she says.

"What?"

"I say when you ga tell me bout the daddy."

"One day." I wish I could tell her. Would she even believe me?

"When?"

"Soon."

There's a click on the line again. "Yeah, Indy, who's the daddy?" Gary's voice is flippant. He could be talking about what to order for dinner tonight. "You even know?"

I hurl the phone away from me, hard as I can. It's swallowed up in the darkness. "Owww!" someone yells—someone real, someone here, not across the phone line. A light flashes on from deep within the beach shrubbery in front of me.

"Who's there? You better not be the bastard who spray-painted my walls. If I catch you!"

Joe.

If I open the door to run into the cabin, she'll know I'm here. I lie flat and hope she thinks it came from someplace else. Except there's no other cabin nearby.

"Who's that up there?" Footsteps, running, the flashlight swinging back and forth, painting the porch in wide strokes of light. I cower beneath them. *Don't find me, don't find me, don't find* . . . "Who's that there? I got pepper spray, don't even think about trying anything."

"Don't spray," I call out, scrambling to my feet. "It's me, it's me."

"Indira?"

I cover my eyes from the flashlight's glare as Joe steps up onto the porch.

"Sorry." She reaches forward and pulls a string to turn on the porch light. "What you doin out here? It's past nine o'clock," she says. I pull my shirt down fast, but it's too late. She only looks at my belly for a moment before her eyes are on my face again. A moment is all anyone needs to make up their mind. "Let's go in the cabin," Joe says. "We can talk. Now that everything's out in the open." There should be surprise on Joe's face, or at least her usual anger. Instead, she looks tired.

What does she mean, *out in the open*? I wonder as I follow her inside.

"You must be past your first trimester now."

Trimester. The word falls like a rock she's been carrying around for some time. How long has she known? Since we went to Mariner's? Since the day I first set foot over that wall, dripping wet?

"How long you knew?"

She shakes her head. "I ain blind."

I feel naked. If Joe could see, Dion knows, then, too. And Maya, and Susan. I must be an idiot to have thought otherwise.

I pull my bag onto my shoulder. My legs are tired; I don't want to run anymore. I edge toward the doorway, but Joe steps forward, blocking my way, and rests her hand on my arm. I flinch, pulling away, hating myself for doing it, but I can't help it. I have to get out of here before she starts asking more questions.

"I'm going," I hear myself say, my mouth dry. "You ain gotta throw me out."

"Only place you're going is to get dinner." Joe props herself under my arm, guiding me out the door. She is warm, and smells of herbs and Earl Grey tea. "I know you didn't eat tonight. Let's go. You look about ready to collapse." At the mention of food, my stomach lets out a growl—I can't deny it.

Unlike Dion or Smiley, Joe doesn't babble to fill space. She and I walk to the pavilion in silence, my breathing so shallow it might as well not be there, hers loud and deep enough to be its own ocean. The dining area is almost empty, with only a couple of guests left at a table, talking. Joe nods at them as we pass. The women don't seem to notice me, too deep in their own conversation. We cut through the back and into the kitchen, where Joe turns on lights and yanks open the door of the massive fridge. She moves so confidently, dishing out two plates of food and pushing them into the oven to heat up. I wait for the questions I know will come.

"I had Dion young," she says instead. "I was about your age, I guess. Seventeen. Girls didn't get pregnant in my family, and if you did you got married off quick. I didn't want no husband, and everyone was after me to do something. Get rid of it. Give it up for adoption. At one point, my family was pushing for my auntie to raise the baby. Bring it up as her child." Her brow is furrowed as she speaks, the memory jostling something in her. It's not the same, I want to say. She probably ran off with some high school boyfriend and forgot to use protection. "What's that look?" she says abruptly, reading my mind.

"Nothing," I say guiltily. "What did you do?"

"Well, obviously I kept him. Ain nobody was gonna make me give up my baby. I lost a lot of other things, though. I had to quit school, cause in those days they didn't have the special classes for teen mothers. I had a scholarship to go off to college; I lost that. Even though I still wanted to get my degree, even though I finished high school after, as soon as they found out, they took my award and gave it to some little flat-bellied girl who they thought was smart enough not to get herself pregnant."

"That sucks."

"It did suck." She opens the oven, testing the food with the back of her hand. "Half my family disowned me, they told me to stop coming to church until my shame had passed. I surely did stop." She closes the oven door with a bang. "When I went to the hospital, the nurses talked to me so bad. Tell me, 'What you screamin for? Bet you scream when you was getting it!' Tell me 'You need to learn. It feel good when he was givin it to you, but it hurt now.'"

Why is she telling me this? To scare me? To warn me? To show me what to expect? I go over to the sink and start washing dishes to give myself something to do. To drown out Joe's words.

"I had a hard time after, and I left home when he was a year old." Her voice reaches me over the sound of the running water, the clink of pots and plates. "I worked at one of the hotels over on Paradise Island, cleaning the rooms to get by. I rented from this miserable woman who used to cuss me for being a mother so young, and no husband, but she never charged me to look after Dion. I learned about yoga from two guests who would go and practice on that quiet end of Cabbage Beach, before they built the new hotel. When their stay was over, they left a yoga book in their room. It took a lot of years of hard work after that, but you see us here now." She glances out the window at one of Dion's defiant vegetable patches. "Tell me something, Indira. How old are you, really?"

I turn the water pressure up. "Eighteen."

"Come on, now. I told you my whole story. Least you could do is be honest with me."

"Sixteen." It comes out as a hoarse whisper.

She comes over, turns the tap off. "And when was your birthday?"

I take my hands out of the water, drying them on my clothes. "March."

She looks away from me, shaking her head. "So when this happened, you were fifteen."

"I'm not what everyone thinks."

"And what does everyone think, Indira?"

"That I'm a screw-up. Even people who don't know my mamma think I'm the same as her, some girl who gone and got in problems. They think it's my destiny. That's what you thought when you first saw me. You didn't even ask questions, you already *knew* what I was."

"The first day—"

"You knew I was somebody who didn't belong here, you knew I was a troublemaker. You told Dion so, in front of me. You were ready to throw me out before I even stepped in."

"You appeared out of nowhere, dripping wet, the day after we had graffiti appear on the side of the office," Joe explains. She opens the oven and pulls out the plates with a pot holder, then sets them down on the counter and hands me a clean fork. "I might have been in a bad mood that day," she says in a voice that is almost apologetic.

"And a bunch of days after," I say.

She raises her eyebrows at that, but instead of answering, she bows her head over the food, murmuring a quick prayer, then opens her eyes. She's quiet, working something out. "Here's the deal. You're underage."

"Sixteen's old enough," I say. It is. It's going to have to be.

"Sixteen's the age of consent. If the baby's father was older than fifteen, he committed a crime."

She might be right, but age of consent doesn't matter when it's all against your will. Anyway, right now what I want is to start over someplace safe. I need Joe to see that. "What if you don't pay me? I could stay here and work for my rent."

Joe sighs. "You can't leave your family. You need to be

with a parent or legal guardian, which I'm not. If something happens, I'm responsible."

"I don't have no place else to go."

"Yes, but you can't just stay here—"

"You want me go now?" I push my untouched plate away, starting to get up.

"You wanna let me finish?" Her voice is abrupt, but her hand on my arm is light, stopping me. "Sit down. If we can't talk, I can't do anything for you. You can't stay here if I'm responsible, unless I know things are fine with you. And your baby. So first off, if you stay here, even overnight, you got to get checked by a real doctor."

"Only doctor I could afford is a fake one."

She glares at me. Then, strangely, her mouth twists like she's found something interesting between her teeth. I think she's trying to hold back a smile. "Know what? Your mouth almost faster than mine. I'll get you checked by my doctor *friend* who won't charge. Make sure you're healthy."

"I'm fine."

"And the baby? You have to be realistic, Indira. You away from your home, I doubt you've been taking any proper care of yourself. What if something goes wrong? I have to think of the retreat. How that headline ga look in the newspaper? 'Runaway teen mother loses baby.' 'Stillborn found dumped in trash at yoga retreat.' You think I want that?"

"Yeah, well, I'm not my mamma. I told you, I'm fine." I stand up and haul my bag over my shoulder.

Joe's voice is quieter now. "I don't know your history. I don't know why you're here, why you don't want to go home. I don't know your mamma, but I know this: you are not fine."

One of the bag's straps gives without warning, ripping apart at the side where once it was carefully stitched. The rest of the bag opens, spilling my belongings out onto the tiles. I gather them up quickly, the old duct tape bra, underwear, toothbrush, everything. I scramble to find the pregnancy book, then remember I don't have it anymore.

Joe reaches down, closes her fingers around the one sound strap, and lifts the bag.

"I'm *fine*," I say again, my voice cracking.

"You ain fine. But you will be. First step, you'll finish eating and stay here tonight. You'll need that cottage swept out, and some towels and sheets. In the morning, you get checked by the doctor. No arguments. Agreed?" She doesn't wait for my answer, is already walking through the doorway and outside, down the path, carrying my bag back to the cabin for me. She's brisk and determined, like she cares. Like Grammy.

15

THE CLINIC SIGN MOCKS me in the morning's half-light.
Dr. A. Palmer, Dr. C. Adderley, Dr. S. Johnson. Unbelievable.
Of all the doctors' offices in all of Nassau, Joe's friend had to
work at this one.

"All right," Joe says. She hops out of the driver's side of
the jeep, all business, and closes the door. "Ready?"

"I can't go in there."

"You can do this."

After what I did yesterday? No way.

Joe rests her arm against the ledge of her open window.
"Then I have to drive you home. I can call Dion and find out
where you live."

That almost makes me desperate enough to tell Joe about
setting off the alarm, and pretending to be Marcy. Maybe I
don't have to. Maybe Joe's taking me to see one of the other
two doctors. "Which doctor is it?"

"Palmer."

I turn away from Joe, wishing for an escape. But to where?

"She's a friend of mine," Joe continues. "She's good. She's gonna see you confidentially, check and make sure everything is fine. And she's not gonna charge."

"I can't see her."

"We've already been through this, Indira. If you're under my care, even unofficially, I'm responsible not only for you, but also for your child."

It's so real when she says it. *Your child.*

The door to the office swings open, and I'm out of time to hide or explain; Dr. Palmer comes out in a T-shirt and jeans. She looks like she didn't plan to be here; she came in just for me.

"Morning." Dr. Palmer waves at Joe. "I got your message. You all come in."

I have no choice. I reach for my bag, its broken strap freshly bandaged up with duct tape, and get out. The ground feels unsteady.

"This is Indira, my young friend I told you about," Joe says to Dr. Palmer as we reach the door.

There's a brief flash of surprise across the doctor's face; then it's gone and she smiles vaguely, the recognition disguised. "I'm Dr. Palmer," she says, ushering us in with a wide wave of her arm, like we're stopping by for a cool drink and a slice of cake.

"I'll be out here if you need me," Joe says, settling into one of the waiting room chairs.

"We have a patient this early?" another voice calls from down the hallway. A face appears, smiling. It's the same nurse who took my form yesterday. Her gaze lands on me. "Hold on, where I know you from? You're that girl!" She turns to Dr. Palmer. "Remember? She filled out paperwork as Sharice Ferguson, for the procedure with Dr. Adderley." The nurse lowers her voice. "The termination?" The nurse's frown deepens as she brandishes a file. I look quickly at Joe, whose face is unreadable.

"All right, Nurse Mackey," Dr. Palmer says firmly, and takes the file. "It's under control. Come on back, Indira. Let's see what's going on."

In the room, Dr. Palmer sits on a stool and opens up the file. I take a seat on the end of the examination table. "Now, is Indira your real name?"

I nod.

She draws a neat line through Mamma's name and writes in mine. "It says here you're nineteen." She peers over her glasses at me. "Is that correct?"

"No."

"How old are you?"

"Sixteen."

"Is anything on this form true?"

"My last name."

"You know a doctor could lose their license, performing procedures on a minor who's lied about her age." She tosses the file aside, opens a drawer, and pulls out a fresh form. "Look, how about we start again. Indira?"

"Indy."

"Okay, Indy. You tell me what happened."

That familiar tightness takes over my chest. She could mean anything: what happened to make Joe bring me here two hours before opening on a Saturday; what happened yesterday in this same room, room number two; what happened five months ago; what started long before. An ocean of answers surges up, threatening to drown me. *Just breathe,* I can hear Joe saying. I pull in a little puff of air, let it out, and pick the easiest of the answers: what happened yesterday.

"My friend set up the appointment for me. For the . . ."

"The termination," she says gently.

"Yes." I look over at the new form, blank except for my name.

"And you pretended to be Marcy, and then you ran out." She doesn't add any commentary; I'm thankful for that. "Is there anything else you need to tell me?"

I shake my head.

"So what can I do for you? Are you keeping this baby or not?"

"Joe said I had to have a checkup or I can't stay by her."

"I'm not asking Joe. I'm asking *you.*" She leans forward, listening, waiting. I wait too, for a flutter, for some confirmation inside. But there's nothing, and right now, it's just me and Dr. Palmer, asking—not telling, not announcing, not already knowing. Asking. Like what I want actually counts.

"Keeping it."

"All right," she says, and pushes her glasses high up on her nose, signaling that it's time for business. I decide I like her. She goes through the new form, asking about how I'm feeling, when my last period was, how easily or often I go to the bathroom. "The next thing," she says, "is a physical exam to make sure you and the baby are healthy. Normally, I would see my patients starting much earlier than where you seem to be, but we'll make the best of it."

"What kind of physical exam?"

Dr. Palmer smiles reassuringly. "Nothing to worry about. First, I'll do a pelvic exam. I make sure it's quick, and it shouldn't be too uncomfortable. Then I'll check your stomach and see how things are going in there." She leaves, and Nurse Mackey returns to take my blood pressure and weigh and measure me. Nurse Mackey doesn't say much—Dr. Palmer must have said something to her before she came in. When she's done, she hands me a gown and a sheet.

"You'll need to take off your skirt and top and your

underwear," she says, closing the door behind her. I change and lie face-up on the table, with the sheet wrapped around my lower half. When Dr. Palmer returns, I see her start to put on a pair of white gloves, and I close my eyes.

I'm on the beach. Salt air eases in through my nostrils, filling my lungs, making my chest expand. Sky a deep blue higher up above me and farther out, where the water deepens, free of seaweed and rocks.

"You still with me, Indira?" Dr. Palmer's voice shakes me back to this place—stark fluorescent lights, pressed-board ceiling tiles, the smell of disinfectant and harsh soap. Crinkle of examination table paper. Cold medical utensils against me. The doctor looks up from down by my knees. I feel sick.

"Good. That part's done." She takes her gloves off and tosses them, scrubbing her hands in the sink. "Everything looks just fine. Based on your weight and measurements, I'd say you are approximately twenty weeks along."

I sit up, rearranging the sheet tightly over my legs.

"Does the father know you're pregnant yet?"

"It doesn't have a father." I get the feeling I'm going to have to say that many, many times.

"You sure you don't want to—"

"No!"

If she's taken aback, she doesn't show it. "Where were you living before, Indy?" she asks instead.

"By my aunt."

"What about your mother?"

"She's not here."

"Does your aunt know about the baby?"

At one time, I would have said a definite no, that Aunt Patrice would never let me be in the house if she knew. Now I remember her face in the kitchen yesterday, how she ducked Ms. Wilson's calls. I'm not so sure anymore. I shrug.

"You think you can tell her? Or someone else in your family? Someone close to you?"

I think of Grammy in that nursing home, her face distorted with shame. The room's starting to do that shrinking thing. "Maybe," I lie.

"Good. Now, I've written down for you to come back during regular hours and let the technician do an ultrasound for you. I'm sending you for a few blood tests, too, and you'll have to give us a urine sample at the same time." She reaches for the stethoscope on the counter. "I'll need to open the gown now so I can check your stomach," she says, motioning for me to lie back again. She presses different spots on my belly, feeling for something. "Indy, I have to ask you again about the baby's father. Do you know who he is? We need to . . ."

I tune her out, focusing on breathing deeply, eyes on the ceiling. I imagine sand under my toes, imagine my hands, palms pressed together, fingers stretched out, base to base and tip to tip, mirroring each other. I imagine tree pose, feet rooting me down, head stretching up, hair sprouting out like summer leaves, lush and shady.

The room has gone quiet.

"You have any questions for me?" Dr. Palmer asks. At least she's stopped asking about a father, about my family.

"Are you sure it's okay?"

She smiles. "Your baby? Yes. Heard the heartbeat for myself."

Heartbeat. There's a heartbeat. "You did?"

"I asked if you wanted to hear it too, but I think you were distracted. I'll let you listen. Why don't you take a few minutes and get dressed first?" she says, stepping out into the hall.

When Dr. Palmer returns, she has me sit again, with my shirt pulled up, and puts the stethoscope against my belly, listening through the earpieces. She repositions it a few times. "Oh, you've got a real swimmer in there. Bouncing all around the place. Hold on. Hold on. Yes, I found it." She hands me the earpieces, and I put them up to my head. First, nothing special, just a noise like wind or rushing water. Then she adjusts it slightly and the sound comes whooshing in.

Tickythumtickythumtickythumtickythumtickythum-tickythumtickythumtickythum. It's so quick it makes my fastest, in-my-ears heartpound seem like a slow drumbeat.

I close my eyes. This time, I'm not escaping. I'm trying to focus hard, to catch the sound of this thing in me. Every beat is so big, so loud, so *there*. Wanted or not, it's there. Like me. "You hear that? Some people say it's like horses galloping," Dr. Palmer says.

"Is it scared?"

"No, the fetus's heartbeat is always very quick. Perfectly normal for five months in."

I could listen all night, but finally, she reaches for the earpieces, cleaning off the stethoscope and hanging it up. Below her row of instruments, I catch sight of a shelf crammed with books.

"Have you been reading up on what's happening to your body and your baby?" She slides two or three books off the shelf and hands them to me. *The Big Pregnancy Book; Your Baby; The First Nine Months.*

I shake my head. "I already have a book. One from my grammy. She put all her own stories in there."

Dr. Palmer smiles. "She was really looking out for you."

As we walk down the hall together, I feel another flutter again. This is real. This is my baby.

In the car, Joe brings me right back down to earth.

"You thought about what I said? About the father?"

I turn to look out the window, watching us fly past houses.

The island is slowly starting to wake up, people waiting at the bus stop, cars beginning to clog up the roads.

"Well, you need to think about it. Is this person going to be coming by the retreat?"

"No!"

"Good." Joe glances over at me when we stop for a red light. "I might not know your full story, but I know someone's done something wrong, Indira. You were underage, end of story. You need to speak up about it."

Something about Joe's words rubs me the wrong way. I can't tell her everything; I know Joe well enough to understand that if I do, it won't be a single conversation, but the start of many long ones, and I'm not ready for that. But I *am* ready for her to know what kind of person I am. I don't want her to look at me the way Aunt Patrice did. I don't want anyone to see me that way ever again.

"I don't have a boyfriend. You mightn't believe me, but I don't."

"So you broke up with this person?"

"No."

"You're still seeing this person?"

"I *never* had a boyfriend. I was never with anybody that way." I don't mean to say it out loud, and as soon as I do, I know I've said too much. I can see Joe's face change: the scolding look disappears, replaced by surprise and concern.

"What do you mean by that?"

"Nothing."

I can tell she wants to push more, but the light turns green, the car behind her honking furiously. I turn back to the window, letting the breeze whip my face. It's straight driving the rest of the way to the retreat, and even though Joe doesn't ask again, I know it's only because she understands I won't answer. She must sense there's something more, something big. It's a wonder the car doesn't crash; I can feel her staring at me the whole way.

"This yours?" Dion holds out the cell phone to me, an ate-the-whole-rum-cake grin on his face. His forehead is shining in the Saturday-morning sun.

"Oh." I take it, brushing off bits of grass and leaf clippings clinging to the screen. Sand grains are wedged in its grooves. It's a miracle the screen isn't cracked, only a few scrapes on the case. "Thanks."

"I found it there." He points over to a cluster of scrubby beach plants.

"What you was doin? Landscaping the sand?"

"Looking to see who sent what flying in there. You'd be surprised what I find. Once, it was two cups from the kitchen, and a fifty-dollar bill underneath. Next time, a gold necklace inside an empty crab shell."

I wait to see if he'll ask what I'm doing here so early, if he'll mention my being pregnant; if Joe hasn't told him, he must have figured it out on his own. When he says nothing, I slip the phone into my pocket. The battery's dead; I'll charge it later. "So I tried a new pose. Ballerina or something."

"Oh yeah? Helped your balance?" he says, taking my cue.

"I fell out of it three times."

"Man, you ain a pro till you fall out of a pose." He slides a plant out of its pot, its flowers trembling like enormous peachy-pink bells, and drops it carefully into a hole in the ground. "Try it, let me see. Go on, I'll look away while you get into it, if you shame."

"I ain shame of nothing." I tilt forward, lifting one leg off the ground, stretching my body out. There's an instant, fleeting and sweet, between precarious and perfect, where I find a bizarre stillness. Then I feel myself teetering and let go, windmilling my arms to catch balance that only comes when both feet are back on the ground.

"Okay, so it's dancer's pose, not ballerina, so you ain gotta dip and twirl," he chuckles, starting to dig another hole. "First, you gotta clear your mind. Next, pick one thing to stare at. And then you concentrate, and you relax. You don't fight. You bring up the arm on one side. Then you get the balance on that other leg, bring the other hand back to your foot, and you lift slowly and—" He stands up and demonstrates, easy, no big deal. Glances over at me. "Wanna give it another try?"

I shake my head and he laughs as he comes down, taking up his shovel. "Take it easy, girlie," he says. When he's far enough away, I scan left, right. It's clear. Breathing first, then finding a knot on the almond tree's bark. I focus on that while I bring up my right arm. Bend my left leg so my toes point toward the sky. Bring my left hand back and hold that foot. Wobble, then down. Deep breath. Start again. This time, I am up, reaching, arm forward, leg backward, body in the middle, other leg an anchor, holding me. Part of me wants to laugh, to dance, to twist and shake and bounce with pride. The other part wants to stay here, just be. I feel graceful and strong.

"Hey, you're doing it!" Dion calls from across the grove, and breaks out into a jig, shoulders one way, hips the next. As I start to laugh, I feel myself falling out of the pose. I let it happen, the falling, the laughter. Know the ground will surge up to catch me, let me try again.

At lunch, Dion, Maya, Susan, and I pile up plates with lentil stew, brown rice, some of Dion's subversive kale, and pumpkin fritters. We eat sitting on the beach, in the shade. The sea is rough today, the tide creeping up higher and higher, nearing our bare feet.

"You should grow a whole bunch more veggies." Susan

stuffs a forkful of kale into her mouth. "This is better than anything we can buy."

"Hey, give the cook some credit," Maya pipes up.

"Yes, Maya. We all know you could cook," Susan says, pacifying.

"Yeah, well." Dion rests his plate on the sand, crossing his legs. "We got plenty room for more veggies, but you know what a certain someone ga say bout that."

"What?" I ask.

"'This is a yoga retreat, not a farm.'" Maya does a perfect impression of grumpy Joe.

"'The garden,'" Susan says, her words muffled by a fritter, "'is for beauty and serenity.'"

"'Vegetable patches smell like manure,'" Maya chimes in again.

Susan chuckles. "What Joe don't know is, Dion dug up squares of grass all over the place. Peas out behind the kitchen, Swiss chard by the office, ten rows of carrots beside the laundry, and pumpkin in the back of the cabins."

"And manure pile up on all," Dion adds.

Their chatter is homey, making a soft space for me to sink into. In that space, though, problems intrude on my peace. Smiley and her smart ideas. *Get with Churchy, sleep with Churchy, let people think it's Churchy's.* Yet people believe *I'm* the slut. But no one would ever think anything bad of little Smiley. My mind wanders to Grammy, stuck in that awful place with its stale smell. What if something happened to her and I had never told her goodbye? Living in that place must be slowly draining her life away. But she sent me here, she *told* Mamma to do it. And she knew, she gave me that book. That book, which I'm wishing I had now.

"This one already in deep meditation." Dion's voice brings me back to the beach. "What you thinkin about over there?"

"Nothing." I glance over and catch Maya staring at me. "This food is good, Maya."

"Thanks," she says, then turns to Dion. "You wanna bring me another plate of the fritters?"

Dion pops the last forkful of food into his mouth. "Indy, you want anything?" he asks as he gets up. I shake my head.

"I'll come with you," Susan says, following him. When they're out of earshot, Maya edges over close to me.

"How you doin?"

"Fine."

"I have three children, you know."

"That's nice." I try to sound calm. My hands go to my belly and this time I don't stop them. My body feels more and more unfamiliar, rounder, firmer in the middle instead of soft. The baby kicks back in response.

"How many months?" Maya asks softly.

I set my empty plate down on the sand. "Joe told you?"

"I had a hunch. Anybody could see it if they know how to look."

"Apparently everyone know how to look."

"You scared?"

"A little."

"Your mummy here?"

"No," I say. Then I add, "My grammy is, though. In an old folks' home."

"Well, you ain gotta be scared. Your body will know what to do when your time comes. And you ain by yourself, you know. Joe, me, Susan, we all had children. All of us been through it. You can even talk to your grammy."

"Were you scared?" I ask her. "With yours?"

Maya leans back on her elbows, stretching her plump legs out on the sand. "Yes, with my first. My mummy passed when I was in my second month, and I didn't know what to expect. I didn't know Joe and Susan then, and my friends didn't have kids yet. I never felt so alone. But I had a good nurse, she sat and talked with me, and she told me what was going on, how I had to open up to a certain size, and then my body would push and the baby would come out."

"Did it take long?"

"Everybody's different, but the first time can be slow. I was in labor for sixteen hours. Susan, hers was twenty-two."

"Almost a whole day?" Grammy's book didn't say anything about it taking that long. Or maybe I missed that part. I've avoided thinking about what happens in four months, when a whole baby has to come out of *there*.

"Like I tell you, every situation's different." Maya reaches over and pats my arm. "Hang with us. You'll be fine."

"Fresh lunch top-up, delivered right to your table, ma'am." Dion swaggers over, a dried palm leaf draped over his arm like a rustic butler as he presents the plate to Maya.

"Gimme my food. Your silly self," Maya laughs.

"Brought you a drink. Veggie wine." Dion winks at me, handing me a glass of beet juice. "Maya, some guests asking for you, they had some questions about your food."

Maya hoists herself to her feet, dusting the sand off her legs. "Remember what I tell you, Indy," she calls over her shoulder.

Settling back into the sand, I taste the juice.

"How is it?" he asks.

"Sweet."

Dion smiles over at me. "They say that one's good for the mothers."

I sigh, sitting back up. "Anybody around here *don't* know?"

He picks up a sun-bleached seashell, flicking it away. "Nothing stays a secret forever."

I don't think he'd be so carefree about bringing it up if he knew the whole story. Maybe it's okay that he doesn't know. I've finally gotten away from Gary. Maybe it's better if Dion thinks I got this baby with a boyfriend. It'd be easier than telling him what really happened. So far, Grammy knows, and Churchy, and telling them didn't help me one bit. "Really think that's true?" I say. "About secrets?"

"Well, sure. The truth wants to dance in the light."

I think it over. Not all truths are the dancing kind, but maybe they do need to be told and heard, even the ugly ones. Grammy already knows my secret; it's time I know hers. I have to find out why she gave me that book.

"Hey, Dion," I say. "Could I get a ride with you after work? Out to Sunset Home?"

16

THIS TIME, I HURRY through the old folks' home, heading straight for the room.

"Grammy?"

A different woman looks up from the chair. All Grammy's stuff is gone, the cane replaced with a walker. The curtains are drawn against the daylight. My lunch threatens to come back up, and I'm starting to get that tight feeling in my chest. No. I have to do this. I swallow hard.

"Excuse me, you know where the other lady, Ms. Ferguson, went?"

The woman scrutinizes me with beady eyes. A pointy nose juts out of her sunken face.

"I'm her granddaughter, I came to see her." My voice is getting louder. I shouldn't be shouting at her, but why isn't Grammy here? "She was right here last time."

"Nurse! Nurse!" the woman starts calling. "Oh, Nurse. Whoa, Nurse." The same worker from before comes bustling out of a room, clutching a spray bottle and a rag.

"What is it, Ms. Ruth?" the worker asks, irritated. Then she sees me. "Can I help you?"

"My grammy. She was in this room."

"This girl yellin. Get her outta here, Nurse," the woman orders.

"Ms. Ferguson? From the island?" My voice is too loud now. I know I should breathe deeply, but I can't in here. Is Grammy wearing diapers now? Did they move her to another home? Is she even alive—

"Get her out, Nurse. And she pregnant, too, look, you could see she pregnant. What any pregnant girl doin here? Too much fuss. Too loud. You too loud. You and that baby. Too much noise."

"That's fine, Ms. Ruth, you settle down, I'll show her out," the worker says. She turns to me. "Come, let's go. This ain no time to visit, we tryin to get them cleaned up and ready for dinner."

"My day, no pregnant girl would be walkin around like that." The woman stares up at me. "Used to send em to the island where nobody would see, lock em up in the house. What you doin out in public, girl?"

"All right, Ms. Ruth," the worker says firmly. "That's

enough." To me, quietly, she says, "Go out in the hall. This one ga keep goin as long as she could see you."

"I ain deaf, I could hear what y'all sayin. Bringin babies in this place. An someone die here last night too. Take her outta here. Get out."

Someone died? "Where's Ms. Ferguson? Where's my grammy?"

"Go down the hall and to the left." The worker waves her hand, dismissive. I brush past her, round the corner. And there my grandmother is, in a room at the very end. She sits beside a window, dozing. On the bureau, I see something I didn't notice before: a copy of the same picture Mamma sent to Aunt Patrice, but whole. Me in the middle, Grammy on one side, Mamma on the other. In the picture, Grammy seems so much younger, standing upright, her arm circling me. Her mouth is barely open, her lips starting to curl up. She was about to laugh.

"Grammy."

She lifts her head, the sun catching the faint hairs on her face. "Indy?" She blinks, making sense of me. "They been looking for you. Your aunt called here and all. They almost sent out a search party."

"You tell them anything?"

Grammy shakes her head slowly, disagreeing. "I didn't know what to tell them. I wanted to say something, but then what if your aunt didn't believe you were telling the truth? I don't like that woman, Indy. I didn't want to cause more problems for you. Where you been? He come after you again? That Gary?"

I don't want to talk about Gary, or about Aunt Patrice. "How come you in this room?"

Grammy leans back in the chair, letting go of her questions, at least for now. "You know why."

Looking around, I do. The sun makes the room feel a little like home, giving it a memory of the warmth her old kitchen once had.

"A lady died last night and nobody else want to be in here. Ms. Ruth was in the other bed, she wouldn't calm down till they relocated her. I tell them put her in my old bed, let me come in here."

"You ain scared?"

"Scared of what? I burn sage in here when they wasn't looking, put my olive oil on the doorway and read my Psalms. I clear it out, everything's fine now. Sit down, girl."

I settle for leaning against the bureau.

"You holdin ya belly."

I hadn't realized I was doing that. I let my arms fall to my sides awkwardly.

"Oh, Indy," Grammy says, "Oh, my baby," and when she says *baby*, I know she means me and the last of my anger drains away. I don't hate her, I can't hate her. But I still don't understand. Grammy lets out a tired sigh. Then, as if she can read my mind, she leans forward and opens a drawer, taking the book out. She lays it on her lap. "I didn't know."

"What?"

"I didn't know any of it. I never knew Gary was going to be in that house. I never knew he would do such a thing. I was sad to let you go, but I thought you would have been safer here. You know your mamma and her friends. She's in the house now. You wouldn't believe how it look."

"I been there."

"To Mariner's? Oh, Indy. I never would have wanted you to see."

"It ain home no more."

She reaches out a hand. I take it, and her fingers clamp around mine. "Don't hate your mamma for how she is either. I love my baby, but she weak."

"She took your house and sent you here," I say, my voice growing hard.

"She weak. She don't know."

"That ain my problem."

"Watch it, now. If you don't forgive her, it'll eat you alive."

I pull my hand away. Forgive. If she says I have to forgive Gary, I don't know what I'll do. I don't want to forgive. I want the right to be angry. I want someone to pay. Right now, I miss Smiley, her grins and her schemes. She might not get everything, but she would understand my wanting someone to pay. I'll call Smiley later, I decide. I'll tell her, finally. I fumble in my bag for the phone and its cord, then plug it into the wall to charge. I sit on the edge of Grammy's bed, resting the bag on the floor.

"Let me tell you a little something about your mamma," Grammy says. "See, you only ever knew her when she was messed up. She wasn't always so. Listen. Let me tell you."

As she does, I can picture it: Mamma, bored silly in that one-room school. Ditching class, skipping down to the water, sneaking out by the dock, watching the men unload supplies, visitors from Nassau stepping ashore, and Mariner's Cay people coming back from trips to the city, trips to Miami, trips to places even farther away. Her smile quick, her hips wide, her sway strong. Swaying because it feels good to sway. Sway not for whistles, for the calls, the *niceness, niceness, pretty, luscious, sweets, lovely,* but to coax a dance out of walking. Easy laugh, not for attention, really, but for the tickle as it bubbles up your throat, for the way it makes other people laugh too. Never wanting to sit still. Always ready to run out of the house and find something to do. Every time she pass by a guy, he smile. And sometimes the girls smile at her too, just to see that joy unwrapped and let loose.

"Your mamma was a pretty girl, but she was lazy. When she reach fourteen, I sent her out to work. She didn't want to put her mind to her books so I say she might as well learn to earn a living. I send her to the neighbor four houses down, a woman who'd had an accident, couldn't get out of bed no more. The husband was the headmaster, and a deacon in the church. Everybody knew them to be good people. Your ma always use to go out smilin and swayin; come back and her face sour. I thought it was because maybe they talk to her bad. I figure she need that, need a little rough treatment to smarten her up, and I never could bring myself to be hard on her, my one baby girl. Your uncle, I brought him up but he was never really mine. I had your ma late in my time. I waited for her for so long.

"One day she come an tell me she don't want go there no more. I figure she was trying to get out of work, want to play round the island, go sneakin with her fast little friends, out looking for parties and boys. Always looking, her. Always looking. You wouldn't understand—you and me, we happy at home. I tell her she have a job, she better go anyway. Well, she went, but she ain come back home on time that afternoon. Come evening, ain nobody seen her. The neighbor, he told me she showed up, cleaned half the house, then left. She came home late that night, wouldn't say a word. I made her go back to work the next day, and the next, and she stayed another month or two, but one day she didn't come home at all, and the man who worked down on the docks came by the house and told me he saw her getting on the boat to Nassau. Anytime I could get my hand on a phone, I called around Nassau and asked, called and asked. No one could tell me where she was.

"For months, all I heard was snippets of things your uncle picked up and passed on to me—word that someone had seen her one place or another in Nassau. Living by this one, sleeping on that one's floor. Then I heard she was pregnant. I thought she would come back to me when her time came, but she stayed right there. Next time I saw her was after she had you. You were four months old and she tell me she was done nursing you. Fact is, I could see she was done with herself, too.

"Indy, she was different. Like somebody gone in her and scrape everything out. She still walk the same way, mouth still twitch and hips still shake, shake more, matter of fact, but the part that make her do them things, the joyful part that was so alive? It was gone. I let her live in the house as long as I could. You remember. Till you was in double digits, she used to stay with us, on and off. But when you started to develop more, I put her out, and all them men who use to come trailin behind her too. I put her out, and you see how she gone downhill. She used to insist on taking you sometimes, say you was her child, not mine. That's how she got her own back on me.

"Indira, I could see the way things was going. That day I came by the apartment above the bar and you were there, outside in your pajamas? I'll never forget that day. I had to tell her send you here, Indy. It was the only way. I know she'll never forgive me. For any of it. And she shouldn't. I shoulda known."

We sit together, in that tired light. The air is dense with Grammy's sadness. When I look over at her, she's shrunken, as if everything she's said is pressing her down. As her story settles over me, I understand. The shame I saw on Grammy's face before wasn't because of me. She's ashamed of herself.

"The neighbor was my daddy?" I ask finally.

"Baby, I ain know. I never confronted him. Soon after your mamma came back, his wife died and he left Mariner's for good. All I know, he start something up in her. He do something that wasn't right. That's why I sent you away. I could see all them men, all them strangers around my good grandchild. And I didn't want see anything happen. Not again. I thought you woulda been safe here. And instead all I do is make the same mistake."

"If you didn't know, how come you gave me that book?"

She shifts forward in her chair, looking right at me. "When you unwrapped it? Let me guess. First day you set foot here."

"Maybe."

Grammy traces book's cover with her fingers. "I remember when I started writing in this. Your uncle had sent a letter to say people had told him your mamma was pregnant. The night I got that letter, I stayed up till dawn. Couldn't sleep. I took out this book, my one book from my time. I went through, cover to cover, and I wrote everything I could find in my mind to tell her about having a baby. I figure, I couldn't teach her how to live straight, I might as well tell her how to carry. When I was done, I gave it to someone on the boat and sent it to your uncle, tell him next time he hear where she was, carry it to her. I sent so many things for her on the boat, every time I knew someone coming down to Nassau. But whenever your uncle went looking at a new address, she'd already moved on. Finally, he sent it back to me. By the time her and that book crossed paths, she was back in Mariner's, staying with me. She never even looked at it."

Grammy flips it open, reading to herself. "You reach this chapter, 'Preparing the Home'?"

I shake my head. She beckons me over. I hesitate, but it's Grammy and her arm's stretched out toward me. I move closer to her chair and she begins to read aloud.

"'Now, baby, I'm not there, so I made you a list of all the things you should put together before your child comes. First, get yourself some diapers. I used the cloth ones, but you might not have time to wash them. You'll need something in the hospital, and as soon as you come home. Second, get some clothes. A hat, a good stock of onesies, shirts, and pants. The color doesn't matter. If you have a girl, just put a bow on her head. My mind tells me it's a girl. Third, receiving blankets, for when the baby spits up, or when somebody wants to hold her.

294

Fourth, at least a couple of good, big bras. When your milk come, you'll want to have your bubbies held up. I never had those, but you can keep your chest shape better if you have that support. Fifth, someplace for her to sleep. Doesn't have to be a fancy crib: for a time, I padded a wood box with soft blankets, and that was good for you. There's more you can get, but you don't need all the bottles and the pacifiers and whatnot. That's fluff. Just a few simple things, and love, is enough. Baby, you make sure you love her. No matter how you might feel now, you love her. That's the most important thing.'"

Grammy keeps reading, to herself now, and I look over her shoulder. At the top of the page on how to settle the baby, she's written about which teas to make to soothe me, and what comforted Mamma when she was little—being bounced gently when she was sleepy, being rocked when she was sick. Reading her words, I can picture it now. Grammy sitting out on the rocks, a tiny Mamma on her lap, the two of them watching the waves. Grammy dancing around the living room singing "Funky Nassau" with Mamma in her arms.

Grammy raises her eyes to meet mine. Tired eyes. For the first time, even in here, she looks old, really old. She shakes her head as though trying to get something out of it. "I wanted you to see. I only ever wanted the best for you, even before you was born. And for your mamma, too. You only ever know her as a whole knot of mistakes. She wasn't always that way, Indy. She's my baby too. I know her from before I could see her, I loved her from before I first felt her kick."

I reach out and take the book from Grammy's lap, running my thumb along the softened edges of its pages. "How come you didn't just give this to me? Why you wanted me to wait and open it?"

"It wasn't the time. But I didn't know when I was going to see you next. I wanted to tell you, when the time was right, that I loved you from before you was born because I love the girl you come from. No matter what. Don't mind how broke up she is now. She is precious to me. Same as you." Grammy leans forward, resting her hand on my belly. "And you."

The door pushes open, and the worker sticks her head around it, looking less annoyed this time. "We're serving dinner, Ms. Eunice," she says. "Time for your granddaughter to say goodbye."

Grammy pulls me close for a hug. I sink into her embrace. "You forgive me, Indy?"

Holding on to her, all I feel is relief, knowing she saw me as something more than Mamma, knowing she believed in a different life for me. Anyone who can look at Mamma and still see a trace of a girl who loved to laugh, loved to dance—a girl who's innocent and free—must be able to see the real me.

"Yes, Grammy."

"And Indy?" Grammy whispers, clinging to me. "You can't

stay in that house no more. You have anyplace else to go?"

I hang on to Grammy even tighter. "I found this yoga retreat, and the lady in charge, Joe, is helping me."

"She's letting you stay with her?"

"Yes, Grammy."

I feel her relax a little then. "Good. That's good."

It's hard to let Grammy go, but when I do, picking up the bag—even with its patched-up handle—feels right, like I'm taking a part of her along with me. I tuck my phone and the charger into my bag.

"You take care of that book," Grammy says. I kiss her cheek.

"Love you, Grammy," I say, holding the book to my chest. "I'll come back soon."

Partway down the dirt track to the retreat, I stop and listen. There are no footsteps, no suspicious rustling in the overgrowth. Instead, I hear crickets singing, the way they did wherever we were in Mariner's. Farther back in the bush, splashes of red poinciana blossoms interrupt the green. Closer in, lilac flowers crop up on scrubby plants. I reach down and scoop one up, stroking the petals. Soft and thin, like damp paper. Maybe like baby skin.

I don't want to be scared to walk down the street by myself anymore, scared to sleep alone. Scared to be a mother, scared of what the baby will come out to be. Half of it will be Gary. But what about me? I'm half Mamma and half who knows what—maybe the neighbor, maybe some other man who thought she was put on this earth to be used. I'm not Mamma, and I'm sure not my father, whoever he was. I'm something altogether different, and this thing, this baby, maybe it'll be something different too.

I bring my hand to my stomach, right where Grammy touched, where she rested her hand when she said *and you.* Mamma isn't worthless. I might not forgive her, but I understand that. She's worth something to Grammy, same way I am, and the baby in me. Mamma's more than what people see now, more than the stinking mess rotting away in the old house. I think of whoever made Mamma pregnant with me, and right there, with Grammy's words in my ear, the memory of her touch on my belly, I see it. No matter how much I might want to put everything that happened behind me, I can't just start over and keep quiet. Gary can't get away with this. I pick up my pace, hurrying toward the retreat.

The office is empty. I turn my cell on, put it on silent, and set it down beside the office phone. More missed calls and messages have come in since it charged. Churchy, Smiley, Aunt Patrice. I don't care; they can all wait. My phone pings, brightening with an incoming message. I ignore it, going to the voice recorder. On the office phone, I dial the house number from memory. I put the call on speakerphone. The line rings four times before there's the click of an answer.

"Hello."

I press Record on my cell phone. The bars measuring the volume of sound flutter, telling me it's picking this up. I feel panic rising, and breathe, breathe past it. He can't hurt me through the phone. "It's me."

"Doubles." Gary's voice is surprised and slow and sleepy, like I've woken him up from a nap. "Smiley ain here. Mummy ready to kill you. You lucky she ain home. You know how much trouble you cause?"

The clock in the office says 5:37. Smiley and Aunt Patrice will be on their way home from her volleyball game soon. I have to hurry. "I called for you."

"What happen, you miss me, ay?"

"I need help from you."

"Help? With what?"

I swallow. "You know what. With the situation."

There's a pause so long I think the call's been cut off. I check my phone: it's still recording. "What makes you think I want to help?" he says, finally. "You the one got yourself in problems—"

"If I have it, I'll do a paternity test, and everybody will know."

"Know what?" A sneer in his voice.

"That it was you. And I was underage, too."

"Stop talkin crap." His voice is alert now. "Everybody could see you old enough—"

"I need to deal with it."

There's a pause. "So what you tellin me for?"

"I have to pay for it."

He coughs. "Use what you got."

"I spent it."

"I give you four hundred and you spend it?"

Sharing a space with him, even a phone line, makes me want to step out of my skin and leave it there, a withered husk. *Just keep him talking,* I tell myself.

"I need a doctor who could get rid of it."

"So?" I hear the fridge door open, the familiar rustling of foil. "What this have to do with me? You got in trouble. Who ga be surprised? Like mummy, like daughter." I hear the pop of him opening a can. I can almost smell the sourness of beer on his breath. "You might not be here if she had made a little trip to the doctor herself. And that would be a shame." He takes a long, noisy gulp from the can. I almost hang up right then. Inside me, the baby is still. I put a hand on my belly, breathe in, breathe out. I have to focus. "My buddy run the bar up there," Gary continues. "In Mariner's. Tell me your ma's be tear right up on rum, let anybody carry her home. Somebody different every night—"

"Make an appointment for me."

"You crazy?"

"Make it for tomorrow." My voice quavers. *No,* I tell myself. *I can do this.*

"You got a lot of nerve, ya know. Who the hell you think you is?"

"I'll do the paternity test."

"How you ga do that? And guess what, you already got four hundred outta me. You think I have more money for you?"

I say nothing.

"You ain worth that much."

Again, I bite my lip. Let the silence sit.

"Even if you keep it, it could be anyone own. And you sleepin out now. You know you can't come back this way. My mummy would have your head on a stick. She goin to the police for you, you know. You probably goin to jail."

"Guess we'll wait and find out when I have the test." I remember what Joe said. "And you might be the one going to jail." He's quiet. Just breathe, I tell myself. Out, in.

"Which doctor you want?" His voice is furious and low.

I hesitate. The only one I know is Dr. Palmer. I take a gamble. "You don't know anyone?"

He swears, but he doesn't say no. "I'll call you back," he says through clenched teeth.

"I want to be on the other line."

"For what?"

"To know if you booked it."

He exhales sharply and there's a brief click; maybe he's hung up. Then another click and he's reconnected. A phone rings twice before a woman answers.

"Hey, Lydia. This Gary." He sounds so amiable, so polite. This must be how he moves through life most of the time. I think back to that first day in Nassau. The laugh. The wide smile.

I look at my cell again; still recording.

"Gary who?"

"You know which Gary. From the hotel."

"Oh, right, right." She laughs, as though she's happy to hear from him. "What's up?"

"I have a little problem. You want to help me out? You could talk?"

"What happened this time?" She sounds amused, and slightly impatient. "Do I even want to know?"

"I need you to sort out a time for someone to come in."

"Come on, man. What I tell you bout being careless?"

"Don't worry about that." The slightest shake in his voice.

"We booked. Not till next month."

I hold my breath, watching anxiously as my phone picks up their voices. "Look here, this an emergency. Monday, man. Or Tuesday."

The woman sighs.

"Come on, sweetie."

"I'll try to fit her in at four o'clock on Monday. And make sure she come on time, we don't stay open for anyone who's late."

"Charge it to my credit card now, so she could be in and out fast as possible," he says, then rattles the number off.

"All right, she's set," the woman says. "Now look here, Gary—"

"Come on, don't give me a hard time." He's all fake suaveness again. "This the first time—"

"Second time."

"That was a while ago."

"Just watch yourself. All right?" Her voice is light, like she's talking to a friend, dropping gentle advice.

"All right. Thanks, honey."

"Don't 'honey' me. Make sure she get here on time." She hangs up.

"You happy?" Gary says. In an instant, his voice has switched, every pretense of pleasantness gone. "You hear what time you gotta be there, you hear it done paid for. And I don't want ever see your face again. Wherever you gone, you better stay there."

"I plan to," I snap, before he hangs up. I did it. My hand shakes as I clatter the retreat's phone down into place, but I did it. I pick up my cell phone. I press Stop.

17

WAKING IN THE DARK, it takes a second to remember I'm back in the cabin. I can't place what woke me in this silent room. The door's closed and latched, I'm alone and safe. Then there's a *ding* as my phone's screen illuminates with a new message. As I reach for it, it beeps and shudders again. I'm still not ready to talk to anyone. I go to the recording and start to play it back, just to make sure it's still there. At the sound of Gary's voice, I stop it. I have what I need. Maybe now, finally, I can be free of him.

I'm still tired, but after hearing Gary, even on a recording, sleep is the last thing on my mind. I start to scroll through the dozens of unread messages waiting for me.

Yesterday, 7:06 p.m. Smiley: **When you comin home, big head? Mummy havin a hot fit in here.**

Yesterday, 9:23 p.m. Smiley: **I lonely, lol!**

Today, 2:44 p.m. **Coming to my game today? Playing soon.**

5:35. **You missed it.**

6:15. **Mummy so pissed at you, Gary told her you called and said you were OK but you weren't coming back. Is that true? Only me and him here if you want to come by. He in his room. Gettin drunk, lol.** It's the last text. A missed call at 8:32 p.m. Two more right after that. I check my voice mail, straining to listen; it's barely audible through Smiley's crying. Crying? She never cries. I make out the words *happen* and *do* and *me*. The phone's screen flashes. She's calling again.

"Smiley?"

"Indy." Her voice is folded in on itself. There's odd background noise.

"Where you is?"

"I by the Tasty Spot." She's crying now.

"What happen? You in trouble?"

"Come for me," she sobs.

I'm already running out of the cabin, heading for the center of the retreat. "What happen? Aunt Patrice can't come?"

"It's, Gary, it's . . . he . . ."

The call drops. I take the office stairs two at a time. "Joe?" No answer; the office is empty, but I can see the jeep in the parking lot. The keys are hung up by the desk. I take them and rush out to the vehicle, climb in, turning the key. It starts up tentatively, like it knows I shouldn't be doing this, then roars, understanding we have to. I can't drive, really; my foot fumbles for the gas pedal, then the brakes, dust flying behind me, a cloud that hides the view through the back windshield. I swerve down the side road, then onto the main street, struggling to stay in the lane. At the restaurant's intersection, I slow down to look for Smiley. A car behind me honks and I turn in. Where is she? Nobody's outside; there are just a handful of cars, the lot slightly lit up by the glow from inside. I pull up farther. There she is—around the side of the building, sitting on the steps with Churchy, his arm protectively around her. Parked right in front, engine still running, is a big black truck. The door is flung open. Gary jumps out, running toward them. Churchy leaps up, recognizing him. His body is tense, bristling for a fight.

I lean on the horn, a warning cry sent up through the night. I should have told her to look out for the jeep. *Please, Smiley, know it's me.* She and Churchy see me, but Gary's head snaps around too. He changes direction, heading my way. Churchy is faster; he grabs Gary by the shirt, stopping him. He shoves Gary hard, making him fight to keep his balance.

"Hurry up, hurry up," I urge Smiley as she sprints for the jeep. Behind her, Churchy tackles Gary, this time knocking him to the ground, pinning him down.

"Smiley, come on! Mummy ga kill you!" Gary yells, struggling against Churchy's hold. "Don't be stupid, hear? Don't be like Indy." I watch Churchy draw his arm back; his fist connects with Gary's face just as Smiley leaps into the jeep, slamming the door. I put the jeep in reverse and spin around, tires squealing against the pavement as I pull out of the parking lot. In the rearview mirror, I glimpse Gary scrambling back into the truck. Then I turn, and turn again, before he can follow me. Beside me, Smiley's wailing.

"What happen?" I ask. "What he do to you?" I turn down another street, heading back to the retreat.

"I was watching TV and I guess I fell asleep. Daddy still away on his trip, Mummy was out late at her women's meeting again. Gary was in his room drinking. All I know, I wake up and he beside me on the sofa. He had his hand on my leg. The lights was off, only the TV was still on. Then he start sayin all kinda funny things, how he make the appointment even though he already give me money, an Mummy ain ga stand for no baby in her house. He keep callin me Doubles, and I keep tellin him I'm Smiley. I try to get up, I ask him what he doin an he wouldn let me go. He tell me don't fight. Say he know I like it, know I miss our secret, an don't worry cause if I ain deal with it yet ain nothin could happen. Then he push me down an I couldn get up. I was fightin him off, Indy, tellin him I'm Smiley, I'm his sister, I slap him, I scratch him, everything, an he wouldn stop tryin to press up on me. I knee him right in the groin an he tumble back, cryin, throw his whole wallet at me. Look. This where he was grabbin me." She turns on the jeep's light to show me the bright red mark on her leg. Looking at it, I nearly run into a car ahead that's come out of nowhere. I swerve and keep going.

We finally reach the dead-end road back to the retreat. No headlights behind us, no dust but ours. I turn in, finally, and park.

"That's my brother . . ." As Smiley starts to talk, her voice catches, and she leans over and curls into me. We hold on to each other in the safety of the jeep.

"What else he do, Smiley? That's everything?"

"That's everything. But Indy . . ." Her voice tapers off as she looks up at me. "How come you didn't tell me?"

She asks like telling would have been an easy thing. Before I can answer, we hear footsteps on the gravel driveway.

"Indira?" It's Joe. She shines her flashlight in through the window. "You took my jeep?"

"I had an emergency."

Smiley sits up, realizing Joe and I know each other. "Ma'am, you gotta help us!"

"No, Smiley!" I don't want her saying it, not here, not to Joe. I don't want all my ugly to come out in this peaceful place.

"Ma'am, it was my brother, he attacked me cause he thought I was her, he grab me here, and he keep calling me by her name, and then Churchy punch him in his face, and you have to help."

Joe looks from her to me, and comprehension slowly starts to dawn on her face.

"Okay, well, I already called the police when I saw the jeep was gone. They're on their way now."

"You gotta help, you gotta help," Smiley urges. "I need to call my parents. I want my daddy."

"Come into the office," Joe says. "Let's call him from there." Smiley's out of the jeep in a flash, plastered to Joe's side like she's known her forever. "Indira?" Joe reaches through the open window, and I offer her the keys. She doesn't take them, just keeps her hand outstretched, palm open, until I put my hand in hers. "Whatever happened, we'll get to the bottom of it."

There it is again. Another flutter. Then a kick. I close my eyes, then blink them open, wiping them. I have to tell her everything, even if I'm not sure where to begin. I have to, for Smiley. For me.

"I'll meet you in the office," I say, pulling my hand away. Joe nods.

After they've gone, I climb out of the jeep. I take the path the other way, heading back to the cabins. When I reach mine, I pause at the door before going in.

I turn on the light and look around the room. Everything I

own is in here: that tired straw bag, one handle taped together. A stack of clothes. *The Pregnancy Book*. One thing doesn't belong—the garbage bag, shoved off to one side, stuffed full of those awful clothes. It's time. I know what to do with it now. I pick it up and slide my hand into my pocket, feeling for the cell phone. Still there. I steel myself, then open the door and step out into the night.

The office is painted with the flashing blue and red lights of a police car. Joe's sitting on the steps.

"Apparently your uncle is out of town, and we can't get ahold of your aunt. I'll keep trying."

"Oh."

"Think she'll want you to go back?"

I shake my head. "She doesn't want me in her house."

"Maybe that's better."

"What about Smiley?"

Joe rubs her forehead, thinking. "Your cousin? I don't know, Indira. That might depend on whether this Gary's going to continue to be in the house." She shifts on the step, making room for me to sit beside her. "There's a policewoman inside, talking to her now."

I drop the garbage bag onto the grass and sit. "Can I talk to her too?"

"Definitely. She needs a statement from you next." Joe looks at the garbage bag. "What's that?"

"Something from when Gary . . ." I can't finish the sentence, and she nods, as if she already understands.

I can hear Smiley's voice drifting out from inside the office, and a woman speaking, steady and subdued.

"Indira." Joe's tone is even. "Is it true? What your cousin says about Gary?"

I close my eyes. Breathe in, filling my lungs, letting the air expand me, then letting it out, letting go.

"Did this Gary get you pregnant?"

I open my eyes. She's looking at me, waiting.

Breathe in. Expand, then let go. I nod my head, but it feels wrong. *Get you pregnant* is what your boyfriend does by mistake. This is something different, something I'm struggling to say out loud. There's movement from in the office then, and Smiley saves me, appearing at the top of the stairs. She looks as shaken as I feel.

Joe stands up. "You want me to go in with you, Indy?" she asks.

"Yes."

Joe walks into the office with me, beckoning Smiley to join us.

The officer sits behind Joe's desk. Smiley slumps into a chair off to one side, leaving Joe and me to sit across from the policewoman.

"I'm Officer Pinder," she says. "I have some questions for you. We'll start easy. What's your full name?"

"Indira May Ferguson."

"Age?"

"Sixteen."

"And your current address?"

I look over at Joe, who nods.

"Here."

The officer keeps going: When did I come to Nassau? Where are my parents? Who are my aunt and uncle? Then come the harder questions, the ones about Gary. What happened, and when, and where. And for the first time, I say it out loud, all of it, not just a few choked words or a whisper. I start with that first day he came to the house. Then I tell her about the first time he came into the living room when I was alone there, and the time without the condom, and all the times with one—before then and afterward—and the truck and the bathroom, and the clinic that day with Churchy, and what Gary did in the kitchen when I got to the house. The policewoman's pen scratches furiously across her notepad, transforming my words from secrets I carry around inside into a real story with a shape, a thing I can point to and say *This is true.* I put my hand into my pocket, bring out my cell phone. I glance over at Smiley, who's been silent this whole time; tonight, she's been changed. Seeing her this way, so frightened and small, I know I can do this. I play the recording for them all. Last, I hold up the garbage bag I brought and explain what's inside.

The policewoman writes down everything I say, then clicks the cap back onto her pen, signaling an end.

"I'll take all of this," she says, gathering up the phone and the garbage bag. She takes Smiley's phone, too. "Who's acting as your guardian, Indira?"

"I'm her guardian." Joe speaks up for the first time.

"Do Cecile's parents know she's here?"

Joe answers no, she's called them but can't get through. Smiley comes over, arms folded, determined. "I stayin with Indy." She reaches over for my hand, her warm fingers curling around mine. It's as comforting as all those nights I slept in her room, chair wedged under the doorknob, her snores lulling me toward sleep.

Officer Pinder closes her notebook. "Joe, you need to take them both in to see a doctor, tonight. Routine, in this type of case. I need to call for backup and head over to your house, Cecile, and to this restaurant. I want to see if this Gary is still there. We need to speak with him. And to the other young man, Churchy."

The drive to Dr. Palmer's office is quiet. Smiley goes in first, while Joe and I sit in silence. After Smiley's exam, I overhear the doctor use the word *intact*.

"You don't have to see me again, right?" I ask Dr. Palmer when she's done with Smiley.

"I really do, Indira. I can't force you to have an examination, but it would be helpful, for the police. And for you."

"Let me come with you," Smiley says, reaching for my hand.

After the examination is done, Dr. Palmer asks Smiley to go out into the waiting area. She pushes the door closed, then passes me a stack of papers.

"This is a brochure for the Women's Center," she says, tapping the one on top, which has the word *counseling* sprawled across the front. I listen while she explains that she has a friend, Nicola, who works there. Under the brochure is a piece of paper covered with Dr. Palmer's handwriting.

"What's this?"

"That's the contact information for a lawyer I know. She can talk to you about legal things. In case you want to press charges. You can call or email her there. And Indy?"

I look up at Dr. Palmer.

"I encourage you to press charges. I'll be there to help you in court. And you know Joe's by your side all the way."

I scan the page. *Friend of mine. Stephanie Brown. Legal advice.* I can't absorb all of this, all these people, all these things to do. I offer the page back to Dr. Palmer.

"Take it," she says kindly. "Look at it when you're ready. I've already spoken to Nicola and Mrs. Brown. Both of them will get ahold of you through Joe."

"What's the rest?"

"A flyer for a parenting class. The dates of your follow-up appointments." Dr. Palmer smiles. "We'll get through this, Indira. You'll see."

When we return to the retreat, none of us can rest. It's after eleven, but I don't want to go to the cottage, and Joe's in no rush to disappear either. We sit in the office, where she makes us tea, then calls again for Aunt Patrice.

"I can't get through," Joe says. "I'm sure she's worried, she's probably trying to get you on your cell phone. You try her." When Smiley shakes her head, Joe hands the phone to her anyway. "I don't feel good about you being here and her not knowing," she tells Smiley. I don't say what my fear is: that Gary will see the missed calls on the house phone and figure out this is where we are, that he'll come looking for us. For me. Joe gets on the phone again, this time calling the rest of the people who work at the retreat. Says the same thing to each one. "We have a situation here. The guests are all fine but I need the staff, urgently." I wonder if she's thinking about Gary coming here too.

One by one, everyone starts filtering in. Maya first, curlers in her hair, two children in pajamas trailing behind her.

"I don't know what you think I supposed to do in this mysterious situation," she says, grudgingly taking a cup of tea.

Susan comes next, with her husband, a fat, shy man who stays outside, watching the parking lot. As the room fills, I slip out to sit in the cool night air. Smiley joins me, leaning against my side.

"How come you never told me?"

"I was scared . . . and ashamed." There's another thing I've never said aloud.

"Ashamed of what? He's the disgusting one."

"I guess, that it happened to me." I try to find the right words. "What he did? It made me feel like less than nothing."

Smiley slips her arm through mine, the way she did when we first met, on the dock. "Well, that wasn't your fault. And you could have told Mummy."

I don't want to tell her what I really think about that. "I don't think Aunt Patrice would have believed me," I say instead.

"Really?" Smiley sounds doubtful. "Anyway, you got me."

We sit there, our backs against the office wall. Smiley dozes off, and I listen to her breathing, rhythmic and deep. She's never done yoga a day in her life, and yet after tonight, she can sound so at peace. How come she's so brave, so free from shame? Maybe because he did less to her? But that first day, he did less to me, too. A handful of flesh at my waist. And I still felt this way.

And then it occurs to me. This *did* happen to her. Smiley. A little of what happened to me. And she's Miss Perpetual Joy, the volleyball star with the laugh that lights up the room, daughter of the church-choir woman. I hate that this happened to her. And I'm grateful that she told. But no one can say now that this happened to me because of Mamma, because I'm just like her. It happened, but not because it was me.

The last person to arrive is Dion. He sits down on the ground opposite us. "What's going on, Indy?" he asks. "Not that guy with the black truck again?"

Smiley sits up, rubbing her eyes. "You know Gary?"

"We've crossed paths."

Something clicks. "Remember that day? When we almost hit your jeep?" I ask quietly.

"Of course. What, he giving you problems again?"

"Would you tell the police about that?"

"The police? Yeah. I mean . . . what happened? Of course, yeah, yeah." He looks from me to Smiley, but he asks nothing more. I get up and go back into the office, borrow the phone, dial the policewoman's number. I get her voice mail. While I dial again, I see Joe walk out to the deck. On the phone, there's still no answer. I leave her a message.

"Hi, Officer Pinder, it's Indy. I found someone else who said he would talk to you. Can you call me back, please?"

Dion comes to stand beside me. "Try her again."

I dial again, and again, and again. Nothing. She must be busy. Or it's too late. Or she's forgotten me.

When I hang up, I go outside to see what Joe's doing. The others follow. She's laid out mats on the deck, as if we're expecting a class.

"What we supposed to be doing?" Smiley asks.

"Come on. Maya, Susan?" Joe steps onto a mat. Maya groans.

Susan sucks her teeth. "You really wake me up to come out here and do yoga, and it's almost midnight?"

Joe brings her hands together at her chest. "We had an emergency. We needed backup. So back us up. Right, Indy?"

I hesitate. Then I step onto the deck, choosing one of the mats.

"Right."

18

WHEN YOU KNOW A storm's coming, you can batten down and hide away, or you can try to outrun the rain. Or there's option three: stand your ground, face the weather, and hope your roots keep you in place.

I'm in warrior two pose, feet wide apart, front knee bent, fingers cutting through the air, when I don't see, but hear, a change, a shift in the wind. A quick sucking in of air. Smiley's gasp.

The truck pulls into the driveway. Gravel dances out of its way. I stand up too fast and bump into Maya. Joe stops too; Susan and Dion turn to look. We all stand frozen on the deck, as if held by a spell.

The driver's door opens, then slams shut. Gary's bald head glints in the headlights as he walks around the front of the truck. Susan's husband approaches Gary, slow; his voice carries through the quiet night.

"Hey, man. Need something?"

Before Gary can answer, the passenger door opens and Aunt Patrice gets out, walking toward us. "Who's in charge here? Where's my daughter?"

Joe steps off her mat, and the spell is broken. Smiley holds my arm tightly and we stand together. Behind us, Maya and Susan stand too.

"She's right here. Why don't we all stay calm? We should talk about why she came, and what happened tonight." Joe stops in front of Aunt Patrice.

"Excuse me." Aunt Patrice brushes past her. "Cecile, you come here right now. Staying out all night? Where you get this from? From her?" She jabs a thumb at me.

"You know what he do? You know what he do?" Smiley's still holding on to me. "He try—"

"She's a minor." Gary interrupts Smiley, stepping forward. "Y'all can't have my sister here and not send her home."

"She *is* a minor. Exactly." Joe's voice starts to shake, angry. "And so"—she points my way—"is she."

"I can't control Indira. She old enough, she made her choice. My daughter is here, I came to get her," Aunt Patrice says. "Come here, Cecile."

Smiley doesn't move, pressed up so close she's almost behind me.

Joe cuts in. "It doesn't look like she wants to go. Don't you want to know why?"

"Don't matter if she wants to go or not. This my child. This other one here, she wild, just like her ma. But she ain ga ruin my one good daughter. And neither are you."

"Indira always causing problems anyway," Gary adds. He shifts from one foot to the other. It's not a laugh and smile situation. He seems lost as to what to do. More lost than me. I catch Dion's eye. *Go on—tell them,* he seems to say.

I wish I could close my eyes and wait until all this has gone away. But there are things I can't wish into the air; I'm here, someplace I finally want to be, but Smiley has to go back there, to that house. I can't let Gary hurt her or anyone else ever again. On purpose or by mistake or whatever excuse he might come up with next. I have to say something. For Smiley. For the laughing, swaying girl Mamma once was. For the baby I'm carrying.

And for me.

"Come here." Aunt Patrice steps around Joe, reaching for Smiley, who darts out of the way. I inhale. *Make the right moves to get out.* Hold it. Exhale.

"I'm pregnant, Aunt Patrice."

Everything stops; no pounding-in-ears heartbeat, only my voice, ringing out. "Gary is the—" I don't want to say *father,* don't want to give him that tie to me, to the baby. "He's the one who did it," I say, holding her gaze. "He made me."

The group is silent, as if they no longer exist. Aunt Patrice looks away, her mouth twisted. She did know, after all.

"This is nonsense." She speaks to the empty space beside me. "What kind of lie you talking?" She shakes her head back and forth, trying to dislodge what she's heard. I can see her starting to buckle under the weight of the truth spoken out loud.

"You don't believe her, do you?" Gary says, his voice whiny and high. "You know she's trouble. And you know what her ma like, you know the two of them loose. Y'all don't believe her." He tries to address everyone now. He gives a little laugh, but it's choked short. "Man, Mummy, you can't believe her. You know she lyin."

"I ain lyin," I say. I take a deep breath and make my mouth form the words my mind's never let me even think, before now. "You raped me."

Gary's eyes dart around, seeking an ally among the faces. "Man, her ma is whore and all. You know what them type a people like, you can't trust what they say."

Dion steps forward until he is standing right beside me. "I believe Indy."

Maya is silent, but I feel her hand come to rest on my shoulder. Smiley shuffles closer to me.

"The police have already talked to the girls. It's you they need to speak to, Gary," Joe says.

"I ain gotta stand here for this." Gary starts to back up, stumbling over his own feet. "Y'all lyin. Y'all lyin about me!"

"It's the truth. I told the police, and I recorded you when you made the appointment to get rid of the baby, so everybody could hear." I'm trembling, but I go on. "And I gave them your pants from after what you did to me in the kitchen, and that money. Everybody ga see."

Gary turns to run, but Susan's husband blocks his way. "If you say it's a lie, you got nothing to be scared of. You can wait here and talk to the police."

"It's the truth," I say again. "You raped me. And you were gonna rape Smiley tonight too."

"Gary?" Aunt Patrice whispers, suddenly afraid. He mutters something, but a siren's wail, growing louder and louder, drowns out his words. "Gary, how could you bring this shame on me?" Aunt Patrice says. She disgusts me.

As the police car pulls up the driveway, lights flashing, I turn my back on the crowd, even Smiley. "Baby, why you didn't tell me?" I hear Aunt Patrice ask her. Behind me, I hear car doors open and shut. Officer Pinder's voice says to Gary and Aunt Patrice, "Come this way, I have some questions for both of you." Even though they're the same words she said to me, she sounds less kind this time. But I don't stay to watch. I've done my part—right now, I want to be away from all this. I head down the path, through the trees, and toward the openness of the water, the flat horizon, the clear air.

When I reach the beach, I breathe in. And breathe out.

I touch my belly. My baby's in there, kicking out. Gently, I press back.

And I bring my hands up to my chest. I need to be calm, need to move through this moment so I can get to the next. I can hear sirens screaming again, through the trees. Inhale—arms up. Exhale—hands down to the ground, bending forward. Right leg back, in a low lunge; then the left. I close my eyes, holding plank pose. Inhale, exhale, and push into upward dog. Then back again; downward dog. I step forward as the sirens grow faint. Something in my chest loosens for the first time in months and lets me breathe right. There are voices, coming closer. I don't stop.

"We need to bring her in to go over her statement again." A man's voice carries from somewhere off through the trees.

"Wait till morning," Joe says. "Please. That's enough for tonight." The voices fade away.

In the night, alone, I glide through poses as I remember them, moving slowly. Ahead of me, the water is dark and smooth, an unrumpled sheet; it blends seamlessly into the sky. I bring my hands together at my chest, standing perfectly still. I am home.

Then I raise my arms up to that sea-sky. I begin again.

EPILOGUE

ON THE FRONT PORCH of my little cabin, I bounce her lightly. Sometimes she's what I imagine Mamma was, mouth wide and upturned, all sweetness and mischief. She looks away from me, down the path, and I follow her gaze. Through the trees, Churchy appears, his backpack clasped in his arms faithfully.

"Who's that?" I say, getting to my feet. "That's Churchy, bringing us something nice to eat?" I say it loud enough for him to hear and he laughs, a string of music unsnagged. In my arms, she laughs too, her voice a clear bell. My breath catches, then comes right back. I kiss the smooth dome of her forehead as Churchy steps onto the porch.

"I got b-biology homework, and math," he says, ever the serious tutor; he's determined to see me graduate next year, coming by twice a week to help me study. "And your grammy send a message. She say wh-when y'all coming to visit? She miss her great-grandbaby."

"We'll come on Sunday."

He produces a pocket-sized teddy bear from inside the bag before setting it down, then bends over, resting the toy on her belly. She grins up at him and reaches for his glasses, and he evades her grip, gently catching a plump hand and pretending to nibble it.

"You brought homework? That's it?" I say, passing her into his waiting arms. I dig through the bag and my hand finds the cool of a glass bowl. "Aha!" The foil covering it crinkles as I pull it out.

"Some homemade sugar apple custard. For s-s-somebody sweet."

I flash Churchy a smile as I set the bowl down on the porch, reaching for her again. "Did you tell Churchy thank you?" I ask her. She is frowning and thoughtful, a little Grammy. Then she squeals at me, grabbing for my nose, and her eyes crinkle and her face is brand-new. My heart skips, and it's a good skip, a love skip.

"Look at you," I tell her, now and every chance I get. "Your own beautiful self."

ACKNOWLEDGMENTS

First, all my thanks and love to my parents, Janice M. Mather and Kingsley O. Mather. You sponsored years of study, allowed me peace and space to write, and let me print off ten forests worth of half-spun stories. Daddy, I wish you were here to see the full fruit. To my siblings, Steven Mather, Carole Henry, and Dr. Andrea Mather, you kept me in encouraging words, must-read books, fancy stationery, and amusing fountain pens. To my niece and sister-author, Rebecca Henry, for inspiration simply by being yourself. (You're next.)

In the unfurling of manuscript to real, solid book, I am deeply indebted to my wonderful editor, Catherine Laudone, for seeing and choosing this story, and for bringing joy in times of deep revision. You edited with wisdom and care, gently showing me the places where there was room to grow. Thank you.

To my agent, Rachel Letofsky—meeting you was a true game changer. You believed in Indy's story, and you believed in me. You are a champion, and we are grateful. I look forward to many more years of working together.

To the wonderful designers who unfurled beauty (outside and within), and to all at Simon & Schuster Books for Young Readers; thank you for the many ways in which you helped bring this book to fruition.

ACKNOWLEDGMENTS

To the CookeMcDermid Agency team, thank you for your commitment to me.

To the 2015 HarperCollinsPublishersLtd/UBC Prize for Best New Fiction judges and readers: I am thankful that you granted me a place on the 2015 shortlist, and opened many doors.

Alison Acheson, my advisor, instructor, butt-kicker, and friend—you were there in the very beginning. You are a blessing. Thanks, too, to the classmates and friends at the University of British Columbia, who read through the very early versions of this book.

To my dear friend, Crystal Lehky, for your honest reading and tireless cheering.

There are many others—friends, teachers, librarians, readers of story scraps, hearers of poems, speakers of encouragements, sharers of books—to whom I owe thanks for seeds planted, sprouts tended.

Most especially, to my husband and love, Jason Rondquist. You bring the sunshine, you stand with me in the rain.

Let the harvest begin.

TURN THE PAGE FOR
A SNEAK PEEK AT
JANICE LYNN MATHER'S
NEXT NOVEL,
FACING THE SUN.

KEEKEE

PINDER STREET TOTES SOFT breezes and ocean bird calls. There are stray dogs and dusty children darting between yards, music blaring from car speakers or cellphones. For a place far east of everywhere, Pinder Street beats fast.

But when I turn onto my father's road, with its old-paved asphalt, bleached white by the sun, I step into a different Nassau than the one I inhabit during the week. Here, there is yellow pine forest for miles. It looks monochrome at first, but if you stop and look, stubby palms begin to show themselves, their fronds like hands waving at their gangly friends, and little ferns and sharp sisal plants push up out of rocky ground. I wonder, not for the first time, how it would be to step off the road and walk into that forest, to keep moving until the bag melts away and my shoes disappear. Moving until my feet stop walking and my arms stop their swing, until sun streams around and through me and birds hover around my hair, then dive in. Moving until no one I was responsible for knew how to find me.

"If I walked out, could I become a pine?" I say, the words taking shape in my mind.

> "If I walked out, could I become a pine,
> legs fusing and feet unfurling pale roots the color of
> my palms?
> Would my toes curl and shoot into the soil
> and pull up food?"

As I speak, I drop my bag onto the cracked street, sinking down to sit. I look out, and up.

> "I would
> reach up my arms and feel the tiny twigs shoot out
> from where
> I had elbows. My hair would turn to needles that,
> dropping, would only let my ownly babies and
> a few more trusted friends grow.
> If I walked out, I could
> become a pine among the pines,
> standing tall and aloof, sun reaching through me and
> my closest kin, casting shadows to the sky."

A cough behind me makes me turn suddenly.

"My little poet," Dad says, and I get up, hugging him. There is always that small bit of shy that grows up during the week, pulled out on Sunday afternoon and replaced by a wide grin and free laughter by the time I have to leave. But like jasmine weed on a fence, it snakes up again by Wednesday, calls and texts too weak to keep its leaves from spreading open, its tendrils from catching hold of my heart. Dad picks up my bag, grunts as though it's filled with concrete blocks, and says, "So, y'all fighting on the beach now."

"Who tell you that?"

"I was talking to Toons." He begins striding toward the house. He's tall himself, though wide-shouldered and thick. I'm used to running so I keep up with him easily. "Say a little trouble gone down. You wasn't in that, ay?"

"In what? He's the one causing problems. Too busy cutting up with Faith to think straight."

"Isn't he with Paulette?"

You'd think he knew these people from when they were small. Sometimes I think he knows them, through my stories, better than he knows me. "And?" I challenge.

Dad shakes his head. "Well, y'all made it away safe."

"Barely. Nia almost got left behind."

"She did? She's that slow?"

I shrug. "The guy was fast." We're at the house, now; Dad

turns up the driveway, stepping over and around fallen guavas that litter the ground, fermenting and half-nibbled by rats.

"Well, you keep outta trouble up there. Don't be in places where you don't belong."

"That's our beach, though."

Dad unlocks the door and the smell of cake barrels out. "No, baby, that's always been private land. Just sat empty so long nobody thought they'd ever build out that way. Now the owner sell it, everyone up in arms."

"It's not empty. The church has stuff there every day."

"Oh, that's what that old place is now?"

"Always was. You'd know if you ever came through to see me there," I tease, kicking off my shoes and welcoming the quiet. No Toons thundering in, no Angel laughing and Sammy murmuring. No voices whispering in the thick of darkness. No three soft raps on the door before dawn. It's bliss.

"Not always, babes. Used to be a bunch of things. But times change. Anyway, listen," he says, stepping into the kitchen, "I want talk to you about that summer program. You fill out the application?"

I follow him, inhaling the scent of butter and slow-roasted sugar. The room is alive with sunshine, the sink piled high with bowls and spoons. "That's lemon cake?"

"Pound." He opens the oven door and slides a knife into the cake's soft center, then eases the blade out, holding it up to the light. "It's an opportunity. You like to write, even though I've never seen any of these mysterious poems on paper." He drops the knife into the sink, then closes the oven again, letting the cake bake a bit more.

I cross my arms and lean back against the counter. "You gonna be there?"

"I already tell you," he says impatiently, "I'm on the admissions committee, not teaching."

"Cause if my one and only daddy was gonna be there . . ."

"I'm serious, KeeKee."

I don't get my father sometimes. He'll be smooth and easygoing one minute, then all business the next. "I don't think my poems would . . . fit."

"You have any of them with you?"

"No, I left them all in a folder at home," I lie.

"You should have brought them," he says seriously. "I'd drive you over there right now, but this cake . . ."

There it is. There's always some excuse why he can't come to Pinder Street. Suddenly, the kitchen is too small. "I could go in the studio?"

"Sure."

As I step out the back door, he lets out a sigh that fills the air and pushes out past me, following me through the grove of dilly trees to the low, shaded shack. Let him be disappointed. He's not the only one. I push the studio door open and sink onto his favorite carved stool. I've been sitting on it from the time I needed to be hoisted up onto it. I run my hand over the smooth sides, left pinky finding the knot in the wood that used to be a tree, right forefinger slipping into the old split. He might as well have come out and said it: Angel won't let him come around. If someone wants something bad enough, though, they go ahead, even without permission.

He's never heard a whole poem from me, only caught fragments spat out in between the time when he sneaks up behind me to listen and the moment when I realize he's there. Yet he thinks he knows they're good enough to earn me a spot in this program. He doesn't know that when I've tried putting them on a page, the words wilt and flop sideways like flowers cut too long. Doesn't know that I'm scared about leaving home for a whole summer, about leaving a world of people behind who count on me. People who need me to serve their grits in the morning and fold their clothes at night, to stand by them no matter what comes to our home. But how could he know if my poems are good, know what I really want for this summer, when he doesn't even know *me*?

NIA

IT'S STILL AND HOT at the dining table. The rest of Pinder
Street is fragrant with Sunday meals —aromas of baked chops,
ribs and rice, potato salad, and macaroni drifting in through
our window from all over.

Mamma sets a plate of cold sandwiches down in front of
me. A rubbery finger of sausage pokes out from between the
bread.

"Any mayonnaise?" I ask, as if that will save this meal.

"Spoils too fast." Mamma slides the hot sauce over to me
and selects a sandwich, nibbling at the crust. "Mmmm." She
licks her fingers as if dry slam bam with almost-stale bread is
spicy battered bird deep-fried and seasoned right. Over her
shoulder, the radio blares a dreary love song. I'm hungry now,
a dull ache in my belly. Slam bam it is. I lean over and take
a piece, looking over at the Newbeat Summer Arts Program

pamphlet held to the side of the rusty beige filing cabinet with an aqua, gold, and black *Happy Independence Day* magnet. The picture of a circle of girls on a beach taunts me.

"Nia?"

I look up at my mother at the other end of the table. "Yes, ma'am?"

"I asked if you're almost finished with the paper for today. Mr. Rahming's granddaughters are coming at three for me to help them with their reading."

I look over at the bulky gray computer monitor, glowing white with this week's Pinder Street Press. "Mmmhmm." My eyes drift up to the pamphlet again. "Mamma, you thought any more about if I could go to that thing this summer?" I force my voice to sound casual.

"Mmm." Mamma reaches for the newspaper. "I don't know about that, Nia. Why you wanna spend the summer away from your friends?"

"Well, KeeKee's applying too," I say. Mamma scratches her chin, turning to the business section. "And it's a chance to experience more of the Bahamas," I add, trying to sound patriotic.

"Come." She tosses the newspaper down. "Pass this form, lemme see."

I spring up out of my chair too fast to be nonchalant, snatching the pamphlet off the cabinet so fast the magnet goes flying. "It's just a short ferry ride away, they have dorms and it's all girls, focused on the creative arts—"

"I don't know what other type arts there are," she interrupts.

Culinary arts, I think, but keep my mouth shut and rummage in my school bag, taking the application out. I pass it to Mamma. "They do writing, painting, sculpture, dance, theatre—you have small classes in your own specialty, and they have an on-site farm where they grow their own food—"

"Organic and free range, no doubt." Mamma scans the page. "Only one page on this application?"

"You attach a sample of your work to it so they can see. That's the most important part."

She flips the paper over to scrutinize the back. "Who is judging the applications to this seasonal nirvana?"

I ignore her sarcasm and push on. "It's a bunch of people. Mr. Lewis from the Nassau Journal, Mrs. Strachan from the university's art department, Ms. Johnson from the art gallery, Mr. Wright, Mrs. Symonette—"

"Mr. Wright?" Mamma looks up abruptly.

"Um . . ." I should have left him out, I think, mentally kicking myself. It's too late now; I might as well not play dumb. "I think he's an architect."

"KeeKee's daddy." Mamma gets up, her back to me as she opens the cupboard.

"But it's a great opportunity, it would look good on a college application, I could learn independence and maturity and—"

"And bring world peace, no doubt." She bangs a glass down on the counter.

"So, can you sign my application for me?"

"Nia, what makes you think I'm sending you out of my sight for six weeks with no one around who I know—"

"But I told you, KeeKee's gonna be there."

"If she gets in." Her voice drifts back to me over the clink of glasses, then of water pouring over ice.

I try again. "That's six weeks you don't have to worry about me—"

"If you think your being off the island staying with strangers is a way for me to worry less—"

"You can't at least think about it?"

Mamma comes back in, setting a glass of water down beside me. I don't want a drink. I want out. I want something other than the cloying routine of a Sunday afternoon spent with Mamma and her papers and her glasses of water and her cold sausage sandwiches. Mamma doesn't answer. Even if she did, she'd just say I'm whining. I take a deep breath and get up to go sit at the computer. I need a minute to gather my ammo. I scan this week's stories: a profile on Danny Ferguson across the street, who won a martial arts trophy; a summary of the protest we went to in Rawson Square; a school essay on Dame Doris Johnson that Mamma made me tweak into something half fit for other people to read; a piece on the school band playing on Friday. Everything about it is so everyday, so unimportant. So small.

Mamma comes and peers over my shoulder, then taps her finger against the screen. "Read this. What you wrote about the protest."

I sigh. "'There was a small group of people who got together in Rawson Square to opposition against—'"

"To protest against, or oppose."

"'To oppose against—'"

"Listen, girl. To *oppose*. Start the sentence again."

"Mamma, you ain ga even answer me?"

"Girl, your head too much in the clouds to see news if it knocked you right in the eye. You doing your work or you nagging me?"

I want to snap back that I don't care about news, that this stupid paper was Mamma's idea all along. Instead, I bite back those words. "Please can I go? Please, please, please?" I fling my arms around her, squeezing tight. "Can I?"

She relinquishes a grudging laugh, squirming away. "I'll think about it—"

"Yes!" I knock the chair over, jumping up and down. "Thank you, thank you, thank you!" I squeeze her, hanging onto her like she's my lifeboat out of boredom.

"Ease up, I said I'd think about it."

"And you know you have to decide by—"

"I saw the deadline, Nia. I can read. Now, can you?"

I bound back to the table. "It's finished," I say, reaching for the form to look at it again.

"The protest?" Mamma slides the application out of my reach. "Oh, forget it. Put the clothes on to wash so you can hang them up before night."

I smack a kiss on her cheek, then start gathering the laundry together. There's a perfectly good washer just across the yard, but it's Angel's, so it's anathema. Usually, I complain about having to tote a heavy hamper of clothes all the way down to the Armbrister house to use their older, less spacious machine, but today, the load is light. I swing the front door open and almost bump into a man in a suit, coming up the porch steps.

"Oh—sorry!" I say. He gives me a businesslike little nod, making a beeline for our door. A man? Come to us? "Excuse me, can I help you?" I ask, turning around.

"Is your mother in, young lady?" he asks, in a serious voice that tells me this isn't a social call.

"Yes," I say, even though Mamma would swat me for announcing her availability without checking who it is first. "Mamma!" I call through the window. "Someone here to see you."

Mamma appears immediately, as if she's been listening. "Can I help you?" she asks, standing in the doorway.

"Marvin Knowles." He extends a hand, which Mamma shakes formally. "MP for Eastern Heights."

"I know you." Mamma withdraws her hand, folding her arms. "Faith's uncle. Y'all used to live on the end of the triplex over there."

"Oh, yes, it's been some years. I didn't think anyone remembered me from the old days."

Mamma's lips are pursed, as if she's tasting something bitter. "What brings you to my doorstep?"

"Just making some courtesy visits through the neighborhood," Mr. Knowles continues. He fiddles with the collar of his suit, adjusting the tie. It fits him evenly, and the fabric looks smooth, not like Eve's daddy's suits, which are always a little rumpled, even when he wears one instead of a plain white bush jacket and pants. "Meeting our constituents." He produces a business card from his pocket.

"Reintroducing. On a Sunday," Mamma says, suddenly devout.

"Yes—reintroducing. It's always good to see old friends. Just coming through to chat with folks about the development up by the beach. Big things are coming for Pinder Street."

"Proposed." Mamma uses her reporter voice as she corrects him. He frowns, a frown Faith has inherited.

"Pardon me?"

"Things are proposed for Pinder Street, Mr. Knowles. The sale hasn't been officially approved yet, has it?"

He laughs, a hearty, fat laugh, as if his mouth is full of candy. "You're sharp, Mrs.—"

"They call me Teacher. Anything else, Mr. Knowles?" Mamma's voice is stretched thin.

"Actually, yes. We had some teenagers causing trouble down at the beach on Friday. I just want to make sure the parents are aware the property is private land."

"What type of trouble?" Mamma asks.

"I can't really go into the details, but I know the property owner is concerned about the level of security on the premises. I believe they may be willing to call the police if trespassing continues to be a problem."

"What about the after-school group they have at the church?" I point out.

"Yes, and I'm sure the Tuesday morning seniors reading group will be glad to have some officers join them," Mamma says dryly.

"I, uh—well, my understanding is all regularly scheduled activities are continuing as normal."

"For how long?"

"I don't have any information around time frames but of course, I want to look out for the interests of my constituents, of all ages. Just going through the neighborhood so persons are aware."

"I'm sure." Mamma taps the card on her leg. "Was that it, Mr. Knowles?"

"That's it." The man bobs his head. "A pleasure." We watch him scurrying down the path, then over to go up to KeeKee's house, as though walking the long way earns him points over cutting across the grass like everyone else. I don't turn back to look at Mamma, only hurry away down the road, toward Eve's house, where Mr. Knowles has no doubt already been. I have no reason to be nervous, I tell myself. I didn't do anything wrong. And none of this will matter when I'm gone. Just so long as Mamma's in a good mood when she looks at my application again. So long as she says yes.

RIVETED

BY *simon teen* ♥

BELIEVE IN YOUR SHELF

Visit RivetedLit.com & connect with us on social to:

DISCOVER NEW YA READS

READ BOOKS FOR FREE

DISCUSS YOUR FAVORITES

SHARE YOUR IDEAS

ENTER SWEEPSTAKES FOR THE CHANCE TO WIN BOOKS

Follow @SimonTeen on

to stay up to date with all things Riveted!